Dear Reader,

Home, family, community and love. These are the values we cherish most in our lives–the ideals that ground us, comfort us, move us. They certainly provide the perfect inspiration around which to build a romance collection that will touch the heart.

And so we are thrilled to have the opportunity to introduce you to the Harlequin Heartwarming collection. Each of these special stories is a wholesome, heartfelt romance imbued with the traditional values so important to you. They are books you can share proudly with friends and family. And the authors featured in this collection are some of the most talented storytellers writing today, including favorites such as Brenda Novak, Janice Kay Johnson, Jillian Hart and Patricia Davids. We've selected these stories especially for you based on their overriding qualities of emotion and tenderness, and they center around your favorite themes–children, weddings, second chances, the reunion of families, the quest to find a true home and, of course, sweet romance.

So curl up in your favorite chair, relax and prepare for a heartwarming reading experience!

Sincerely,

The Editors

JUDITH BOWEN

is an award-winning romance writer particularly known for her Men of Glory series in Harlequin Superromance. She grew up in Alberta and knows its landscape intimately, as this book attests. Prior to becoming a novelist, she worked as a journalist. Judith now makes her home in Vancouver, British Columbia.

HARLEQUIN HEARTWARMING

Judith Bowen

The Rancher and the Schoolteacher

Recycling programs for this product may not exist in your area.

ISBN-13: 978-0-373-36566-1

THE RANCHER AND THE SCHOOLTEACHER

This edition published by arrangement with Harlequin Books S.A.

For questions and comments about the quality of this book please contact us at Customer_eCare@Harlequin.ca.

www.Harlequin.com

Printed in U.S.A.

The Rancher and the Schoolteacher

To Patrick

CHAPTER ONE

"YOU'RE PRISCILLA PRESCOTT?"

There was a man at the door, a very tall man wearing jeans and boots and a broad-brimmed hat and carrying a small child on his back, monkey style. The child peeked over one broad shoulder to smile impishly at her.

"Yes," Cilla replied, willing her cheeks to cool. "Yes, I am she." She saw the cowboy's face twist a little at her perfect grammar. At least she presumed that was what had caused the sudden tightness of the mouth—a very handsome mouth, she observed—just before he smiled again. A very handsome smile, too.

"Of the *Blue Owl* Montessori Preschool?"

"Yes," Cilla replied airily, desperately wanting to reach up and make sure she'd tucked all the flyaway ends of her hair into her quick elastic-secured bun. She'd been washing up her painting tools when the door-bell rang and had made the world's fastest change of clothing, whipping off her jeans and T-shirt in the tiny utility room and slipping on her sundress in less than ten seconds. It might be a potential student at the door, and she couldn't afford to miss even one. School started in another week, and any late registrations were more than welcome.

"Well, Marigold," the cowboy drawled, aiming his comment at the little blond girl clinging to his back with both arms around his neck and scowling now at Cilla through overlong bangs. "I guess we're here, honey."

"Hello, Marigold," Cilla said gently and smiled. She didn't step forward and offer her hand, as she would have done if the child had been standing before her. For her trouble, she got an even darker frown.

"Now, come on down, Marigold," the cowboy ordered. Cilla presumed he was the father of this ragamuffin. "Off!"

"Ain't going to!"

"Aren't," the man corrected with a sly glance at Cilla, as though to make sure she understood that he knew bad grammar when he heard it. "Sure, you are," he continued amiably, raising up with one large hand to grab the child. She scooted over to his other shoulder.

"Ain't!"

He made a great show of trying to grab her on his shoulder, then reached up and grasped the child by one bare foot. "Ha—gotcha!"

The girl yelled, then started to giggle. "Stop, you're tickling, Uncle Jeroo!"

Jeroo? Cilla watched with amazement as the man, who'd stand an inch or two over six feet in his stockings, clearly all muscle and sinew from a lifetime spent working with horses and cattle somewhere in the hills around Glory, plucked the girl from his back. He then held her upside down, gripping the child securely by both ankles.

The girl's face turned pink and she caught at her uncle's hands. "Swing me, swing me, *puh-leeeese!*"

"Nope." The uncle shot Cilla a pleased grin and she did her best to look respectable. Concerned. Mildly interested. The way the director of the town's new preschool should.

She saw one of her newest—she hoped—students hanging upside down, no shoes on, in need of a good wash and a hairbrush, giggling her little self silly.

Cilla suppressed a grin. "Come in, Marigold. Would you like to show your uncle the schoolroom?"

The man flipped the girl right side up and

set her down, and she turned alert blue eyes on Cilla, who'd remained at the door. The girl pushed back her shaggy blond hair with both hands. *"School?"* she asked, her voice awed.

"Yes, this is the new school I'm opening here in Glory for little girls like you." Cilla smiled and stepped back.

"And boys?" the girl asked.

"Yes, little boys, too. Bring your uncle in and you can have a look around. Marigold's a very pretty name. I'd like to hear more about how you got your pretty name—"

"It's a *school,* Uncle Jeroo!" the girl interrupted and marched inside. "Not a place for babies, so *there*—"

The adults exchanged a look.

"Babies?" Cilla repeated.

"Her mother told her it was a nursery school. I guess Marigold objected. *Nursery* is what her ma calls the room they've got for the new baby at home," he said.

"Oh." Cilla was shocked to see bald interest on the man's face as they spoke. Interest—in her. She held out her hand politely. "I'm Cilla Prescott. The teacher. And you're...?"

"Jeremiah Blake, ma'am, at your service." He doffed his hat with his other hand and bent slightly over her palm, as though he intended to kiss it, before she hastily pulled it away. As he straightened, he replaced his hat and grinned. A smooth, practiced, almost theatrical gesture.

"Marigold's uncle, I understand?" she said.

"That's right. Her ma and dad—Cal Blake's my brother—are away right now, and I'm taking care of the bean sprout out at the Diamond 8. I'm the ranch manager there." His cool blue eyes, rimmed with the blackest lashes she'd ever seen, met hers. Almost in challenge, she felt.

"I'd have thought you'd be too busy on a ranch to look after a small child."

"Oh, it's not just me, ma'am," he interrupted with a lazy smile. "There's me and the Pings, Georgie and his uncle—they're cooking for me at present, since my cook took off and since my brother's shut his place down for a couple weeks' holiday. And then there's half a dozen hands in the bunkhouse, sometimes more, always somebody ready and willing to saddle up Marigold's pony when she wants him for a—"

"Strangers?" Cilla frowned. She hardly thought a bunch of ranch hands were qualified to take care of a little girl.

"They're not strangers to me," he replied

amiably. He took off his hat again, revealing thick, dark-brown hair. Almost black. Shiny in the afternoon sun. “Shall we go in, ma’am? Have that look around?”

“Yes.” Cilla took a quick breath as she led the way inside. She didn’t think for a moment that her cheeks were less flushed now than when she’d raced for the door.

Marigold was standing happily at the materials table, pouring dry cornmeal from one container to another, Cilla noted with pleasure. She’d filled the bin with cornmeal only this morning, to find out how much she’d need. The Montessori method of educating young children took a hands-on approach. Children were encouraged to explore their world with all the senses, at their own individual pace.

“Whew! I smell fresh paint.”

Cilla tried a light laugh. If the townsfolk, including this man, only knew how much her new venture was based on a wing and a prayer. And she was the entire staff at present—janitor, teacher, organizer, carpenter. “Actually, I’ve just finished painting the small room I’m going to be using to store supplies.” It was more of a combined staff washroom, utility and supplies room. And it wasn't small—it was *tiny*.

"Uh-huh." Jeremiah Blake was looking skeptically around the schoolroom. Cilla hadn't set up the furniture yet, so boxes were stacked here and there. A world map covered one wall and a large calendar with September exposed hung on another. The squares on the calendar had no numbers. When school started, she'd practice the days of the week with the children and they'd put up the new number for the new day.

"How many kids you got signed up?" he asked, studying the room as he walked around.

"Thirteen so far," Cilla replied. "Will Marigold be attending?" she added, wishing she didn't sound quite so hopeful.

"Her ma says so. Her dad isn't crazy about the idea. Figures kids her age should play, not go to school."

"I see." Cilla felt her hackles rise. She believed every child should have every opportunity available, and that included socializing with more than a bunkhouse full of cowboys. "And are you of the same opinion, Mr. Blake?"

"Do I agree, you mean?" he asked with a

grin. "Yeah, I guess I do. Although I don't have any children myself. I'm not married." He paused and looked at her, as though to let that fact sink in deeply. She felt her cheeks flame again. "But if I did, I'd probably prefer to see them running around catching frogs and making mudpies before I'd see them all dressed up to go to school."

"I see," Cilla said again, resolving not to get into an argument with Marigold's uncle before she'd even filled in a registration form. "Shall I take down a few particulars from you? I believe Marigold is content where she is."

"Sure," he agreed and took a step toward her. "Let's take down the particulars," he mimicked. "Oh, and *Miss* Prescott?"

"Yes, Mr. Blake?"

"Do call me Jeremiah. Or Jem."

"All right. Jeremiah it is. And I'm Cilla. I expect the children to call me by my first name. It's part of the equality and respect that is so essential to the Montessori program."

After that rather stiff little speech, which he appeared to follow raptly, she led him to what would be her office when school started. She had stacks of boxes in there, too, but she knew just where to find the registration forms. They could discuss the form in the classroom and keep an eye on Marigold at the same time. Cilla was acutely aware of Jeremiah, walking right behind.

He paused at the door to her office, which reeked of paint fumes. "Man, you've been painting in here, too." He strode over to the window and wrenched it open.

She looked up as she put her hand on a registration form. "I just shut that and locked it. I was going to leave soon."

"You don't need to worry about leaving a window open in this town. Nobody's going to break in."

"Is that a fact? What—no crime in Glory?" She couldn't resist.

"Oh, we've got our share. But what's to steal in here?" He glanced around. "A bunch of pencil crayons?"

Cilla didn't reply. She left the window open and hurried back to the classroom, sitting down at one of the tiny wooden chairs. Very carefully, Jeremiah sat in one across from her.

There weren't many questions on her information sheet. She passed over a sheaf of papers for the cowboy to take home to Marigold's parents. There was a brochure explaining her school and its aims, some information on Maria Montessori, the Italian doctor and founder of this method of teaching children, a form for medical information.

"What's this?" Jeremiah held up one sheet, a pale yellow one.

Cilla wished he hadn't. "Er, it's a volunteer sign-up sheet. I'm hoping the parents will sign up for various jobs that need doing around the school."

"What sort of jobs?" He looked interested. Too interested.

"Oh, mowing the grass, keeping up the playground, helping me cut out materials, weekend work bees, that sort of thing." Cilla was embarrassed, although she knew she shouldn't be. She even had a proposal for a charity auction in the middle of September with another Glory arts venture, a new dance school.

She'd so hoped that she'd be able to run Blue Owl free and clear, but her capital hadn't lasted as long as her ideas had. The old building she'd rented had required a lot more updating than she'd planned on, and the furniture, mostly new, had cost a fortune. Like many preschools, hers would be forced to count on parent participation. As for drawing a salary, that would have to come later.

She'd received a small inheritance from her great-aunt and kept back part of it for living expenses, but that would have to last her until the school showed some profit. By Christmas, she hoped. All the rest of her money, money she'd begged and borrowed, had been plowed into the preschool.

She'd had no support from her family. Considering the way they'd scoffed at her initial plans to open a Montessori school, she figured she'd die before she'd ask for their help. The Prescott girls, in her parents' and grandparents' opinions, were born to learn French and German, to host marvelous parties, to draw and paint and arrange flowers. If they didn't marry a rich man, they were expected to marry a diplomat or at least someone in the foreign service.

Mary, her oldest sister, had gone along with it, marrying a man more or less picked out by their father, although Mary insisted she was in love with Talbot Potter. And her middle sister, Jeanne, had given up her nursing career at the request of her fiancé, a stodgy Italian industrialist in glass fixtures or women's stockings or some sort of hideous manufacturing enterprise. They were to be married in November, and then Jeanne was moving to Florence. Cilla had no idea when she'd see her again.

Great-aunt Martina had left the three sisters each a modest legacy when she died the year before. Cilla's grief over the loss of her favorite aunt was tempered by knowing that she'd put her inheritance to a purpose her great-aunt would have approved—her own business. Martina von Schelling had married into money, as expected by the family, but her husband was already an old man when she married him and he died within ten years of their wedding. After that, she went into business for herself in Germany. She'd specialized in designing and producing outrageous fake furs and had been wildly successful. Her will had endowed various animal foundations and educational groups, as well as each of her nieces.

Cilla didn't know what Mary and Jeanne had done with theirs, but nearly every cent of her legacy had been spent fulfilling her dream of teaching young children in her own nursery school. She'd had the training, from a Swiss institute, and the experience, from her first Montessori teaching jobs in Ontario; now she had the means, as well. Her first task had been to settle on a location. Why she'd chosen Glory she wasn't sure, except that when she'd researched smaller centers in Alberta that lacked educational facilities for small children, Glory had seemed the likeliest of the list. It wasn't far from Calgary—she thought she'd hate living in a small town if she couldn't escape to the city occasionally. But it was far enough that there was no question of her living at home, which her parents would have tried to insist on if she'd stayed in the city, even though she was nearly twenty-seven. Her father, a scion of an old London, Ontario, family who had moved west with his company's head office, a man used to money and a generous patron of the arts, was very protective of what he referred to as "his girls." He included her mother in that list. And her mother, a Swiss-born woman who'd grown up in Europe, was, in Cilla's view, extremely old-fashioned.

Glory had offered another advantage: there'd been a building available immediately, a rental building already zoned for commercial use, which allowed her to run a school without going through a lengthy and costly rezoning process. Now, following Jeremiah's gaze up to the spotted and waterstained ceiling with its newly installed and requisite water sprinklers, Cilla wondered if she'd made the right choice. Perhaps she shouldn't have been so hasty in her decision to lease what many would regard as a ramshackle building, with sloping floors and cracking plaster. But the price had been right. And, after so many delays already, she refused to wait another year.

"Well—I guess the two of us had better hit the road," Jeremiah said finally. "Marigold, hon?"

He took his niece by the hand. It was a touching picture, the big, tough-looking cowboy and the tiny blond waif. Now that Cilla knew the circumstances, she realized why the child looked so neglected. Obviously Uncle *Jeroo* didn't know how to style a young girl's hair into a neat ponytail or a braid.

"Would you like me to give you a ponytail, Marigold?" she asked impulsively.

The girl frowned, felt her unkempt locks with both hands again, then brightened and nodded. "Yes, please."

Jeremiah shot the child a surprised look. "You would?"

"Uh-huh." The little girl smiled up at her uncle, nodding vigorously.

"You never let me brush it for you, hon," he complained.

"That's cuz you always do it funny."

"I do?" He seemed so taken aback by her remark that Cilla laughed out loud.

"I've got a few new combs in my desk," she said. "I keep them on hand for the children to use."

She retrieved a large-toothed yellow comb and sat on the small chair again, while Marigold happily positioned herself between Cilla's knees. Gently Cilla began to comb out the child's tangles.

"So, tell me how you got such a nice name."

"My momma gave it to me," the child replied simply. "It's a flower. My real first name's Anna, but everybody calls me Marigold cuz Uncle Jeroo started to, when I was a baby. I even remember, even though my nanny said it's 'mm-possible."

"You have a nanny?"

"Yes. She's Letty, but she's visitin' her sisters 'n' stuff now, way far away. She used to be my mommy's nanny when my mommy was a little girl. Now she's mine. She's got a boyfriend! He's *old,*" the girl announced proudly, with a glance at her uncle.

"I see." The Cal Blake family sounded

interesting, a little different from the usual ranch family. "How old are you now, Marigold?"

"I'm four-goin'-on-five."

"Do you know when your birthday is?"

"Uh-huh. It's March."

So the child had turned four fairly recently. Hardly "goin'-on-five." Still, she fit into Cilla's program for older children. Cilla didn't accept children who weren't three yet. She would have eight three-year-olds and six four- and five-year-olds. It was enough for one teacher, even if she divided the children for two half-day sessions.

Cilla produced a covered elastic from her dress pocket and cinched the girl's hair into a bouncy blond ponytail. "There! All done."

She was shocked to see the expression on Jeremiah's face as she glanced up. He'd been watching them intently and had a curious look on his handsome features. Soft. Very appealing.

Cilla stood hastily. "The first day of school is next Tuesday, just for an hour in the morning. Will you be here, Marigold?" After the girl's initial reluctance, she wasn't sure. Nor did it sound as though the father was in favor.

"Yup." The girl took her uncle's hand again

and swung it. "I'm big, Uncle Jeroo. I'm telling Dad that. I'm going to *school.*"

"You too big to ride on my back?" he teased.

"No way!" she cried, and he swung her up onto his shoulder again, the way they'd arrived.

Cilla saw them to the door and waved as they got into a pickup and began to reverse from the curb. Jeremiah honked his horn and she spotted the girl waving madly from her place in the passenger seat.

Cilla went into the classroom. The spurt of energy she'd felt when she'd begun painting early that morning had faded. Meeting Jeremiah, liking the way he smiled at her, a smile she'd received many times from men—brought back a lot of memories. Many of them pleasant.

She sighed. She'd always had a lively social life and once had thought she was actually in love. With one of her fellow students in Lucerne. Sebastian. A long-haired, wild and crazy Welshman. She smiled, remembering. Sebastian—had he married? Had he moved to Australia as he'd wanted to?

But a relationship of any kind was strictly out of the question now. She didn't have the time for it. Not until she'd made a success of Blue Owl. The school was her absolute first priority. Her pride demanded it. She surveyed the room before flicking off the lights and wished that it held the same appeal as it had that morning. Cilla locked the door, then remembered the open window in her office. She went back in and shut the window firmly. Pencil crayons, indeed! On *her* budget, she couldn't afford to lose even a paper clip.

She locked up again and began walking toward the street that led to her new apartment, a small furnished place on the second floor of a big house.

The next year was to be firmly dedicated to establishing her school. That was her business and personal plan. She had plenty of obstacles in her way without the added complication of a man in her life—not least the fact that she barely had enough students to open her doors, certainly not enough to hire another teacher yet to reduce her workload.

What about marriage, though, and children? She'd always wanted children of her own someday. And a man. The right man. When? Well, she could only concentrate on one thing, one goal, at a time. Great-aunt Martina's money had been the sudden stroke of luck that allowed her to pursue this dream. Do it all on her own. Prove something to her family. To herself.

But meeting Jeremiah Blake today, noticing the way he regarded her—as a woman, an attractive woman—had reminded her of some of her other goals. The ones she'd put on hold. Since she'd moved to Glory five weeks ago, she'd noticed local men looking at her in a certain interested way. She was flattered, naturally. Even though she was in no position to return any of that interest.

But maybe it wasn't her at all. She heaved a sigh as she walked. Maybe the town of Glory was just short on single women.

JEREMIAH DROVE UP to the Grizzly Drive-in and ordered maple-walnut doubleheaders for himself and his niece. Marigold was thrilled. He'd never met a kid who didn't love going to this Glory landmark, an edifice fashioned in the shape of a huge bear's head, with Ma Perkins taking orders from the drive-through window set inside the snarling concrete teeth.

"Hello, Marigold, honey!" the gray-haired woman called through Jeremiah's open window.

"Hi!" the girl shouted, bouncing up and

down on the seat beside him. "Guess what? Guess what? I'm going to school!"

"Uh-huh. The new kiddie school in town?"

Jeremiah nodded. "Yeah. We had a look this afternoon. Marigold likes it."

"How about you?" the keen-eyed proprietress shot back.

"Kiddie school?" Jeremiah grinned. "No opinion."

"How about that teacher, though? Priscilla Prescott. She's somethin' else, I hear."

"Oh?" Jeremiah accepted the ice cream cones she handed across and passed one to his niece. "Says who?" It annoyed him that word was out on the new preschool teacher. But why wouldn't it be? She'd obviously been in town for a few weeks already.

"Oh, this one and that one," Ma said, grinning. "I'll never tell." She winked. "Don't tell me you never noticed."

Jeremiah shrugged and gave her some money.

"Come on, Jeremiah Blake!" Ma Perkins scoffed, ringing it up in the old-fashioned cash register with a resounding clang. "You can't tell me a young fellow like yourself doesn't know about a pretty new miss in town!"

Jeremiah made no reply. He winked and held up his cone. "See ya around, Ma. Don't take any wooden nickels, huh?"

"I won't," she returned with a wave. "Oh, go on with you now—get outta here, Jem!"

Jeremiah drove to the edge of the parking lot, supervised as Marigold got back into her seat belt, then handed the girl her cone again. She settled happily beside him, licking the ice cream energetically. He was glad the seats in his pickup were vinyl. He held his cone in his left hand and drove with his right.

Ma Perkins was right: *Miss* Priscilla Prescott was a fine-looking woman. And not married, either, just as he'd suspected—which was a piece of considerable luck. For him and all the other single guys in Glory. When he'd heard her name from his sister-in-law, he'd just naturally presumed she was some dried-up prune of a spinster, about a hundred years old, with a name like Priscilla.

Cilla.

Now *she* was a whole 'nother story. Blond hair, brown eyes, legs that seemed to go on forever…

And it just happened that he wasn't dating anyone at the present time. Now, wasn't *that* an amazing coincidence? In fact, he hadn't been in a relationship for more than six months, since February, the last time he'd taken Dana Willetts to Banff to ski. That pretty much spelled the end of a relationship that had never been all that promising to start with.

Since Dana—and he hadn't felt the slightest emotion beyond faint relief when she'd phoned him and told him it was over, she was seeing someone else—he hadn't bothered. He was getting tired of never having a relationship that lasted beyond four or five months. He was nearly thirty-three and had a responsible position in life, and maybe it was time he settled down and got married. Lots of people, including his brother and sister-in-law, told him he should. Except how was that going to happen when he never managed to meet the right woman?

Not that he didn't give every woman he met a fighting chance. In fact, right now he was seriously thinking of giving Miss Priscilla Prescott an opportunity to get to know him.

Looked like she'd bitten off a little more than she could chew trying to set up that preschool of hers in the old Buffalo Head Hardware building. The location was fine, facing the river, with a park across the street and a playground. It was just that the building should've been torn down years ago. It had high ceilings, which would make it difficult if not impossible to heat in the winter, the squeaky old floors sloped this way and that, and the siding on the outside, weathered tongue-and-groove, could stand a coat of paint.

Jeremiah finished his cone and glanced at his niece. Marigold was ice cream from her nose to her tummy button. Her ma would have a fit if she could see her now. Jeremiah didn't mind; he'd just hose off the kid when they got back to the ranch. He'd done it before.

Jeremiah prided himself on his attitude toward life. He'd never met a problem he couldn't solve—with the exception, currently, of this woman thing. But that, he was pretty sure, was just temporary. Generally, he could work at a problem and figure it out. Whether it had to do with ranching or anything else.

He thought of the cartons stacked up in the new preschool, the smell of fresh paint in the air. He recalled the flustered look on Cilla Prescott's face when she'd opened the door. She was doing her best to appear cool and collected, when he'd obviously caught her in the middle of painting her office.

She was a one-woman show, no matter how much she tried to pretend otherwise. She was trying to do everything herself. Jeremiah respected that. Maybe she didn't have the spare cash to hire a helper or two. She definitely seemed to have way too much to do before school opened next week. He'd see if he could give her some help.

After all, what were neighbors for? And living only ten miles out of town like he did, they *were* practically neighbors...weren't they?

CHAPTER TWO

CILLA HAD PLANNED to be back at the school by eight o'clock the next morning, but she woke late and then decided to have a lazy breakfast. She hadn't cut herself much slack in the hectic schedule she'd set to get her school off the ground. She could use the break, she decided.

She'd rented a two-bedroom apartment on the top floor of her landlady's house. Mrs. Vandenbroek, an elderly Dutch widow, hesitated to rent to her at first, saying she'd lost her last few tenants to marriage and didn't want to lose another one. Never mind, Cilla had told her, she had no plans to get married, at least not for a few more years.

"Oh, *ja,*" Mrs. Vandenbroek said with resignation in her voice. "That's what they all say."

So Cilla had moved in, grateful at finding a furnished place on such short notice. Since then—the middle of July—she'd been busy supervising improvements to the old hardware building, ordering supplies, composing ads to solicit pupils, painting, traveling back and forth between the small town of Glory and Calgary, and doing what seemed like a million other things.

No wonder she'd slept in.

When she finally made her way to the school she got another surprise. There were half a dozen cowboys sitting on the grass outside the school, apparently waiting for her arrival.

"Miss Prescott?" One of the older men climbed to his feet and doffed his hat. He wore scuffed boots and new jeans and a flannel shirt.

"Yes?"

"We're ready to give you a hand this morning, ma'am."

"A hand?" Cilla looked from his sunburned face to the deeply tanned and lined faces of the others, all turned toward her. One chewed a stem of grass philosophically and another had an unlit cigarette hanging from his lower lip. They regarded her intently.

"Yes, ma'am. The boss said you could use some help painting and moving stuff around."

"Your boss wouldn't happen to be Jeremiah Blake, would he?" The truth slowly dawned.

What an astonishing idea—he'd sent these men to help her!

"Yes, ma'am. The boss said your school could use a coat of paint on the outside, too. That what you want us to do, ma'am?" The cowboy twisted his sweat-stained broad-brimmed hat in his gnarled hands. He looked worried.

Her reception hadn't exactly been welcoming, she realized. She stepped forward, smiling, and held out her hand. "Well, am I glad to see you! Your boss is absolutely right, I definitely could use some help."

The cowboy shook her hand. His grip was like dry rusted iron. "Pete McGinty, ma'am, number-two cow boss on the Diamond 8. You're not to mention nothin' about payin' us, neither. The boss said this was a donation from the Diamond 8."

"Fine. Lovely. Excellent." Cilla smiled and shook each man's hand in turn—Henry, Tom with the grass stem, Wallace, Slim and Charlie with the unlit cigarette, in addition to Pete. "Well? Shall I give you all something to do?"

Cilla had a few words for Jeremiah Blake the next time she saw him and only two of them would be "thank you." She appreciated the help, no question, but she did think he could have asked her first. Before sending over a crew the way he had, and putting her on the spot. What if she'd gone to Calgary this morning? Or had hired a crew of her own?

But considering the sheer good luck of the offer of help coming when it did, Cilla didn't waste any time on thinking about what hadn't happened. She had too much to do. *Don't look a gift horse in the mouth, and all that,* she mused.

Jeremiah was right—the outside of the old place needed a lift. She sent Pete and Henry to the hardware store to bring back enough paint to give the building's exterior a coat. She specified that she wanted barn-red for the exterior and bright blue for the door and trim, and to charge it to her account. The blue would go with the name of her school—Blue Owl—a character from a favorite book when she was a child. Tom and Slim she put to work moving boxes from the main schoolroom to her office and the storeroom, so the room would be empty when the carpet-layers arrived later that morning. Cilla had only remembered after breakfast that the carpet was being delivered today, and she'd had no idea how she was going to clear the room in time for the carpet people to work on it.

Wallace volunteered to cut the grass out front, using the mower he'd stowed in the back of one of the pickups the men had driven. He finished that within the hour, and then Cilla asked him to build a cover for the sandbox she'd set up in the play area that had once been the hardware store's parking lot. She'd already had the small playground fenced. The equipment was scanty, just the sandbox and some climbing bars, but she hoped that the fund-raising she had planned for the fall would allow her to purchase more.

The carpet-layers arrived just before noon, and Cilla insisted on taking all the Diamond 8 cowboys out for lunch. They hemmed and hawed when she challenged them to pick a restaurant and said she'd pay. Finally, reluctantly making their decision, they ended up at the Glory Hotel, at the small restaurant on the main floor, facing the street.

It was a hot-beef-sandwich-and-apple-pie sort of place. Cilla was very aware of the interest from other diners when they trooped in together and she requested a table for seven. She was also aware that the men would have been more comfortable filing into the hotel tavern for a meal, but that they wouldn't dream of suggesting it.

While they waited for the waitress to prepare a table, Cilla continued arguing with Pete McGinty, who said his boss wasn't going to be happy when he heard she'd bought them lunch. No sir, lunch was supposed to be on him, and "that's an order."

"Guess what, Pete?" she asked, her cheeks warm. "I don't care *what* your boss says—it's my treat. Jeremiah Blake can take his order and jump in the lake, as far as I'm concerned. You're not working for him today, you're working for *me,* right?"

Henry guffawed and Wallace smiled and looked sideways at his companions.

"I'll be sure and tell him, ma'am," Pete said with a slow smile and a twinkle in his sharp blue eyes. "Shall I tell him to take off his boots before he jumps?"

The men guffawed again.

"You can tell him that's up to him," she replied tartly, to another round of amusement.

Cilla got the feeling that her manner had impressed them. She also got the distinct feeling that not too many of them would have gone against the boss's orders on their own. Maybe Henry, who seemed to refer to Jeremiah more as a son or a close relative than an employer.

Turned out they'd obeyed orders, after all. Following a meal of the soup du jour—cream of chicken—and steaks and fries all round, except for Cilla who had a club sandwich and a salad, Pete excused himself, mumbling that he had to see a man about a dog. Cilla assumed he meant he was looking for the men's room.

But when she asked for the check, the waitress told her it had already been taken care of.

"Pete?" she asked archly. "Know anything about this?"

Pete cleared his throat, his face brick-red under his sunburn. "Aw, Miss Cilla, you don't want us gettin' fired, do you?" Although they'd enjoyed the fun they'd had at the expense of their boss, they obviously had no intention of letting her pay. Period. As ordered.

Pete stood, holding his hat carefully at his side. "Come on, boys. Let's see if we can finish the job this afternoon or we'll be back here arguing with the schoolteacher tomorrow. And I got a feeling she might just get the best of us if we give her another chance."

Cilla decided to accept gracefully. None of these men were used to taking directions from a woman. Probably none of them had let a member of the fair sex pay for her own meal in their entire lives. It was the western way with a certain kind of man.

The steamroller kind. Like Jeremiah Blake.

That afternoon, Wallace helped Pete and Henry paint, and by the time five o'clock rolled around, the outside of the building was finished, with only the trim remaining. Cilla was thrilled at the progress. While the three cowboys painted, the others had been busy inside, arranging the furniture on the newly laid carpet. They set up bookshelves for her and installed coat hooks in the little reception area where the children would keep their outdoor clothes and boots and knapsacks. One of them fixed the dripping faucet in the boys' washroom—Cilla had had to have a second washroom installed to meet regulations—and another picked up a few large plants she'd bought earlier at the florist's and hauled them into the classroom for her.

When the men had gone, Cilla made herself a cup of tea and sat quietly at the big windows looking onto the street and, across the street, the river. She could hear the shouts of children somewhere in the distance, and a bird calling. She'd already seen some geese heading south. A beautiful sight but sad, as it always meant summer was nearly over.

She gazed slowly around the room. It was completely changed from the day before, when it had been clogged with boxes while she painted the storeroom and her office. Now, the storeroom was fitted with adjustable shelves and the supply boxes had been transferred to them. Her office was almost ready. She had a large tree-trained hibiscus in there, which would do very well with the northwest light in her office. She still needed curtains, but she'd order them or make them up herself. It wouldn't be more than a day's work. She could borrow her landlady's sewing machine.

Cilla looked critically at the floor in the schoolroom. The new carpet hid a lot of sins. She couldn't even tell where the floor sloped anymore. And the huge elephant foot plant in one corner, the weeping fig by the door and the pots of ivy and spider plants she'd hung on the walls and, with Henry's help, from the ceiling, gave the whole room a fresh new look. Everything was falling into place. Finally.

If she could get hold of a secondhand refrigerator and stove so she could set up a kitchen nook near the back door sink, she'd be well prepared. Part of the curriculum she'd planned for the children was to make simple meals, mainly soups and muffins and salads that they could help with and could invite their parents to share.

She drained her cup, thinking wryly that she'd better not mention it to Marigold's uncle, or he'd have kitchen planners in the next day.

Jeremiah Blake. She wasn't sure how to take him. He was certainly…interesting.

She shook her head at the way her mind had wandered and decided to call it a day. When she got back to her apartment, the phone was ringing. Cilla hurried to answer, certain it would be one of her sisters calling to check on her progress.

"Cilla?"

It was a man with a very deep voice.

"Speaking," she replied coolly. *Jeremiah Blake.*

"Jeremiah here. Uh, how did it go today? With the boys?"

"You mean with the six men who were waiting for me when I got to the school this morning?"

He laughed. “Yeah. That’s who I meant. Everything work out okay?”

“Well—” Cilla hesitated. She didn’t want to appear ungrateful….

“Anything wrong?” His swift question was concerned.

“Oh, no. Not at all. It was—well, it was very good of you to send them over,” she said, wishing she didn’t sound so formal. “I appreciate it very, very much.”

“But?”

“But what?”

“I can hear a *but* in there somewhere. You might as well spit it out.”

“Well, I have to say I was surprised. And I must also say that I wish you’d mentioned it to me. Ahead of time.”

“Would you have agreed?”

“Probably not—”

“Well, there you go. Why mention it, then?”

Cilla didn’t answer. He had a point. But she wasn’t used to dealing with people this way.

“Listen, I’ve got a proposition for you,” he said.

“You do?”

“Yeah. Let me take you to dinner tonight. Somewhere quiet. Casual. You must be tired after bossing those cowboys around all day. We can talk and—"

"Jeremiah," she interrupted, almost putting her free hand over her other ear to block his voice out. What a man!

"Yes?"

"I *am* tired. I am very, very tired. And the last thing I want is to go out—"

"With me?"

"With anyone," she said firmly. That was being polite, at least. After all, it wasn't *him,* it was any man.

"We could order in. I could pick up some Chinese food, maybe a pizza—"

"Thank you for asking, but the answer is no." She needed to be completely clear with this man. "I appreciate what you've done for me, I appreciate your sending over the men to help me today, but I am not interested in having any kind of relationship with you. I am not interested in dating you. I am not interested in dating anyone."

"Ever?"

"No, not ever. But for now. While I get established in Glory and get my school running. I don't have time for anything else."

She heard a long, low whistle over the phone. "That's putting it directly."

"That's what I feel I have to be with you—direct," she said, smiling a little. He didn't sound the least bit put off. "You are a very persistent man."

"Well, okay. I can take no for an answer."

"Can you?" She allowed herself to smile. After all, he couldn't see her smiling.

"Yes, for today. But I'll be asking again. Just so you know, Miss Cilla."

"And I'll be saying *no* again, Mr. Blake. Just so *you* know."

"Nothing personal, though, right?"

"Right. Nothing personal."

With a laugh, he said goodbye and hung up. Cilla looked at the black receiver in her hand for a few seconds, then hung up, too, shaking her head. She went into her small bathroom to run a bath. That was what she needed, a long, relaxing soak. Some music, maybe flute, a few strings.

She turned on her stereo in the living room, then went into the plain utilitarian kitchen with the dining nook between stove, sink and living room—she'd had no time to even personalize her place yet—and opened the fridge. Not much there. She checked the freezer compartment and pulled out a frozen pasta dinner and set it on the counter to defrost. She'd zap it when she got out of the tub. That would be her dinner. By herself.

But she locked the apartment doors before she got in the tub, even though she knew Mrs. Vandenbroek was home downstairs. And she locked the bathroom door, even though she was the only one in the apartment.

Somehow she could see Jeremiah Blake bursting into her kitchen laden with a bag of burgers. She wasn't entirely convinced he knew what *no* meant. At least not as it applied to him.

NOW, WHY HAD HE done that? He'd only called to find out how today had gone. He hadn't actually thought of asking her for dinner until he had her on the line. Hadn't planned to. It was too soon to be asking her out, way too soon.

Man, she was tough! Jeremiah hung up the phone in amazement. He wasn't used to a woman refusing his invitations. All the same, he felt good that she'd turned him down the way she had. It meant she was worth pursuing. Actually, come to think of it, he was actually pleased. She'd said it wasn't him—she'd said she had no interest in dating *any-*

one. If she turned him down, she'd turn down any guy who asked.

That gave him a chance to change her mind. He just needed some time. And he needed to get in there and persuade her before some other hot-to-trot single guy did.

Then he moved from the phone and muttered softly under his breath. What was he doing even entertaining a notion like that? Just because there was a new woman in town didn't mean he had to waste all day thinking about her. He had a ranch to manage. A meeting with his employers in Calgary next week, the business partners who owned the Diamond 8 and paid him to run it. Marigold's parents were due back home after supper this evening. He had to take the sprout back to Cal's place, along with Henry J. Hilton, his brother's foreman, whom Jeremiah had "borrowed" for the crew he'd assembled to help Cilla. He'd made sure he sent over only the elderly and the married. No way was he giving any single guys extra chances.

Henry was not only elderly, he was in love already. He'd been courting Letty Esperanza, the sprout's Filipina nanny, since she'd arrived with his brother's wife, way back before Marigold was born. Jeremiah had never seen a man so besotted. Jeremiah hoped Letty would soften one day and return Henry's affection. He and his brother had grown up with Henry and the old saddle bum had always been more like a favorite uncle than a hired hand.

Jeremiah reminded himself that he had other things on the go, too. Serious things. Stock to ship. Feed to buy. Mooning over the new woman in town, like some teenage kid, was the last thing he should be doing.

"YOU KNOW THE TROUBLE with you, Jeremiah?" His sister-in-law was winding a ball of wool while her daughter stood holding the skein of yarn patiently.

Jeremiah wondered how long that would last. "What, Nina?" He made a face at his nephew, not quite six months. William, or Sweet William, as his mother called him. The baby giggled. This kid, at least, appreciated his talents. He made another face.

"You're too hot and cold with women. You rush them off their feet, then when you run into any kind of complication, you cool off, and next thing you know they're gone."

"So?" Jeremiah looked up. "I thought women liked to be rushed off their feet."

"Not if you don't really mean it."

"But I do always mean it. At first," he added, grinning.

"That's it. You mean it at first, and that might be fine when you're a kid, but you're not a kid anymore." She gave him a severe look and Marigold dropped one side of the skein. Nina waited for her daughter to pick it up again. "You should settle down, you know. Think about marriage. At your age, women expect you to be serious, not just out for a good time like some teenager."

"Well, that's true." Jeremiah got up and ran one hand through his hair. Time for a haircut, he noted absently. He was tired of the subject of women. Better get a haircut before the big meeting in Calgary.

"Where's McCallum?" His brother had been in when he brought Marigold and Henry back, but he'd gone out a few minutes after they arrived.

"Where do you think? He's checking his mare. Cal figures Willow's ready to deliver any day, although the vet says not for at least another week." Nina sounded resigned. Jeremiah knew she'd been happy to get her husband away from horses and ranch life for even a short time. They'd gone out to British Columbia to visit her parents, who lived in Vancouver. Marigold had said she wanted to stay with her uncle Jeroo and her uncle Jeroo was always happy to oblige.

Uncle Jeroo. He smiled. The sprout had been calling him that since she'd learned to talk. Jeremiah had never realized how much fun kids could be until he'd had a niece and nephew of his own.

"Maybe I'll stop by the barn and see him on my way out."

"You're going already?" Nina glanced up, concerned. Jeremiah smiled; his brother had had a major stroke of luck the day Nina came into his life. Not many men got that lucky.

"I thought you'd stay for a cup of tea and a piece of cake when Cal comes in."

"No, I've got to be heading home. Need my beauty sleep—the kid plumb wore me out this week," he teased, tousling his niece's head when she grinned up at him. She was careful not to drop the yarn, he noted. Real mother-and-daughter picture they made.

He thought of Cilla Prescott combing out Marigold's hair and talking softly to her. It seemed he had women and kids, motherhood and babies, on his mind these days.

"If you want, I can take Marigold to school next week." He looked at his sister-in-law.

"I'll take her," Nina said firmly. "Besides, haven't you got a meeting on Tuesday? I want to talk to the teacher about helping out with the fund-raising she's got planned for the fall. That charity auction sounds exciting. I saw something in *The Plain Dealer* about it, a combined fund-raiser for the school and Jen Beaton's new dance academy. She sounds like a real go-getter, this Prescott woman. A real asset to the community."

Jeremiah settled his hat on his head. "She's that, all right. Well, see you later."

He opened the door and stepped outside, stopping when he heard Nina call his name. He poked his head back in. "Uh-huh?"

"She wouldn't happen to be young and pretty, would she?"

"Oh, yeah. She's that all right, too. Like you said, an asset." He laughed as he closed the door behind him.

Single. Pretty. Full of spark and spunk. And not interested in a relationship, not with him or with any man. What a waste.

He couldn't quite get away from the idea that he was just the guy to change her mind about that...

Charity auction, huh? They'd need donations, wouldn't they? They'd need stuff to sell so they could raise the money they wanted.

Goods. Services.

He could offer a day's work—to the right buyer. Jeremiah smiled and lowered the visor on his pickup window as he turned northwest toward the Diamond 8. The sun spilled like molten gold over the Rockies, ready to set.

Now *there* was an idea worth thinking about. He'd see if he couldn't donate himself.

CHAPTER THREE

"NOW THAT WE'VE DEALT with the figures on this year's returns, I'd like to bring up another matter, Jem." Bat Middleton, the eldest of the six partners who owned the Diamond 8, one of the largest spreads in the High River-Glory-Pincher Creek area, looked around the polished walnut table in the center of a Palliser Hotel meeting room. Warm September sunshine streamed through the multipaned windows and glinted on the silver coffee service that had been brought in a few minutes earlier by the hotel staff.

"You mean about the manager's place?" Earl Whitford asked. He was a Calgary lawyer, a fairly new partner who'd recently bought out one of the original owners, Sven Gunnarsen. He looked up from stirring his coffee.

Jeremiah didn't say anything although he was surprised there was another item to be discussed this afternoon. He figured they'd pretty well covered everything in the past four hours. It had been a lengthy meeting already, starting with a leisurely lunch served in the conference room. He was looking forward to knocking off soon and having a shower and shave, then making some phone calls and maybe checking out the Calgary nightlife. Take his mind off the young, single, pretty Cilla Prescott.

"What about the manager's house, exactly, Bat?" Jeremiah asked, leaning forward. What Earl had referred to as the manager's place had been a burned-out shell of a building when Jeremiah took over the ranch five years before. The old house—or what remained of it—had been bulldozed and now wild roses grew abundantly on the knoll where it had sat. Jeremiah lived in a small building that was once the harness maker's combination workshop and dwelling, back in the days when the ranch had relied solely on horses. The arrangement suited him just fine. He didn't mind the smell of neat's-foot oil and sawdust that had seeped into the timbers. Matter of fact, he liked it.

"It's time we did something about replacing that house, Jem. I know you might not think it's necessary now, but if you were to get married, if you brought a woman out to the Diamond 8 one of these days—"

"Hey, Bat. Let's worry about that when we have to," Jeremiah said with a laugh. He leaned back in his chair.

"No, seriously." The old man's steely blue eyes met his. "The Diamond 8 ought to have a proper ranch manager's house, just like all the other big ranches. We could draw up some plans—with your input, of course, Jem—and we could put it out to bids and get started this fall. Before it snows. What do you think, boys?" He glanced around the long table. There were nods and a low rumble of assent.

Jeremiah shrugged. "Well, if you insist. I can't see that it has much priority, though. I'd rather see that money go into a new silo or a tractor or maybe a few new bulls—"

"What about it, Blake? You got any plans in that direction?" It was Bill Pickett, a rancher himself down in the Strachan area. "Marriage, I mean. You're not getting any younger, y'know. None of us are." A ripple of well-fed, contented mirth spread around the table.

"No plans, Bill. But you have a point. After all—" he shrugged "—time could come you'd want someone else to take over. Maybe you'd look for a manager who's already equipped with a wife...."

"Now, don't go gettin' your shorts in a knot, son," Bat Middleton interrupted. "You know we're pleased with the way you're runnin' the Diamond 8. But it's our job to look ahead a little. Plan. I say we get busy on rebuilding the manager's house—all in favor?"

There was a chorus of assent. The business meeting was over.

The men stood around talking for a while, and a few of them wandered off. Some were staying for dinner in the hotel. One man, a financial specialist from Winnipeg, was flying back that night. Jeremiah had checked in for the evening, although he could easily have driven home. He felt restless, had felt that way for the past week...ever since he met Cilla Prescott. A night on the town could be the change he was looking for.

He decided to call a woman he'd dated more than a year ago. She wasn't home. Then he phoned Dana's cousin, Tracy Billings, who he was pretty sure had had her eye on him the last time they'd met at a wedding he and Dana had gone to. She was happy to hear from him, but she had plans. He called his buddy, Austin Shot-on-both-sides, a member of the Blood Tribe he'd once rodeoed with who was now working for a farm implement distributor. Austin had tickets to the Calgary Stampeders–B.C. Lions game that evening and didn't think he could get another one for Jeremiah. Besides, he had a girl.

Jeremiah showered and shaved and went to Bailey's, a well-known downtown rib and steak house for dinner. By himself. It was filled with men. In a lot of ways, Calgary was a man's town—certainly as it pertained to his interests and concerns, which were mainly ranching, agricultural equipment, sports and banks. The city wasn't known as Cowtown for nothing.

Still restless, he decided to wander over to another place on the Macleod Trail. This one blazed with neon and hummed with music and laughter. The parking lot was crammed full of pickups and utility vehicles. Inside, it was packed and noisy and a band was playing a popular swing tune over the clink of glasses and the buzz of conversation. Real cowboys and the drugstore variety swung their partners on the small dance floor. The stand-up bar was crowded. Jeremiah edged into a gap between two truck drivers and ordered a drink. The truckers were talking brake linings, a subject he knew nothing about, so Jeremiah took his drink over to a table and sat down with a man he recognized from High River. A tool pusher for one of the oil and gas exploration companies working in that area.

After the man went home to his family, Jeremiah stayed for another hour, but when no one came in that he knew or caught his attention, he gave up and left. Back in the parking lot, he discovered his truck was out of gas. Some prankster had siphoned it dry while he was inside. That was the last straw. Jeremiah yelled and slammed the steering wheel with both hands, then yelled again as pain shot up his wrists. The nearest gas station wasn't more than two blocks away, on the strip, but he wasn't going to walk over there and drag back a can of gas.

Forget it. Jeremiah locked his truck and headed for the nearest city bus stop on the east side of the Macleod Trail, heading north. He dug in his jeans pocket for change. He was looking for new experiences, wasn't he?

He'd take the bus back to his hotel. He'd never done *that* before.

The truck could wait. He'd get a taxi and pick it up tomorrow on his way home.

CILLA THOUGHT Marigold's mother was going to be a treasure. The very first day of school, when the children only stayed an hour to familiarize themselves with the classroom, Nina Blake offered to chair the auction committee. Cilla had assumed she'd have to do some phoning for volunteers and had been dreading it.

"I know what it's like being a newcomer," Nina confided in her when she picked up her daughter. "I was one myself not so many years ago. Between Cal and me, we can round up a lot of donations from local merchants. Services, too. Even some stuff from the ranchers and farmers, I'm sure."

"Like what?" Cilla had asked, curious as to what the ranchers could donate.

"Oh, hay. Feed grain. Maybe a foal or a calf." Nina smiled. "This is a ranch and farm town, so there's always a market for that sort of thing. I'll talk to Jen Beaton and see what she's got in mind. And I know her mother will help out—have you met Donna yet?"

Cilla shook her head. Jennifer Beaton was the young dance teacher who'd formed the Glory Academy of Dance and Theatre Arts the previous spring. Cilla didn't think she looked a day over sixteen, although she was apparently at least twenty. Jennifer's youth and enthusiasm made Cilla feel positively ancient at twenty-six. She'd seen a poster promoting the dance academy at the library and thought it might be a good idea to organize some fund-raising together. Jennifer had been pleased at her suggestion of a charity auction.

"Oh, you'll love Donna. Everybody does. Now come on, honey," Nina said to her daughter, "let's go home and tell Daddy all about your first day at preschool. Hurry—the baby's sleeping in the car." Nina Blake, impossibly fresh and beautiful in a cool green matching cotton skirt and top, herded her small daughter along the street to where they'd parked.

Marigold was the last to go. Cilla went back into the empty classroom and breathed a sigh of relief. Mostly, she felt like kicking off her shoes and doing a little jig, right there in the middle of the room, with only Hammy the hamster looking on. Hammy had been a donation from one of the children that day. Luckily, Cilla had planned for a class pet of some kind and—also luckily—a show of hands had revealed that no one was allergic to hamsters.

And she had fifteen paying students! At

the last minute, a thin, pale boy had been produced by a caregiver of some sort, a distant cousin, she'd said. The cousin had said her charge, Rory Goodland, was four and would like to come to the school. She said it had been his idea…so, here they were. The woman had given Cilla a check for four months' tuition, until Christmas.

Cilla had thought it was an odd way of doing things—not even waiting to see if the boy fit in at school—but she'd been so glad to get another student she hadn't questioned it much.

She hadn't yet had a chance to look over the paperwork the woman had filled out before leaving Rory for the short orientation period. The boy seemed very shy, and had stuck to her like a burr the whole time, eyeing the other children suspiciously. They'd ignored him, generally, although Marigold had spoken to him a few times and had graciously offered to share her plasticine with him. He'd shaken his head, reluctant, it seemed, to leave Cilla's side.

The boy hadn't said a spontaneous word that she could remember. He'd repeated his name for the other children and had nodded solemnly when she'd asked if he liked going to school. At her next question—whether he had any brothers or sisters—he'd stared at her for a few seconds, green eyes huge, and then shaken his head slowly.

Odd, she thought again, standing stock-still, her shoes off and her toes digging into the carpet. It was almost as though he wasn't sure, that he'd had to think about whether or not he had siblings.

She walked into her office and glanced at the registration form the woman had filled out. It was carelessly done, in a pen that had leaked ink and left blotches. No, she saw, Rory Goodland didn't have any brothers or sisters.

She wished she knew someone in the community well enough to talk to about the children, just in a general way. She'd like to know a little more about them than the dry facts presented on a registration form. Well, that would have to wait. She'd get to know them all eventually.

Her school was going to be a success. She could hardly wait to tell her parents. She knew they wanted the best for her, even if they found it hard to believe that teaching in her own preschool in a little hick town was what *she* wanted. Luckily Jeanne was getting married soon. That kept her mother busy, anyway.

The next day, Marigold's uncle arrived to pick up his niece from school. Cilla was busy with the other children and only nodded to him briefly. He looked just about as handsome and impressive as she'd remembered from the week before. There was no opportunity for conversation, which was just as well.

The following day, Jeremiah again appeared at the stroke of 3:15. Was he making a habit of this? Cilla had divided the school day into two sections and had the three-year-olds in the morning and the fours and fives—there were only two fives—in the afternoon.

This time he hung around outside with the mothers and the children until nearly everyone had gone. Then he approached her in the doorway, just as she shook little Rory's hand and said goodbye. The welcoming and departing handshakes and the eye contact were part of the Montessori way of establishing a relationship of trust and quiet respect with each individual child. Most of the children still found it funny to shake hands with an adult and giggled at the ceremony. Not little Rory Goodland. He was as solemn then as he was throughout the day. Hard to believe that—as his caregiver had stated—it had been his idea to come to preschool.

"Afternoon, Miss Cilla," Jeremiah said, stepping up and doffing his hat in the semi-theatrical way she remembered. "How are you this fine September afternoon?"

"Very well, thank you, sir." Two could play at this game. "And you?"

"Oh, could be better," he drawled giving her a cheeky look. "Could be better." He turned to gaze down the sidewalk, in the direction Rory and his cousin had taken. They'd nearly reached the end of the block already. "That the Goodland tyke?"

"Yes. If you mean Rory Goodland, that is." Cilla frowned. "You know him?"

"Know the family," Jeremiah replied, turning to face her again. He didn't offer any more, and although Cilla was dying to ask him about the child, she knew it wasn't appropriate.

"So, er, did you have something you wanted to see me about, Mr.—"

"Jeremiah," he inserted.

"—Jeremiah," she finished weakly. There was something so intimate about using this man's first name.

"That's better." He drew himself up to his

full height and looked down at her seriously. "I'm here to deliver an important message."

"A message?" She could barely restrain an answering smile. He was such a goof! But what a handsome goof. "From whom?"

"Whom? Er, from my sister-in-law. Nina Blake. Marigold's mother. My brother, Cal's, wife."

"Uh-huh."

"Well, as you know, Miss Cilla, my sister-in-law is helping out with that fund-raiser you'd planned, you and Jen Beaton. Nina says to tell you she's got everything under control and a date picked out for the auction."

"Great!" Now Cilla really couldn't restrain her smile. Having someone organize the auction for her was a godsend. And to find that Marigold's mother had worked so fast at organizing it was even better news.

"She asked me to tell you she'll be calling this evening to go over some details. Apparently she's rounded up a committee of volunteers to scare up donations, as well as getting plenty of stuff herself."

"Wonderful! Please thank her for me. Or I will myself, when I speak to her this evening." Curiosity got the better of her. "Did she—well, did she mention what kind of items she'd managed to have donated?"

"Nope. But I do know one item that'll be going for a good price."

"Oh? What's that?" Cilla interrupted breathlessly. A weekend in a fancy hotel? A season's pass to the local ski hill? A catered dinner for two in the winner's own home? A gift certificate from an airline?

"Me, ma'am," he said with a grin, replacing his hat. He cocked his two thumbs in his belt buckle and winked at her. "Jeremiah P. Blake. I figured this was such a worthwhile cause that the Diamond 8 ought to make a substantial contribution. So I'll be going on the block myself, along with a few other local cowboys."

"You're *what?*" Cilla was so surprised she stepped back a pace.

"Donating myself," Jeremiah repeated. "My services, so to speak." He quickly added, "As an escort, a day laborer, fence builder, whatever. Nina hasn't quite figured that out yet."

"You mean—your sister-in-law approves?" Cilla didn't know what to think.

"Oh, sure she does. She's all for it," he finished. He seemed quite pleased with himself.

"I don't mean to sound arrogant, but she figures she'll get some pretty brisk bidding on me."

"I can imagine," Cilla said dryly. The man had a huge opinion of himself, no question. "Well, thank you for letting me know."

He nodded. "Just thought I'd tell you ahead of time so you could take a look in your piggy bank, maybe count up your nickels and dimes…."

"Forget it!"

Jeremiah pretended to duck. Laughing, he looked around the small grassy front yard. "Okay, where's that bean sprout?" Marigold had climbed the big Norway maple at the corner of the lot. Cilla could see that the girl had already taken the knees out of her nice white tights. "Marigold! Come on down. Uncle Jeroo's gonna take you to the Grizzly place—"

"That's bribery!" Cilla gasped.

"Incentive." He shot her an amused look. "She comes down when I say, I take her for ice cream. Incentive. Modern management technique, you should know that."

Cilla had to laugh. Marigold hastily scrambled down the tree and marched over to her uncle. "Ready, Uncle Jeroo!"

"See?" He winked at Cilla. "Get in the

truck, honey. I have to say something to your teacher."

"You can say it in front of me. I won't tell," the girl said, hands on small hips.

"Nope. This is grown-up stuff. Scram!" She raced off to Jeremiah's pickup, parked on the street.

"I can't imagine what more you could have to say to me," Cilla began cautiously.

"Just this." He leaned against the door frame, so that he was very close. She controlled the impulse she had to step back again. She wasn't going to show him, not by so much as an inch, that he had her off balance. "You ready to change your mind about going out with me?" he murmured.

"Not yet." She might have known—

"Any idea when?"

"Maybe never."

"Never say never, Cilla." He was completely unflappable, just kept that easy grin on his handsome face. "I'm a persistent kind of guy."

"I can see that."

"I just want to make sure you know my intentions haven't changed—before some other guy gets in ahead of me."

"I guess you'll just have to trust me on that,

Jeremiah," she said softly, hoping her eyes weren't dancing with the merriment she felt inside. "I'm a big girl. I can make my own decisions. But I can't promise anything, if that's what you mean."

"Oh, no promises. Just wanted you to know what I have in mind. Eventually."

"I can't promise that some other man might not make a more attractive offer," she said, as seriously as she could manage. "That I might not find another man more appealing."

He winked. "That's the least of my worries." With that parting comment, he turned and strolled toward his truck, stopping to wave briefly as he exited the gate and carefully closed it behind him.

What a man! What an ego! she thought as she went back inside the school. What—what self-confidence!

Never say never. Indeed.

CHAPTER FOUR

THE MORNING of the auction dawned clear and cold. Even though it was only a few weeks into September, Mrs. Vandenbroek's back garden had already had a touch of frost. The petunias that had lined the neat borders of the concrete sidewalk had succumbed to an overnight frost a few days previously, and after briefly mourning them, Mrs. Vandenbroek cheerfully ripped them out and raked over the flower beds in preparation for spring. Some years, she'd confided, she had petunias blooming until the end of October.

Not this year.

Cilla had a huge list of things to do today. Her last meeting with the head of the fund-raising committee, Nina Blake, and her cosponsor, Jennifer Beaton, had been Wednesday evening. Cilla hoped that no crisis had sprung up between then and today—Saturday.

Nina had nixed the idea of holding the

auction at the Blue Owl premises. She didn't think the room would hold enough chairs, and she was determined to get a big turnout for the auction. Nor was there enough parking around the old hardware building. Jennifer's leased dance studio, above a row of shops on Main Street, was definitely too small. They decided to rent the Canadian Legion hall at an expense that had made Cilla hold her breath.

"Don't worry, Cilla, we'll get it all back and plenty more," Nina had said reassuringly. "Besides, I'm going to see if I can knock them down fifty dollars or so. After all, it's for a good cause."

A Good Cause. That's what the auction had come to be known as in the community, Cilla feared. The weekly newspaper, *The Plain Dealer,* had done a front-page story on the upcoming event last Saturday. The photographer had insisted on pictures of her and Jennifer, and there they were in grainy black-and-white, looking quite silly in the middle of the empty schoolroom.

At least, Cilla felt she looked silly; Jennifer, as usual, was graceful and lovely in her long skirt and silk top. Cilla thought she herself appeared positively frumpy in her striped shirtwaist, cardigan sweater and sensible shoes.

What was happening to her? She seemed more and more to have taken on the role of old-fashioned schoolmarm. If only she'd let down her hair for the photograph, looked a little more relaxed, casual. But there she was, hair tucked up into a neat roll at the back of her head, careful smile on her prim mouth. Where was the elegant, fun-loving dynamo she used to be? Well, she thought wryly, she was still a dynamo. She had to be, with all that needed doing.

She was a bit lonely, though. She missed her sisters. And her parents, difficult as that was to admit. And her friends in Calgary. She'd sent everyone invitations to the auction tonight and had her fingers crossed that maybe one of her sisters would come. Although she'd grown to like Nina and Jennifer very much and had gained several other new friends in the community, her self-imposed exile from any kind of social life was beginning to pall. If she hadn't been so busy with the initial days of school, getting to know the children, and the hectic meetings to finalize the auction, she would probably have stolen off to Calgary this weekend, stayed with her sister Mary and gone to a concert or a first-run movie. She might even have gone out with one of the several men she'd been seeing off and on since her arrival back in Alberta after her last teaching stint in Toronto. Not that any of them particularly interested her, beyond providing occasional companionship to a restaurant or a movie.

Jeremiah Blake had been uncharacteristically silent the past two weeks. She'd run into him at the deli once, with an attractive woman. Other than that she hadn't seen or heard anything of him, except what she'd gleaned from his sister-in-law regarding the crew he'd rounded up for the charity auction. Nina was pleased with his efforts. She said Jeremiah had convinced several cowboys at his ranch and at various others to contribute by auctioning themselves off for any variety of services, from squiring someone to the next community dance, to fixing a leaky roof or spading a garden. The cowboys were all bachelors, and Nina thought it would be an excellent fund-raiser. So did Jennifer. Cilla didn't dare express her doubts.

But maybe she was wrong. Maybe the single women of Glory would line up to place bids on some of these cowboys. Maybe boots and belt buckles and brawn had a rural appeal all their own. She had to admit that a fine-looking specimen of manhood—someone like Jeremiah Blake—suited jeans and hand-tooled boots and chambray shirts, but to her mind, it was an image that belonged on a tourist poster or a beef ad in a glossy magazine, not in some real woman's life. *I mean—a cowboy? In this day and age?* She wasn't a snob, but she just couldn't imagine what she'd have to say to a man like Jeremiah or any of the other ranch hands on offer. She knew nothing about cows or horses or—or hay. Things that, presumably, they found riveting. Her background was entirely different.

Backgrounds were important. Her parents, for instance, who had what she considered a very good marriage, came from backgrounds that were only superficially different. He was a born-and-bred Eastern Canadian from a wealthy family, who'd been brought up in relative ease and had gone to the best colleges and universities in preparation for a life in business or the law. Ilsa Prescott, her mother, although of European background, had also been raised in a privileged atmosphere. That meant they'd grown up with a great deal in common, including their love of art and music. Their manners, their enjoyment of the world of literature and fine foods—there were dozens of things her parents shared that had to do with a similarity of background and education.

One day, Cilla fully expected to marry a man of a background much the same as hers. It was just that, unlike her sisters, she intended to pursue her own dreams and goals before marriage. That was why establishing Blue Owl School had been so important to her. Independence from her family was important. Standing on her own two feet was important. Living up to what her great-aunt Martina would have expected of her was important.

But she was no romantic. She had no silly ideas about meeting Mr. Right out here on some ranch in the hills around Glory. Eventually, she expected she'd fit back into city life somewhere, perhaps establish another Montessori school wherever she decided to put down roots. Eventually, she would settle down to a life similar to her sisters', with the exception that she'd be pursuing a teaching career as well as marriage and motherhood.

Why was she here in Glory at all? Because Glory needed a preschool, and it needed the kind of preschool she and Aunt Martina believed in.

First on the list today was to make sure she had all the supplies for decorating the hall. Two parents, the Gordons, little Carla's mom and dad, would be showing up around noon to help her, and she hoped they'd be nimble enough to climb on the ladders to tack up the crepe paper streamers and balloons. She was a little giddy about heights.

On the way to the co-op to buy supplies, Cilla stopped at the deli to pick up a cup of take-out coffee. She glanced around quickly when she entered. No Jeremiah Blake this time. Just a couple of girls from the library on their breaks, and the postmistress, Myrna Schultz, sitting over a cup of coffee and the *Calgary Herald.*

A week ago, when she'd happened on him, Jeremiah had been standing at the counter waiting for his order. She'd been right beside him before she noticed him in the crush of lunchtime customers. She'd only had a few minutes; the morning class left at half past eleven and the afternoon class started at one o'clock and she had to clean up after the younger children's session and get ready for the older ones.

"Hello there, stranger!" he'd greeted her.

She was shocked to find that Jeremiah's

warm smile and dancing eyes had her toes tingling immediately.

"Hello," she'd responded, rather weakly, then returned her attention to the woman who'd taken her order. Cilla was clutching a number 17 in her hand. Jeremiah held number 16. "How are you?"

"Oh, very well, ma'am. Very well." He was teasing her. She'd glanced his way again, almost afraid to meet those knowing blue eyes. It was as though he saw inside her, as though he knew every thought that flickered madly through her mind.

"How's the sprout doin' in school?" he asked. It was a casual question. No more than friendly.

"She seems to like it very much," Cilla replied. It was true; Marigold was a special child. Forthright, sensitive, intelligent. "She's made some friends already."

"The Goodland boy?" Jeremiah asked, frowning.

Cilla met his gaze. "Yes," she said. "Little Rory. I'm pleased she's singled him out, because so many of the children seem to ignore him."

Jeremiah sighed. "He's quite a case, all right. Poor kid."

"I've been wanting to ask about him," Cilla began.

Jeremiah had shot her a hard look and looked around the deli, obviously checking to see if they were being overheard. "Long story," he muttered. Cilla wanted to ask more, but just then his order was called, with hers right after. She noticed that his tray held two of everything—soup crackers, sandwiches, drinks.

So…he was meeting someone.

"You got time to sit down?" Jeremiah had paused as he turned to take his tray to one of the tables alongside the window.

"No," Cilla had said regretfully. She was sorry to lose this chance to probe Jeremiah about the little Goodland boy. There was something about the quiet child that tore at her heart. "I'm heading straight back to the school."

As she walked toward the door with her take-out bag, she'd spotted an attractive, dark-haired woman sitting alone at a booth by the window. The woman smiled brilliantly, eyes only for the man clearing a path in front of Cilla. So…this was the lunch date?

"Cilla—" She knew Jeremiah wanted to introduce her, but all she wanted was to get out of there. The dark-haired woman looked hungry, all right, and it wasn't for the soup and sandwich she'd brought. "This is Rhonda Maclean, an old buddy of mine."

Not that old, Cilla thought. She'd stopped and smiled, determined to be polite to everyone she met in her new town. "How do you do, Rhonda? I'm Cilla Prescott, the new preschool teacher in town," she said quickly.

"Can you join us for a few minutes, Cilla?" he'd repeated, setting down his tray. His companion clearly wasn't as enthusiastic, but she smiled in a friendly enough fashion.

"Thanks, but I've got to run. See you later," she'd said with a small wave. Now, *why* had she said that? She had no intention of seeing him later. Although, of course, she would. It was a small town.

That had been last Tuesday.

Cilla opened the service door to the Legion hall and flipped on the light switches. The room, decorated in overstock colors of oil paint and fake pecan wood paneling, smelled like beer and old shoes. Yuck. She'd need to open all the doors and windows for the afternoon to air out the place.

She knew she'd definitely see Marigold's uncle this evening when he showed up to be auctioned off to some lucky bidder. Like some bull or prize ram.

Beginning with the nearest window, Cilla gritted her teeth and hammered at the jammed catch with her fist. She couldn't think now why she'd ever agreed to such a ridiculous idea—auctioning off local cowboys and their services! Just like the cattle they raised. It was stupid. *Stupid, stupid, stupid...*

But if it meant money for Blue Owl and for Jennifer's dance academy, that was all that counted. She had to keep track of her priorities. She'd been party to plenty of so-called stupid ideas before, many of which—like Blue Owl—had worked out just fine.

So far.

The parents who'd volunteered to help her were late. Cilla was at the top of a ladder beside the stage, cautiously tacking twisted crepe paper streamers to the wall and trying very hard not to look down when she heard the door open and a woman's voice. Footsteps approached.

"Sarah? Bill? That you?" she called out, clutching at the side of the stage and wishing her knees didn't wobble so badly. That had to be the Gordons, finally. If she wasn't careful, she'd fall off this stupid ladder and then what? "I'm glad you're here. I—"

"Nope. Wrong party," came a deep, familiar baritone.

"Jeremiah!" She grabbed at the framing at the side of the stage and clung to a wall light fixture with the other hand, her heart nearly popping out of her chest. The ladder shuddered from her sudden movement.

"Whoa. Hold on, Miss Cilla." Cilla felt the ladder steady as someone—obviously Jeremiah Blake—secured it.

"You *scared* me!" she managed, breathless, her brain still swimming with fear.

"Man," he said from below, "I just hate it when women say that."

She heard a giggle. Or if not a giggle, a wholly feminine sound. She risked a glance downward, holding firmly to the light fixture. A young woman, wearing a fashionable jacket-and-trouser suit, gazed up, a smooth leather portfolio tucked under her arm. Not Glory style. This—this *cowboy* seemed to be able to produce no end of lovely women to hang on his every word! Where did he find them all?

"Come on down, Cilla," Jeremiah called.

"I'd like you to meet Reta Janeway. She's building me a house."

A house?

Cilla transferred one hand tentatively from the light fixture to the top of the ladder. She hated to let go of the framing, but if she didn't, she wouldn't get back down. Her knees started to wobble again, which in turn made the ladder shake.

"Don't worry, I'm holding you steady," Jeremiah said. "You can climb down. I've got you."

He was directly below her. He ought to have a very good view of her jeans-clad legs and frayed running shoes. Not to mention the well-worn sweatshirt she'd pulled on at the last minute, fearing the hall would be chilly.

"Man, oh man. Are you a sight for sore eyes," Jeremiah said admiringly, still holding her elbow. She was so relieved to be down on the firm tile floor that she didn't care what he said or how he clung to her. "I always knew there was a good-looking woman in there, inside that schoolteacher uniform."

Cilla shot him a poisonous glance, then quickly brushed off her jeans. She mustered a smile and held out her hand to Jeremiah's companion.

"I'm Cilla Prescott. What's this about a house you're building for him?" she asked, determined to stay on a neutral subject.

The other woman smiled and briefly shook her hand. Cilla tried to ignore Jeremiah, who was still studying her. Like some filly...with prospects.

"Even a ponytail!" Jeremiah narrowed his eyes, and Cilla reached up and yanked the elastic from her hair, allowing it to fall around her shoulders. She shook it once, defiantly, to settle it, then sneaked a quick look at Jeremiah. He laughed.

"I'm helping Jeremiah figure out some house plans for the ranch," the woman replied. "Then I'll be drawing them up. I work with a contractor in High River."

"I didn't know you were building a house," Cilla said conversationally, arching one brow. In fact, she knew almost nothing about the man, except that he was singularly irritating.

"A ranch house for the Diamond 8. The owners decided it was time for a new one. The old one burned down a few years ago," he added, by way of explanation. He didn't sound that enthusiastic about the project.

"Uh-huh. So where do you live now, in a tent?"

"Nope." He grinned. "Used to, before I moved up in the world. Then I tried bunkhouse living. Got into too many poker games. Now I live in the Diamond 8's old harness shed. It's been fixed up." He shrugged. "Suits me, but like I said, my bosses decided it's time I got a regular house built." He paused, giving her a knowing look. "In case I get married."

"I see," she said coolly. She wondered if he had anyone in particular in mind. Not that she'd ever ask. There certainly seemed no shortage of candidates. Every time she saw him, he had a different woman in tow. Maybe that meant he'd bring a good price at tonight's auction. She could hope. Where were the Gordons, anyway?

As if in answer to her silent prayer, Sara Gordon walked in, offering her apologies for her husband, who'd had to drive to Calgary unexpectedly. Naturally, Jeremiah volunteered to help, and Cilla could hardly refuse. Reta, it turned out, was staying in town until Monday and Jeremiah had convinced her to come to the charity auction that night. The man had a gift. He'd missed his calling. He should have been a politician or a salesman.

Reta left after meeting Sara Gordon. She,

too, volunteered to help, but Cilla felt on firmer ground refusing her offer. Jeremiah's lady contractor wasn't dressed for it, plus Cilla had plenty of help now.

Cilla contemplated the first job she'd assign Jeremiah. Should she send him up on the ladder? Well, yes, there was the rest of the crepe paper to string up. Get him to move all the chairs out from the storage closet? Assemble the tables? That was actually a job for the Legion staff, who'd be arriving at four o'clock to finish setting up.

"You see that box with the vases in it?" she finally decided. He strolled over and looked into the box she'd pointed to. "These?" He held up one milk-glass vase. Nina had begged and borrowed as many vases as she could from her friends for the table centerpieces.

"Uh-huh. And you see that pail of flowers over by the door?" She'd picked them up from the florist on her way over.

"Uh-huh." Jeremiah started to smile.

"We need the flowers arranged in all those vases, one for each table. Think you can handle that?"

Jeremiah laughed out loud, the glint of a challenge in his eyes. "You bet I can, Miss

Cilla. I figure I can handle just about anything you could throw in my direction."

"Anything you can do, I can do better?" she teased, unable to stop an answering grin. She fastened her ponytail tightly again, ignoring his interest as she did so.

"You got it. Anything you can do, I can do better," he repeated, grinning.

"Well," she said, tossing her ponytail over her left shoulder. "You can start on the flowers and we'll just see about that."

CHAPTER FIVE

THE CROWD for the charity auction was better than even Nina Blake had expected.

The hall was jammed, both with ten-dollar ticket holders for the informal buffet supper catered by the Legion, and for the auction itself, which was scheduled to begin at half past eight. Mort Chavitz, a local farmer, had volunteered to be auctioneer. Cilla wasn't sure "volunteered" was the operative word. More likely Nina Blake—or her husband, Cal—had called in a favor or twisted an arm.

But Mort, a burly, red-faced man sporting closely shaved jowls and a brand-new Calgary Flames cap, seemed enthusiastic about his job. During dinner he jollied the diners and had everyone guessing which item would bring the highest price. All bets seemed to be on a weekend package for two at a hotel in Kananaskis, donated by a principal from a Calgary packing plant. Cilla wondered who had gone so far afield for donations. Donna

Beaton, possibly, Jennifer's lovely and energetic mother, who ran a gift shop in Glory.

Cilla had inspected the long printed list of donated items, as well as checked over the paper-covered tables that lined one side of the hall—the side opposite the buffet table. It held many of the goods to be auctioned, which varied widely. There was a cup-and-saucer from Mrs. Reeves's collection, an assortment of small figurines, a gift basket loaded with bath items, three sacks of top-quality dog food donated by the local vet, a brand-new stepladder from the hardware store and a large rococo mirror from the local glass shop. And much, much more.

Cilla overheard one matron sniffing at the donation made by an acquaintance who ran an antique shop. "Really, I would've thought Gladys could come up with something a little better than *that* old thing!" *That* being a large gate ornament of a jockey holding a house nameplate. Still, some collector would be happy. And, for a buyer with different tastes, there was a family grouping of white plaster ducks, a mother and eight ducklings, all tied together by their wire legs, ready to promenade silently and eternally across some well-dressed Glory lawn.

Cilla saw Jeremiah once during the buffet meal, catching his eye as he surveyed her over the heads of the crowd. She noticed a girl of eighteen or nineteen with long auburn braids beside him. Cradle snatcher! Well... possibly a neighbor or niece, she decided charitably. Then, when she paused at the outer door, where old George Frizzell, the retired publisher of *The Plain Dealer,* was taking admissions, she sensed Jeremiah's presence nearby. She didn't dare look to confirm her suspicion. What was wrong with her, that she was so acutely aware of this man?

A shabbily dressed man shuffled toward the door, his torn and stained shirt and pants at odds with what appeared to be brand-new athletic shoes on bare feet. She felt Jeremiah step nearer, almost protectively, and this time, she did glance his way. He was just behind her, looking toward the open door. "Old Seth Wilbee," he murmured in her ear.

"Got any money, Seth?" boomed Frizzell, preventing the man from sneaking into the hall, as he seemed about to try to do.

"Oh, that poor man!" Cilla murmured, embarrassed on the newcomer's behalf.

"It's a legitimate question," Jeremiah muttered dryly.

"Still, putting him on the spot like that!"

"Oh, takes more than that to bother old Seth," Jeremiah replied. As though to prove Jeremiah's point, the shabby man promptly turned his pants pockets inside out, a comical gesture, and replied to the publisher's query, "Nope! Not a cent!" He grinned widely as though amazed at the finding, and Cilla noticed that he was missing several teeth. His eyes were vague and watery looking, the open trusting gaze of the myopic.

"You checked your piggy bank, Miss Cilla?" Jeremiah murmured, as the byplay between George Frizzell and Seth continued.

"My *what?*" Cilla breathed.

"Your piggy bank. I presume you'll be making bids on one or two of the items this evening," he returned smoothly.

"You mean, on a lawn ornament? Or a bag of dog food?"

"You got a dog?"

"No," she said, laughing softly.

"I was thinking more along the lines of the livestock on offer. The two-legged variety."

Cilla smiled, hoping Jeremiah couldn't see her. "No plans in that direction. Sorry. I'm sure there'll be plenty of takers, though."

He ignored that. "'Course, you could

change your mind and put in a bid, after all. Given the right incentive?"

"I could," she admitted, suddenly aware that he was flirting with her and that she was enjoying it tremendously.

"A woman's prerogative, right?"

"Mmm," she responded noncommittally, realizing with a shock that she should *not* be flirting with this man. Or any man, for that matter. She wasn't in Glory for the social life; she was here to run a business. And the business, so far, was being run on a very thin shoestring. Which was the reason for this evening's event. It needed all her attention.

Jeremiah leaned toward the ticket taker, who was still arguing amiably with old Seth, and tossed the three-dollar auction-only fee onto the table. "I'll keep an eye on him, George. Take him over to the buffet so he can fill his pockets with the leftovers. Nobody'll mind."

"All right." George Frizzell nodded. "And keep him clear of the egg salad, Jeremiah. You know how that can go off without refrigeration."

As Cilla watched Jeremiah disappear into the crowd, his hand on the shabby man's elbow, she heard George speak to her. "You must've seen him around, ma'am." She had, now that he mentioned it. She'd seen the derelict in the delicatessen, going from table to table, earnestly collecting used teabags and putting them in a plastic margarine container. "Seth Wilbee's a town fixture. Lives in a shack he built down the other side of the culvert, has for years. His brother's got a big farm over by Tamarack and could take care of him, only Seth Wilbee don't want taking care of. He's an independent cuss. Just stubborn, I guess."

Independent, stubborn...Cilla was sure she could add a few more adjectives to describe *all* the men of Glory and the surrounding district.

The bidding started promptly at half past eight. Cilla noticed that her landlady, Mrs. Vandenbroek, bought the teacup and saucer. Bidding was slow on the dog food and lawn ornaments and brisk on the stepladder and the tune-up donated by a local garage. The mirror went for a surprisingly high price.

Cilla lost track of the bidding, convinced that the auction was going to do very well for Blue Owl and for Jennifer's dance school, after all. It gave her a huge sense of relief. Nina Blake had done a terrific job of organizing. Cilla and Jennifer had bought a big bouquet of flowers to present to her later in the evening, after the bidding, as a small token of their gratitude.

"Cilla!"

Someone touched her on the arm and she turned. "Mary!" The sisters hugged and Cilla felt her eyes prickle. She blinked hard. "Are Mom and Dad here, too? Talbot?"

"No, Tal's at home, and Mom and Dad had something else on," her sister said, glancing with interest around the room. "I couldn't miss this place, Cill. Every car in town has to be parked outside."

"And pickup," Cilla added. They both laughed. "Did you drive out here alone?" Cilla couldn't believe how thrilled she was that one member of her family had responded to her invitation.

"No, Kirstin came with me—where did she take off to?" Mary stood on tiptoe. Kirstin McPhee was one of the Prescott girls' childhood friends. "Oh, there she is!" Mary laughed and gestured with one hand. "Checking out the cowboys. Wouldn't you know?"

Cilla looked in the direction Mary had indicated. Kirstin McPhee, blond and just a year or two older than Cilla, was twice married and currently divorced. As Mary had said, she was in the middle of a knot of good-looking men in tight jeans, bright shirts and big hats, probably some of the crew Jeremiah had rounded up for the auction. Jeremiah, Cilla noted with satisfaction, wasn't among her admirers.

Cilla squeezed her sister's hand. "I'm so glad you're here, Mary," she whispered. "I miss you and Jeannie and, even Mom and Dad sometimes!" She was only teasing and her sister knew it. Mary squeezed her hand in return, and then Cilla led her over to a table near the wall, where they could keep an eye on the bidding and stay out of the traffic. A few people were still being admitted and a few more were still making trips to the dessert buffet. She noticed Seth Wilbee lounging against a wall at the back. His pockets looked filled to bursting and Cilla saw that he'd acquired a shopping bag somewhere, which also bulged.

"Don't you like Glory?" Mary whispered, an expression of concern on her pretty face.

"Oh, I do. It's just that—well, it's kind of quiet. Compared to what I'm used to," Cilla said reassuringly. She didn't want to get started on the details. But it wasn't that at all;

she enjoyed the peace and quiet. "I do like it," she said, contradicting herself. "Very much." She was surprised to realize that she meant it.

"The school's going all right?" Mary asked, her blue eyes searching Cilla's.

"Oh, yes. Quite well. I've got fifteen students!" Cilla said proudly. "Sixteen, actually. I've got a new one coming in this week."

Mary didn't seem all that impressed. "How many were you counting on?"

Cilla signed. "I'd hoped for twenty. Twenty would have meant a bit of a profit so I could hire another teacher but, well, it'll come, Mary. I truly believe that."

Mary held her gaze for a moment. Then she smiled and patted Cilla's hand. "It will, Sis. Don't you dare fold. Dad's so proud of you—"

"He is?"

"He's telling everyone that he's got a daughter who runs her own business. He's pleased as punch."

That was news to Cilla. She'd had the definite feeling her parents hadn't wanted her to move to a small town and spend her inheritance on starting a preschool. Maybe they'd made the adjustment. Maybe they'd realized she had no intention of wasting her time on the Calgary social circuit that kept them both so busy, attending gallery openings and doing "good works."

"Oh, look! They're bidding on a romantic picnic dinner for two," Mary said, quickly sticking up her hand. "I'm going to bid on that. I'll surprise Talbot with it some nice Sunday afternoon."

There was a flurry of bids, then Mary bid again. An older woman, with steel-gray curls and thick glasses, won it in the end.

"Who's that?" Mary asked.

"I have no idea." Cilla didn't think she'd seen the woman around town before. Maybe she was a visitor.

"I'm glad she got it," Mary whispered. "Good for her if she surprises her husband with a little romance."

"Or boyfriend," Cilla said slyly. Mary hooted with laughter.

"Okay, maybe boyfriend."

But it wasn't so funny when the weekend for two at the luxurious mountain resort in Kananaskis came up for bidding and the gray-haired woman won again, with an outrageous bid, far beyond what Cilla thought the weekend was worth. It was all gravy for her and Jennifer, though. She ignored Mary's groans of disappointment. Mary had bid on the weekend, too, and so far had only succeeded in buying an old-fashioned ivory dresser set, which she said she didn't really need or want.

Cilla bid on two gallons of paint, which she thought she'd use to paint the kitchen and bathroom of her apartment one of these days, when she had a spare few hours. The paint was a bargain at seventeen dollars. Kirstin, who joined them about twenty minutes later, after they'd sat down at a table, was the only bidder on a set of hubcaps for a Buick. She didn't own a Buick but said she didn't care; she'd use them for planters in her garden.

Then—the bachelor auction. The event the crowd had been waiting for. There was a pause while the auctioneer looked toward the side of the stage, the scratchy shriek of a sound system, and finally—with only one false start—the unmistakable strains of a country western tune. Eight cowboys, Jeremiah among them, sashayed onto the stage, all in step. They wore standard cowboy gear, and one or two had on short chaps. Three carried lariats and they all waved their hats in their right hands.

The crowd yelled its approval. Kirstin, to Cilla's horror, stood up and clapped madly, then put two fingers in her mouth and gave an earsplitting wolf whistle. She sat back down, laughing hysterically.

"I'm gonna get one of them!" she announced.

"What?" Mary asked innocuously. "For your backyard?"

"Oh, Kirstin," Cilla said, "you're not! What would you do with a cowboy? You live in Calgary—"

"Oh, I'll think of something," she said slyly and winked. Cilla was glad the lights were down, because she knew she blushed furiously.

The truth was, she was embarrassed for Jeremiah's sake. It was awful to see him up there, waving his hat with the rest of the cowboys and twirling his rope like some parody of a Hollywood cowboy.

With a huge round of applause, the music stopped and the three cowboys carrying lariats threw loops out into the crowd. One snaked their way but thankfully fell harmlessly on the floor in front of them. That would've been the final humiliation, Cilla thought, to be roped like some reluctant heifer.

One large loop landed over the head and shoulders of a teenage boy nearby and he happily allowed himself to be hauled up onto the stage, where he received congratulations for being a good sport, then bolted back down again, ten dollars in his hand from the auctioneer.

"All righteeeee! We're gonna start right here with Henry J. Hilton of the Rocking Bar S," the auctioneer sang out. "Henry's a native of Maple Creek, Saskatchewan, but he's lived right here in southern Alberta most of his life. He's been stove-up, stove-in, busted and tossed more times than most of you can count, but experience means somethin', don't it, Henry? He's an antique, folks, but there's still plenty of rawhide left in the old fella."

The crowd roared.

"Okay, who'll give me a bid on Henry J. Hilton? Five hundred dollars, five hundred? Who'll give me four-fifty-four-fifty-four-fifty-do I have four hundred? Three hundred—"

"Three hundred!" cried one of the spotters helping the auctioneer. It was a dark-complexioned little lady in a print dress. Cilla had seen her earlier, sitting at the Blakes' table. She had one of those ageless faces and could have been thirty or sixty, it was hard to tell.

"All right, who'll give me three-fifty-three-fifty—?"

The bidding went on, until Henry J. Hilton was sold to the lady who'd made the first bid on him, for $475.

Henry beamed as he was led off the stage to be claimed by the woman in the print dress. The crowd cheered when he took off his hat and gave her a big kiss. She blushed and looked down at her hands and said something to him. Grinning, he put his arm around her shoulders. Obviously there was more to this story than Cilla knew.

She was curious. Was Henry this woman's beau? She'd recognized him as one of the men who'd come to Blue Owl to help her set up at the end of August. One of the crew sent by Jeremiah Blake.

Ty McTavish went for $650, and Kirstin was disappointed at being knocked out of the bidding. She'd set herself a limit—which she had now revised, she told Mary and Cilla—of $600. The next good-looking cowboy, Ben Longquist, brought $825, and this time Kirstin was successful.

"Oh, Kirstie, he can't be much over twenty," Mary said, giggling.

"I like 'em young," Kirstin returned, a

twinkle in her green eyes. "They're easier to train, didn't you know?"

She went up to claim her prize, and a few minutes later the bashful young cowboy had joined them at their table.

Next on the block was Lewis Hardin, a dark, handsome man with a big black hat and black jeans. He looked to be in his mid-twenties and had been the lucky one to lasso the teenage boy in the audience.

Ben Longquist watched the bidding with interest. It was brisk, with the Hardin cowboy finally going for just over $500. Cilla noted that the young woman with auburn braids, whom she'd seen accompanying Jeremiah earlier, had won the bidding. She took her prize's hand as she went up to claim him and the two of them disappeared toward one of the exit doors.

"They seem to know each other quite well," Mary murmured, watching them leave.

"That's my sister, Phoebe. She's sweet on Lew, has been for a long while," returned the cowboy Kirstin had claimed, shaking his head slowly. "Mom and Dad aren't keen, though. They're going to have a fit that she bought him with money she's supposed to be saving for college. He's just out of jail."

"Jail!" they all exclaimed as one.

"What for?" Cilla asked.

"Rustling," the young cowboy said matter-of-factly.

Cilla stared at Mary; Mary stared at Kirstin. Kirstin stared back at Cilla. *Rustling?* What were they living in? A Wild West dime novel? All three burst into laughter.

Then Cilla stopped laughing. Jeremiah Blake was the next cowboy up for grabs.

CHAPTER SIX

CILLA FELT A WAVE of acute discomfort roll through her. She desperately wanted Jeremiah to come to his senses and simply step off that stage and go home. Or if that didn't happen, she wanted to buy him herself and tell him to go back to the Diamond 8 and put an end to all this nonsense. Or if *that* wasn't going to happen—and it wasn't, since she had no intention of bidding—she hoped he'd bring the best price of all the cowboys.

Mostly, she wanted this crazy event to be over. It was nearing half past ten, and the organizers had hoped to be finished by now, to allow time for cleanup.

And what if the worst happened? What if no one bid on him at all? Or only reluctantly? Cilla didn't think she could bear it. But she didn't have to worry; the bidding was fast and furious. She tried to see who was bidding, bristling at the presumption of some of these Glory women, but couldn't pick out any single bidder. There seemed to be so many! At one point, she spied the woman she'd seen with him in the deli, grinning and holding her hand up to catch the spotter's eye, then frowning with disappointment as someone went higher.

Good. Cilla didn't want that young dark-haired woman to get him. What was her name—Rhoda something? Rhonda? Cilla didn't want anyone to get Jeremiah.

Anyone except her.

Cilla put both hands to her hot cheeks. She was insane! She was feeling as upset and bothered as if she'd been in a six-furlong event herself. And she wasn't even *in* the bidding race. Her heart sank as she saw the young architect or contractor or whatever, who'd been with Jeremiah earlier in the day, raising her hand. Then Kirstin sneaked in a bid and Cilla actually yelled at her.

"Oops, sorry," her friend apologized, with a quick grin and a glance. "I didn't know you wanted this one."

"I don't!"

But Kirstin didn't pay any attention. Her eyes were back on the stage where, to Cilla's absolute horror and amazement, Jeremiah was doing a sort of chicken dance, waving his elbows, wiggling around and turning around and around to the delight of the crowd. The auctioneer nearly choked, he was laughing so hard.

By now the bidding was already well above a thousand dollars, and quite a few had dropped out. Cilla prayed for this whole thing to end. To her surprise, she saw the gray-haired woman who'd purchased several items earlier still serenely bidding on Jeremiah. Every bid that topped hers, she overtook almost immediately, barely hesitating. The auctioneer finally sang out the magic words—"Going, going, *GONE!*"—and the show was over. The gray-haired woman had bought Jeremiah for a price of just over thirteen hundred dollars. *Thirteen hundred dollars!*

That was by far the highest bid.

Cilla was instantly relieved. At least it wasn't one of these dozens of young, pretty women who'd been bidding so enthusiastically at the beginning. In fact, she wanted to laugh at the way things had turned out. Served him right! The gray-haired woman who'd bought him probably wanted her potatoes dug or her garage roofed or something. But why would the woman, a stranger, have donated so much to the school and the dance academy?

Cilla watched as the buyer—she had to be well into her sixties—made her way to the stage. When she got there, Jeremiah picked her up and twirled her around, to a roar of delight. The woman blushed—Cilla could practically see it from where she sat—then wiped her glasses when Jeremiah set her down. She patted at her skirt, looking quite flustered, and stepped up to the microphone. The auctioneer adjusted it so she could speak.

"Step right up, Bea, and say a few words to the folks," he invited. "Ladies and gentlemen, *Bea Hoople!*"

Bea cleared her throat with a ladylike "ahem." "Well, as you all know, I've been pretty fortunate tonight with my bidding. Luckily I'm retired and I can afford it. Maybe I should run out and buy a lottery ticket now…." There was an appreciative chuckle from the crowd. "I'm thinking maybe I've taken more than my share, although it's all money going to a very good cause. I've got a little great-nephew attending Miss Prescott's Blue Owl school, and he just loves it, so I'm happy to do what I can to contribute."

Now, who would that be? Cilla wondered.

The audience was getting a little restless and someone called out, "What're you gonna do with Jeremiah Blake?" The crowd's murmur swelled.

"You're asking what I intend to do with Jeremiah? Well, you all know me and you know I'm not married, never have been—" there was a burst of laughter "—and I'm well past the stage of wantin' to, either, not to mention I've known young Jeremiah here since he was knee-high to a grasshopper." She shook her head. "Plus, he's altogether on the youngish side for a woman of my years. Now, if I coulda got my hands on Henry Hilton—" the crowd roared again "—I'd probably be singin' a different tune," the woman finished. She was clearly enjoying every second of her few moments in the spotlight.

The audience loved it. Cilla would never have guessed that the conservative-looking older woman in skirt and sweater and old-fashioned bifocals would have been so humorous. Then, to her shock, she heard her own name mentioned.

"Now, if Miss Priscilla Prescott could step up to the stage here, I've got something I'd like to say to her. We're awful proud to have a young lady of her background and training come to our town the way she did, with the interests of all the little Glory children in her heart—"

Cilla blushed scarlet. Kristin and Mary urged her on, and she pushed back her chair and stood, feeling very visible, and walked to the front of the room. This was all her own fault, she thought grimly, for getting involved in A Good Cause.

She walked up the few steps to the stage and shook the auctioneer's hand. Then she shook Bea Hoople's hand. Jeremiah stood back, grinning widely, but didn't move forward.

"So, neighbors and friends, I'd like you to know that I'm handing over Mr. Jeremiah Blake to Miss Priscilla Prescott of the Blue Owl Preschool to use him as she sees fit in fixing up the school."

What?

"I've got nothing for Jeremiah to do myself, and I'm sure Miss Prescott can come up with something. She's got a lot on the go over at that little school, and if she can't think of anything in particular right now, why, I'm sure she can dream something up…." People clapped and laughed and stamped their feet.

Jeremiah stepped forward and before Cilla

could even think of a thing to say—surely she had to respond to this incredibly weird, unforeseen donation—he'd swept her up in his arms, just as he'd done to Bea Hoople.

"Put me down!" she got out through gritted teeth. "This very second."

"And if I don't?" he teased. He was so close. She could see every black lash, every drop of perspiration, every smile line. For safety and support, she'd automatically thrown her arms around his neck, which forced her even closer.

"If I wasn't so well brought up, I'd smack your face," she whispered tersely.

"And if I wasn't such a gentleman, I'd kiss that pretty mouth of yours right here in front of everybody."

Her eyes widened. "You wouldn't dare!" But it didn't come out nearly as emphatically as she would have liked. Of course, he *would* dare, without giving it even a second thought, and she was in enough trouble. Cameras were flashing. Of course—now it would be in the paper, as well. With any luck, none of her family would see it.

He set her back on her feet and stepped back, still grinning.

It was a done deal. There was nothing she could do except be gracious.

"Thank you so much, Miss Hoople. I appreciate your kind gesture and generous donation to the school. I'm sure I can put Jeremiah to good use—" She tried hard to ignore the crowd's knowing laugh. "I was thinking that we need some more play equipment built and the building could probably use a second coat of paint and there are always windows that need cleaning." She added, at the crowd's chuckle, "When he gets that done, I believe Jennifer's new dance studio needs the floor refinished...."

There was another burst of laughter, this time directed at Jeremiah Blake. The laugh was on him.

The evening broke up with a general air of excitement. More than ten thousand dollars had been raised, to be split between Blue Owl and Jennifer's dance academy after the expenses were all paid out. Cilla couldn't have hoped for a better outcome—other than being saddled with Jeremiah Blake and his so-called services. Her share of the money would help pay for extras. Perhaps, by Christmas, she'd have more students.

Mary and Kirstin drove Cilla home. She'd taken her own car back late that afternoon to change her clothes, then had walked to the hall. Speculation was rife during the short drive to Cilla's flat.

"How about Jeannie's wedding? You could have him escort you to that."

"I don't think so," Cilla said dryly. "Could you see him in a tux?"

"Oh, boy," Kirstin moaned, biting her knuckles. "Could I ever!"

Cilla was disgusted. "Honestly, Kirstie, you'd think you'd never seen an ordinary man before."

"I've seen plenty, hon." She turned in the front seat and gave Cilla an exaggerated wink. "But I can always appreciate another one. And your Jeremiah is a lot better than 'ordinary.' *My* cowboy is taking me riding," she said.

"Oh?" That sounded interesting. She hadn't ridden for years. Despite what she'd told the crowd, she really had no idea what to do with Jeremiah. She'd been kidding about the dance studio's floors.

"Yes. Two Sundays at his brother's farm. Or at his boss's ranch up in the foothills somewhere. The Double O—isn't that romantic?"

Mary was braking for Cilla's stop. "You'll think of something, Cill. I think he'd clean up just fine for the wedding, if that's what you decide. Give Mother and Dad a scare. Unless, of course, you'd rather go with one of Dad's prospects." She grinned at Kirstin, who nodded. Mary was referring to the endless stream of suitable men her parents were always introducing to their three daughters—the Promising Prospects. Now, with Mary and Jeanne married or about to be married, the entire pressure was on the youngest Prescott.

Ah, yes, the Promising Prospects. How could she have forgotten? Cilla got out of the car and bent down to Kirstin's open window. "Now, you two go straight home, y'hear?" she teased, shaking her finger at them. "Drive carefully. I'll let you know what I decide about...the cowboy. And thanks for coming out to the auction tonight. Say hello to Mom and Dad."

Waving, she watched them drive away. Then, with a sigh, she walked toward the outside stairway that led to her second-floor apartment. The street was quiet. Quiet and cold, the sky a carpet dusty with stars. She heard the faint, oddly dislocated and despairing sound of the wind chimes that Mrs. Vandenbroek had hung from a post on her back patio, next to a bird feeder. And the poor woman wondered why the birds wouldn't use her feeder.

Nearly midnight. A day of rest ahead of her, Sunday. And then back to work on Monday. Somewhere in there she'd have to think of some way to handle Jeremiah. Because, if she didn't come up with a plan, she was pretty sure he would.

JUST AFTER LUNCH the next day, there was a polite tap at Cilla's door. She opened it. Jeremiah Blake stood on the landing, looking simply wonderful in a Western-cut dress jacket, open-necked white shirt and tan trousers. No jeans, no spurs, no lariat.

"Good morning," he said and took off his hat, giving it an expert twirl on his forefinger before clasping it gently against his chest. He smiled at her expectantly. Cilla was astonished. Astonished enough that she retreated a little, a move he took complete advantage of by stepping inside her kitchen and closing the door behind him.

"Wh-what—"

"You're wondering why I'm all dressed up, huh?" He grinned and tossed his hat onto her kitchen table, which she had just cleared of her breakfast dishes, after a long shower, a manicure and two chapters of her book. She'd started rereading a sentimental favorite, *Pride and Prejudice,* the week before. It had been a heavenly morning.

"Sure, that and a few other things," she replied.

"Well, I've just been to church—"

"Church!" Somehow she hadn't taken him for the church-going type.

He bowed. "Yep. Went with my brother and his wife and Marigold. They got the littlest sprout christened this morning. The boy. I figured, now, if I'm good and go to church today I'll be all prepared for the worst Cilla Prescott can do."

"Said your prayers?" Cilla teased. She couldn't resist. At least she was dressed. An hour earlier and she'd have been in a dressing gown. When she'd heard the knock, she'd assumed it was her landlady coming up to tell her something. Or give her something. Mrs. Vandenbroek often brought her a fresh loaf of homemade bread, or a few carrots or a tomato from her garden.

No matter how she'd offhandedly portrayed him to Mary and Kirstin the previous evening, Jeremiah Blake was undeniably a handsome man. Even without all the cowboy gear—and frankly, she preferred him like this—he was impressive. Black hair, dancing eyes, a tanned complexion, tall, extremely fit…the list went on.

And right now, for whatever reason, he was very interested in being in her kitchen.

"What brings you here this morning, Jeremiah?" she asked bluntly. There was no point in beating around the bush with him; she'd already learned that.

"You and I have a few things to discuss, don't you think?" he said lightly, his eyes searching hers. "I came by to take you for a nice quiet Sunday afternoon drive. We can see a little of the countryside and we can talk about our business arrangement in—"

"Our *business* arrangement?"

"Sure. The way I figure it, I'm worth about two hundred, two hundred and fifty bucks a day. Bea Hoople bid just over thirteen hundred dollars, thirteen hundred and seventy-five to be exact, which works out to about, let's see—" He cast his eyes up to the ceiling as though calculating, but Cilla knew very well he'd done the math hours ago. "That'd be about six and a half days' labor—"

"You said you were worth two hundred and fifty," Cilla quickly got in. She could see where he was headed. "That'd make it a lot less time—"

"Five and a half days," he interrupted, with a shrewd glance. "Which do you figure I'm worth—two hundred or two fifty?"

"Oh, definitely, two hundred and fifty," she said, knowing why his eyes suddenly gleamed. He had her. "Even more," she ventured lamely. Why not?

"Three hundred?" He grinned.

Cilla looked this way and that way, then nodded. "Sure. Three hundred. That'd make it just four days—"

"A little over. Mind you, I hate to take advantage of a situation and overcharge," he drawled. "Two fifty's fair. So that's five and a half days' worth, let's say six—"

"Let's just say five. That's plenty," Cilla shot back.

He grinned again. "Okay, five. So we've got to talk about that. We shouldn't have any trouble deciding, we're getting along just fine so far, don't you think? Look how much we've already got settled."

"I'll get my purse." Somehow or other, they were going to get this straightened out right away. She'd had vague notions about maybe getting him to help set up the play equipment she intended to order with some of her share of the auction proceeds. That would take about a day. Maybe a day and a half. Then, maybe he could arrange for her to go riding—not necessarily go *with* her, just arrange for the horse and tack—which would account for another day. That was it. She'd had no intention of having him around for five days. Six, if he had his way. What in the world did he think she was going to do with him for all that time?

But she hadn't paid for him, had she? Miss Bea Hoople had. And Bea would want Blue Owl to get the full value of her thirteen-hundred-dollar donation.

After all, as the town would say, it had gone to support A Very Good Cause.

CHAPTER SEVEN

JEREMIAH THOUGHT he'd drive Cilla out to the Diamond 8. They'd take the long way, wind up around the village of Black Diamond, then down through Turner Valley and Longview. Let her see some of this foothills range country he loved so well. He'd grown up on the Rocking Bar S, the ranch currently operated by his brother, Cal, and Cal's foreman, Henry J. Hilton. The two orphaned brothers had been raised mainly by their aunt, Louisa Twist, after their uncle had died, and Louisa had left the ranch just before Cal married and brought his wife back from Vancouver. Louisa—Weezie, as Jeremiah liked to call her—had remarried and was now the third Mrs. George Edward Robeson. Her new husband had a passel of grown children and had outlived two wives already.

Bea Hoople was his aunt's closest friend. And man, did he owe her! She'd managed to snag him the opportunity to spend some quality time with Cilla Prescott when it had looked as though there was no chance, even for a persuasive fellow like him. Jeremiah had no delusions. He knew perfectly well that he had a way with women—most women—a way his brother, Cal, had never mastered. And yet look at how things had worked out for boring old Cal. A wonderful wife, father now of two little Blakes, still the fine rancher he'd always been, and yet he'd hardly changed at all. Cal had always been a homebody and still was. He'd always preferred horses over people, and still did.

If things could work out for Cal Blake, they sure could work out for his younger brother.

Jeremiah wasn't entirely sure what he meant by that. He wasn't in the marriage market himself, no matter what people like Bat Middleton and Nina might think, only in the courting game. He wasn't looking for a wife—no way—but if he did feel up to the challenge of the chase, especially when the lady involved made it clear she wasn't interested. Cilla's insistence that she had no interest in men at the moment, never mind marriage, made him all the more determined to change her mind. If not about marriage, certainly about men—well, one man anyway.

Heading to Black Diamond was a start. They'd have coffee, pick up some justifiably famous cinnamon buns at the Prairie Bakery, take in the scenery. He'd show her just what southern Alberta had to offer. He had a sneaking suspicion she wasn't going to be all that impressed, that she was a city gal through and through, but he'd just have to show her she was wrong.

Jeremiah had considered bringing his brand-new Ford truck to town, but had decided on his classic 1962 Chevy pickup, fully restored and shiny cherry-red. He rarely drove it. He'd been working on a classic truck of his own, a 1947 Ford pickup, when he got the job at the Diamond 8 a few years back and had ended up selling it, only half-finished. He had no time for it with his new job. He'd bought the 1962 Chevy pickup, already restored, from a friend.

He noticed Cilla's eyes light up when she spotted it at the curb. A woman after his own heart.

"Yours?" she asked, clearly delighted.

"All mine," Jeremiah said, handing her into the passenger side. He adjusted his hat as he walked around to the driver's door. Was it possible to feel any more pride or pleasure?

He reached for the chrome-plated starter when he got in. "What do you think of her?"

"Her? Meaning the truck, I presume?" she asked wryly.

"Yeah."

"Well," she said, looking around the beautifully restored interior, "it's very...very retro, isn't it? Very cool."

"You could say that," he said, pleased. "I confess I didn't do the work on her, but I bought her from a buddy who did. A perfectionist."

"Like you?"

He considered briefly. He'd never thought of himself that way. "Yeah, like me."

"This is a hobby of yours, classic cars?" she asked, settling in. Jeremiah had to admit he'd chosen the shiny old pickup today for another, less honorable reason. The seats were the old-fashioned bench style, newly upholstered in polished leather. Now and then, dates had been known to slide right over against him on a really sharp corner. Not that he was expecting it to happen this time...

"No cars. Just trucks." He grinned at her as he moved the four-on-the-floor gearshift into second. "It's more than a hobby. I'm a nuts-and-bolts guy. I like getting my hands dirty.

You probably don't know too many guys like that, do you?"

He shot her a sideways glance. She seemed at a loss, so he continued, "If I had more time these days, I'd be restoring something else. But I don't have much spare time anymore."

"I see," she murmured, gazing with interest out the window as they left town, headed north. "Responsibilities. I suppose being a ranch foreman is a busy job."

"Manager," he corrected her. "I manage the Diamond 8 for half a dozen partners. It's a corporate ranch, as a lot of the big ones are these days."

"Oh?" she turned to him, a look of puzzlement on her pretty face. She obviously didn't have a clue about what a ranch really was, except that she probably knew most of the beef she ate came from one. "Where do the partners live?" she asked.

"Oh, here and there. One's from Winnipeg, a couple are in Calgary. Another one runs a ranch himself over toward Strachan."

"Mmm." She'd only been making conversation, tossing the old conversational ball around the court. It was a ball he intended to retrieve and return. Again and again.

He took a deep breath. "So, what about you?"

"Me?" The puzzled expression was back. "I'm a teacher, a preschool teacher. You know that."

"Sure, I know that. But where are you from? Where were you raised?" He was dying to ask if she had a man in her life somewhere, if maybe that was why she was so shy of them here, but he didn't dare.

"My parents live in Calgary. I grew up there, mostly, after we moved from Ontario," she recited politely. "I went to university in Edmonton, got my teaching degree, then went to Switzerland to study the Montessori method. I'd been to Switzerland for my last year of high school."

"Switzerland, huh?" He whistled softly, a reflex.

"Yes." She rolled down the window a little and the breeze lifted her hair. It was warm for early October, and that was one thing about the classic truck—no air-conditioning. "My great-aunt lived over there, my favorite aunt, a widow. One of my mother's aunts. I stayed with her for a year. Then I taught in a couple of schools in Toronto."

It wasn't a lot, but at least she was talking.

"What about books? Huh? Your favorite book? Favorite color? Animal?" He looked at her quickly and caught her surprise.

"Is this part of our business?" she asked.

"No. I just want to know more about you."

He couldn't be more straightforward. Still, she didn't pull back. Somehow, he'd known she wouldn't. Deep down, he was convinced she felt as curious about him as he did about her. Jeremiah understood what went on between a man and a woman, and there was something going on all over the place between him and Cilla Prescott.

"I like to read, yes. Right now I'm rereading *Pride and Prejudice* for the umpteenth time. By Jane Austen. Have you ever read it?"

He thought briefly. "Maybe in high school. Is that the one where the rich guy wouldn't consider marrying her and she wouldn't consider marrying the rich guy, except they did in the end?"

She laughed. It was a delightful sound that sent shivers down his shoulders. "Yes, that's the one. There was a movie a while back."

"I didn't see it."

"Maybe we could go sometime—" She snapped her lips together, as though trying to catch back the suggestion and looked determinedly out the window. *Check. He'd have to rent that one, or buy it in case he ever got her to his house.*

"What are those reddish cows?" she asked, entirely the tourist now.

He glanced out the window to the field beside the road. There wasn't a cow in sight; they were all steers. "Red Angus. They've become pretty popular around here. They do well in the heat, better than the black. Mind you, we haven't been getting too much heat the past few summers. Black Angus are a lot more common. Good mothering breed and top-quality beef."

"And those ones with the white faces? The ones you see everywhere?"

"Herefords. Still the standard range cow in this area. Most ranchers prefer 'em. Not much like the original British breed anymore. Ranchers have done a lot of improving to get the western range cow they want." He sounded like a tour guide.

"You?"

"We raise mainly Herefords. Also some crosses and some exotic breeds."

"Exotic breeds?"

"Maine-Anjou, Charolais, some beefaloes."

"Mmm." There was silence for a while. She

hadn't answered him on her favorite color or animal, but he wasn't going to bring it up again. She also hadn't asked him what a beefalo was, but maybe she'd guessed. He was driving nice and slow, taking his time. He was looking forward to a long, leisurely afternoon drive. Informative. Educational. His aunt Louisa would be proud of him.

He'd read her exactly right. "Okay, your turn," she said, smiling, after a few moments of silence. "Favorite color, animal, book you're reading."

"Red, dogs, especially the mutts my brother's foreman raises. We call 'em Hilton hounds. You met Henry when I sent him over to work on the school."

She nodded. "I remember. He's the one Bea wanted to buy at the auction and then had to take second best."

Second best? He was startled for a moment. "Me? Oh, yeah," he finished lamely. If she only knew…

"So, you've got some of Henry's dogs?"

"I've got three right now. One's a bitch expecting any day. Book? Let's see. Man, that's a tough one. *Sports Illustrated* count?"

She laughed. "No way." She'd actually turned a little, so her back was resting against the passenger door and her attention was directed toward him. He'd finally caught her interest. At least, her curiosity outweighed her determination to keep him at a distance.

"Book, book, let's see...boy!" He was embarrassed. He couldn't remember the last book he'd read. He read a lot of magazines, newspapers, reports, agriculture bulletins, machinery catalogs but...books? "Okay, I remember. It was last winter—"

"Snowed in, huh? Truck out of gas? TV didn't work, nothing to do?" She was enjoying this as much as he was.

"Got it from one of the boys out in the bunkhouse. He recommended it. About an old sunken ship full of gold being found somewhere down there off the United States. *Ship of Gold,* I think it was." He felt better. He'd actually remembered the title. And it'd been a good story.

"You don't read fiction?"

"Nope," he admitted, shooting her a grimace and a quick wink. "I live it."

She laughed. He smiled in response, then returned his full attention to the road. They were getting close to the town of Black Diamond. It was the kind of place you'd miss if you blinked at the wrong time, so he slowed down.

"You feel like a coffee? They build some mighty fine cinnamon buns over at the bakery there."

"With raisins and icing?" She seemed interested.

"With or without," he said, pulling in to the curb right beside the bakery. "You want to come in, pick out your own?"

The bakery was closed. Of course—it was Sunday. He felt like an idiot, then remembered that the coffee shop up the street served pastries from the same bakery. He almost took her arm as they walked, then realized she most likely would not appreciate the gesture. This wasn't a date, he reminded himself. This was business.

Unfortunately, two cowboys he knew were in the coffee shop, trying to gulp down copious quantities of caffeine.

"Who ya got there wit' ya, Jem?" one groggily asked. Jeremiah considered ignoring the request, but Cilla immediately stepped forward and offered her hand.

"How are you? I'm Cilla Prescott, I'm the new preschool teacher in Glory. And you're—?" She glanced at Jeremiah when the first man stared transfixedly into her face, as though he'd seen an angel, and refused to release her hand.

"Chuckie Gonzales, Cilla. Let go of her hand, Chuckie. And that's Morris Jack." He hoped she wouldn't notice Moe's upper plate sitting tidily on a napkin beside his coffee mug.

"Luv'ly gal, Jemmie, m'boy. Luv'ly gal," he muttered, and Jeremiah stepped up to the counter, his hand firmly on Cilla's elbow.

"Never mind them," he murmured in her ear, catching a glorious scent of flowers and something citrusy in her hair. Blond and beautiful and not snagged up in one of those tight buns she favored. Lucky he'd caught her unawares this morning, before she'd had time to starch and primp.

"Some of your crew?" she murmured back, one eyebrow arched and a smile on her pretty pink mouth.

"Not mine. Although I've hired 'em both from time to time. Good workers when they're awake."

They returned to the truck with a coffee for him, a cappuccino for her, both in cardboard containers, and two huge bakery cinnamon buns in a paper bag. His was iced, no raisins; hers was plain, with raisins.

They munched their pastries in silence for a few miles and then Jeremiah noticed Cilla delicately licking the tips of her fingers. "Tissues in the glove box," he said.

She removed a tissue and finished wiping her hands, then picked up her coffee cup and took a sip. "Mmm. Very good."

"Surely you didn't expect cowboy coffee?" he teased.

"Cowboy coffee? What's that?"

"Boiled up once or twice, a shot of cold water to settle the grounds and then poured into a tin mug. Gets pretty rank by the end of the day but cowboys don't care."

"I can imagine."

They were approaching Turner Valley. There wasn't much to see beyond the tourist info cabin, already closed for the season, and the wooden derrick that marked the first gas well in the area, the first and biggest gas field ever discovered in Alberta. The teahouse on the corner had been moved there from another community. It was closed.

Longview was a few miles farther south. By the time they arrived, Jeremiah was beginning to see some of the country through her eyes. The vast open spaces, hills brown now that it was fall, sparsely dotted with cattle. That part was beautiful; he didn't think anyone could disagree. The Longview Hotel dominated the center of the collection of motley buildings that barely passed as a town. The hotel was an establishment surrounded by dusty pickups most nights but deserted on a Sunday. The town's one decent restaurant had a tattered sign nailed to the door outside that flapped in the wind.

Jeremiah knew what was written on the sign. You didn't dare get hungry in Longview unless it was Friday, Saturday or Sunday night, the only times the restaurant was open. Of course, there was always the place up the street, where a guy could fill his belly with the best beef jerky anywhere, made right there. Civic requirements were satisfied by a combination post office–library–town hall, with a big bulletin board outside. That was it. The only sign of life in town this afternoon was a grizzled rancher filling his pickup at the service station on the corner.

Then they were out into wide-open ranch country again, heading south on Highway 22.

"Where are we going?" Cilla asked. She

seemed only mildly curious. "Weren't we going to talk business?"

"I thought we'd stop in at the Diamond 8. I'll show you around a little. Meanwhile, you keep thinking of things you want me to do to fulfill my duties. Six days' worth. Sound okay?"

"Five. Sounds fine."

"Now," he said, feeling confident again, "where were we? You never told me your favorite color."

She smiled. "I never saw a shade of pale blue I didn't like," she said, eyes twinkling.

"Blue, huh? Favorite animal?"

"Cats. I like birds, too. I had a budgie when I was growing up. Of course, cats and birds don't really mix."

Jeremiah gave an exaggerated shudder. "I hate birds. Especially crows and magpies. Don't mind a pheasant on a plate with a nice puddle of gravy, mind you. What about boyfriends?" he slipped in. "You got one?" He was venturing onto dangerous ground.

She hesitated. "No, no boyfriend." Was he getting too personal?

"What about marriage? You ever been engaged?"

"No. You?" Her brown eyes regarded him intently.

"Me?" Jeremiah frowned. He hadn't expected her to turn the tables quite so quickly. "Yes, I was engaged once. Nearly got married, too, only she changed her mind, decided I wasn't that great a prospect, after all. Can't say as I blame her, can you?" He tried to make a joke of it.

"Oh?" She sounded alarmed. He regretted bringing up the subject when he saw her concern. "I'm sorry I asked," she said in a rush. "It's none of my business, and—"

"No, it's okay. I don't mind." He shot her a glance. "That was before I started the job at the Diamond 8 a few years ago. I was pretty shook up at the time, but I'm a big boy. I'm over it now." He grinned.

"I'm sorry," she repeated. "Was—is your, uh, lady friend married now?"

"Matter of fact, she is. She decided to take a chance on a Calgary businessman instead of a foothills cowboy. No hard feelings on my part. I was pretty wild back then."

"And you're not now, of course," she said dryly. He felt like stopping the truck and reaching over and kissing her. She'd decided to take his broken engagement in the spirit he'd hoped she would.

"Nope. Not a bit," he agreed, but he knew she didn't believe him for a minute. Nor should she.

The Diamond 8 was tucked up against a hill that edged the Elk River valley to the southwest, in a spot guaranteed to keep the worst of the winter wind away from the buildings. The drive approaching the ranch was lined by a double row of cottonwoods that had been planted by the original owners at the turn of the century. It was an impressive approach, Jeremiah knew. Fitting. Grand, even. It wasn't his ranch, not in terms of ownership, but no actual owner could be prouder. On each side of the lane, Diamond 8 horses grazed, some mares with foals, others the geldings used mainly as working horses, as were the mares when not in foal. Although a great deal of ranch and range work was done these days with all-terrain vehicles or light planes, there were some jobs that couldn't be done without the help of a horse. And every cowboy, no matter how modern or mechanically inclined, preferred to survey his domain from atop a horse. Jeremiah didn't think that would ever change. At least, he hoped it wouldn't.

When they arrived at the ranch, there was news.

"Tilly's gone and had her pups. Out in back of the machine shed. Looks like five of the little devils this time." That was the greeting from the cook, Marshall Downing, who happened to be walking across the yard as they drove in. Downing had been on and off Jeremiah's payroll over the years. He was the best cook the Diamond 8 had ever employed—when he wasn't on one of his regular fishing vacations.

"Five!" Jeremiah was delighted. He turned to Cilla. "Want to go check 'em out?"

"Of course I do," she said calmly, waiting until he walked around the cab to open her door. It showed she was a woman used to men who performed these little courtesies automatically. A lady. He took note. *Check.* He was going to get it right with her. She was a challenge, no question. But he was up to a challenge.

"Look, we don't have to go see these pups. I mean, if you'd rather we stuck strictly to business...?" he asked. "I know you're not big on dogs. Maybe you're allergic or—"

"I *would* like to deal with our business," she replied matter-of-factly, "but I also think it would be silly not to have a look now that we're here, don't you?"

Tilly seemed suitably pleased with herself in the nest she'd made for her pups in a sandy dugout at the back of the shed where he kept the tractors. She was a wiry, shaggy, grayish mix, not a bit handsome—like a lot of the dogs Henry Hilton bred.

"Is this a cow dog?" Cilla asked, when they came upon the litter. Tilly growled at Cilla, the stranger, and wagged her tail faintly at him.

"You could say that. Henry breeds his dogs for cow sense. Corgis, blue heelers, collies, he tosses anything at all into the mix. Long as they're smart, got plenty of heart, not afraid of cattle and love to work. He also likes medium-size to small, because they don't eat as much and they live longer," Jeremiah said, squatting beside the litter to pat his favorite. Tilly was seven now. This was her third litter.

He noticed Cilla hesitate. Was she afraid? She'd said she was a cat person, not a dog person. It seemed that on nearly every subject they'd covered today, they were opposites. He liked red, she liked blue. He liked dogs, she liked cats. And birds.

Birds? *Nobody* liked birds.

"Here." He handed up a blind, squirming bundle of black and white and tan, under Tilly's watchful eye.

"Oh, what a sweet little darling!" she whispered, gently stroking the pup's blunt head. It thrust its face toward her, triangular pink mouth open, perhaps expecting a feed. Then, as though discovering it was no longer in its mother's tender care, the puppy began to squeal. Tilly immediately stood up, causing the rest of her pups to roll over and paw the air and turn their milky mouths upward searching for the teat they'd lost. They began to squall, causing the poor mother to look from the crying pup in Cilla's hands to the rest of her litter, loyalties torn.

Cilla bent down. "Here," she said comfortingly, "here's your little puppy, Tilly dear. Don't worry, he's safe now. You're all together now, one big happy family."

Still on his knees, Jeremiah smiled at her and she smiled back. It was a simple, happy smile. A natural smile.

Maybe he was wrong. Maybe they *did* have a few things in common.

CHAPTER EIGHT

CILLA DIDN'T SEE Jeremiah again until the following Saturday morning, the day he'd promised to help install the play equipment that she'd ordered from a Lethbridge firm. Delivery was to be made Friday afternoon, after the children had gone home for the day. They'd agreed that installing the playground equipment would take one and a half days of the time he owed her.

The week had been difficult. One of the three-year-olds dropped out of the program. Her mother had decided she wasn't quite ready for preschool, after all.

Cilla had to agree; she'd noticed that the child rarely participated in schoolroom activities and spent a great deal of time lying on a mat, sucking her thumb and watching the other children. The girl had a new baby in the family, Cilla knew, which might have accounted for her inattention and lack of interest. But for whatever reason, she was gone.

Then, on Friday, she'd had a strange experience with Rory Goodland. The slack-jawed, drab-haired woman he called his cousin hadn't come for him until nearly an hour after the other children had left. Nor had she phoned.

Cilla felt sorry for the boy. He'd moped on the steps for a while, elbows on knees, politely resisting when she asked him to come back inside. Then she'd offered him the job of helping her tidy up for the weekend, a task he took on with his usual sober attention to detail. He methodically and thoroughly did everything she asked of him, and when she suggested he feed the hamster, the boy actually smiled, a tiny, hesitant smile that went straight to her heart.

"Do you take him home with you, Teacher?" he asked. Despite her best attempts, he never addressed her as anything but "Teacher."

"Sometimes. Usually I just come down on Saturday or Sunday and see that he's got enough food and water," Cilla answered. "Would you like to take him home with you some weekend?" Occasionally a child would ask for the privilege, and Cilla intended to draw up a weekend schedule soon.

Rory seemed to consider her question for a

long time. Finally he shrugged his thin shoulders. "I guess not," he said sadly.

Cilla wanted to go over and hug him. She didn't dare ask him why. She had no idea what his home life was like. He would know better than she did whether a weekend visit from a hamster was possible. Cilla felt a strange affinity with this child, something she'd never experienced before. Rory was different. But *what* was different about Rory? She couldn't really say.

Eventually, just as the men from the delivery company arrived to unload her order, the "cousin," a woman he addressed as Evelyn, arrived and brusquely collected her charge, without a word of apology for being so late. Rory had trudged off with his little red backpack, a resigned look on his face.

The next day, Cilla made up her mind to ask Jeremiah about the boy. She'd been itching to query someone and somehow she felt that Jeremiah would tell her what he could, without mentioning her curiosity to anyone else. As a new teacher in a small town, she'd hate if anyone thought she was too curious about one of her students.

Jeremiah got to the school just after half past eight. He called her from his truck phone and she told him to go ahead and start unpacking the cartons in the small play area out back, that she'd be there as soon as she'd finished her breakfast.

She downed a glass of fresh orange juice standing at the kitchen counter and ate a toasted bagel on the way, sure she'd find he had a crew of men with him and they'd have the play equipment set up by noon. She didn't think for a minute that he intended to spend a full day on it, a job a high school student with pliers and a screwdriver could have handled. After all, he was a ranch manager, a man with a busy working day, weekend or no weekend.

But he was alone. Wearing jeans and work boots and a tight T-shirt under a jean jacket. He looked fantastic. No other word for it.

It was a gorgeous fall day, clear and crisp. Cilla had pulled on jeans and a woolen sweater over a T-shirt for the short walk to the school. She had tasks she could do in the school but had come prepared to help, if he wanted help.

"Good morning! I didn't realize you planned to come so early," she said, smiling. She was inexplicably pleased to see him and preferred not to examine the feeling too closely.

"No time like the present," he replied with a grin. He took a cardboard take-out cup out of a thermal pack on the passenger seat of his truck. "Here. Fresh cappuccino. Hope I got it right—cinnamon, no sugar?"

"Thank you." She took the cup from him and curled her fingers around it. "That's very thoughtful."

"Not really," he said with a grin. "I can't get started without it. I'm on my second." He held up his cup. Plain coffee from the looks of it. And, if she remembered from last Sunday in Black Diamond, plenty of sugar and cream. Didn't he worry about cholesterol like the rest of the world? Apparently not.

They began to unwrap the cartons of equipment, no small job in itself. Everything was triple-wrapped in brown paper, bubble wrap and cardboard with plastic foam inserts between the pieces. The modules were made of a special hard weatherproof plastic, brightly colored and slightly cheaper than the wood version, which she would've preferred.

It would have to do. She was on a very tight budget, auction or no auction.

"There's got to be a set of instructions in here somewhere," she said, pawing through the box she'd opened. "Have you seen them?"

"Not yet." Methodically, Jeremiah sorted the pieces into different components—braces, uprights, movable parts, bases.

Naturally, the instructions were in the very last box, the one containing all the hardware. The diagrams resembled a cross between some kind of aeronautical device and a doughnut maker. She couldn't see a climbing set and a playhouse at all. Cilla was beginning to panic. This didn't look as simple as she'd expected. She was just grateful Jeremiah was here, thanks to Bea Hoople. Particularly since Cilla had opted to save some money by refusing the set-up package offered by the company.

"Does this make any sense to you?" she asked doubtfully, standing between two empty boxes, scanning the instructions worriedly. She wasn't even sure she had them right side up.

"Here." He took the papers from her and began to examine them. He didn't seem daunted. If anything, his expression was one of genuine interest. He sank slowly onto one of the boxes and continued studying the diagrams.

Cilla left. She went into the building and reviewed her activity sheet for the following week. There wasn't enough time on school days to do the extras, like gathering supplies or preparing materials. More than once she'd stayed late into the night to get ready for the next day, or had come in on the weekend. She didn't mind how one-sided her life had become, she told herself. She'd made a promise that she'd give Blue Owl her best shot, no matter what. If that meant a year with almost no social life, outside of conferences with parents or school-related functions or occasional trips to Calgary, so be it.

She glanced out the window to where Jeremiah Blake still sat, deep in thought over the plans, and sighed. It was going to be hard. One fact Cilla had to admit after the Sunday trip to the Diamond 8 was that she liked Jeremiah. She wasn't in the habit of deluding herself about that sort of thing.

She liked him very much. She liked talking to him, she'd enjoyed being with him Sunday afternoon, she'd enjoyed their banter. And, on a less social, more disturbing level, she was desperately attracted to him. Of course, that was all it was. And she hadn't been involved with a man in ages. Three years? Since Sebastian? She'd had one brief boyfriend during her stint in Toronto.

When push came to shove, she and Jeremiah had different opinions on nearly every topic under the sun. He was politically conservative—he'd told her he voted straight Tory; she was liberal. He had a high-school education and a couple of years of agricultural college; she'd gone to a finishing school in Switzerland and had a university degree. He'd grown up an orphan, raised by his aunt and older brother; she'd grown up in the lap of luxury in a close-knit, loving family.

Everything! He had one brother and she had two sisters. He liked red, she liked blue. Did that mean he was hot and she was cold? Maybe. But if so, it was going to stay that way.

Luckily, he appeared to be the perfect gentleman. He hadn't made the slightest move on her during their drive or at his ranch. He'd been polite and considerate. And beyond the startling conversational gambit of questioning her preferences, he hadn't pried or poked into her life at all. He seemed to have accepted her strictures about a relationship. She wasn't sure she could have held off a determined assault from a man like him.

Of course, he didn't have to *do* anything, did he? Not really. She just had to spend time with him to realize how attractive and appealing he was, which was exactly what had happened since Bea Hoople's unexpected donation.

She walked back outside, into the sunshine. He looked up, a pleased expression on his face. "I've figured this thing out."

"I'm glad one of us has," she replied. "I knew it wasn't going to be me."

"Trust me. This'll be a piece of cake." Jeremiah stood and they decided on a location for the climbing bars. He began assembling the base. She handed him screwdrivers and other tools he'd brought with him and they set to work.

Maybe they *were* total opposites, she thought. But that might have a bright side. After all, she wouldn't have deciphered these instructions in a month of Sundays, as her grandmother Prescott used to say. And he had.

CILLA DIDN'T HAVE an opportunity to ask Jeremiah about the Goodland boy until they were sitting over lunch at the Glory Hotel Café.

Cilla would have preferred Molly McClung's, the deli where she usually had lunch, and was surprised when Jeremiah suggested the hotel restaurant. It was where she'd gone with the crew he'd sent over that first day. The clientele was mainly men, all of whom looked up when they walked in. Jeremiah nodded left and right. Obviously it was a crowd he knew well. The slightest shadow of a doubt crossed her mind. Was this why he'd chosen the café? So that he could make it clear the new teacher was a personal friend? Stake his turf, so to speak? The human male equivalent of marking his territory? Cilla smiled to herself; she'd watched altogether too many movies.

He insisted on buying her lunch, which she refused, so they ended up compromising. She'd buy his; he'd buy hers.

Cilla knew the compromise was ridiculous, but somehow that was what she liked about it and why she agreed in the end. Sheer zaniness.

Over the beef noodle soup, she broached the subject. "You seem to know the Goodland boy."

"I do." He nodded. "Don't know the kid all that well, but know the family. Or what's left of it."

Cilla stared at him. "What does that mean?"

"Rory's never mentioned his mom or dad? A sister?"

"No," Cilla replied, slowly shaking her head. She thought back to when she'd asked the children about their families the first day. She'd been surprised at how he'd hesitated before answering, almost as if he didn't know.

"Well, they're dead—"

"Dead?"

"Yeah. Freakiest accident you could imagine. They'd just been notified of a big win in some sweepstakes, and the parents and sister were on their way to Edmonton to claim it when they were rear-ended by a tractor trailer and they were all killed. Including the truck driver." Jeremiah shook his head, frowning.

"Oh, my," Cilla whispered, shocked beyond belief. "That poor, poor boy." The waitress approached then, bringing their sandwiches—a double cheeseburger with fries for him, a cream cheese and tomato on brown with potato salad for her.

Jeremiah thanked her, then shook his head again. "The whole town feels sorry for the little guy, but there's not much anyone can do."

"Well, what about this—this *Evelyn?*" Cilla leaned forward, her hunger forgotten. "Who's she?"

"Evelyn? Oh, that's Evelyn Bell. She's a second cousin of the kid's, his mother's cousin.

She's been saddled with him since the accident, although I don't think she's crazy about the idea. She's got five kids of her own."

"Saddled? That's crazy!" Cilla was at a loss. "Surely there's *someone* else who wants him—"

"That's for sure." Jeremiah grimaced. "There's another second cousin, even more unsuitable than Evelyn Bell. Then there's Rory's uncle Phil. He's the town drunk. One of 'em, anyway. Glory's got several. Phil Goodland never married and, believe me, is in no position to raise a kid."

"So why do they want Rory? I don't get it." Cilla picked up half her sandwich and took a bite. It was surprisingly tasty. The brown bread was very fresh. Jeremiah's fries looked good, but no way was she reaching over and trying one.

Jeremiah glanced to the right and the left, as though checking to see if anyone was listening to their conversation. Then he leaned toward her, elbows on the table, and said softly, "Because the kid might be rich, that's why."

Cilla swallowed and frowned. "Rich?"

"The sweepstakes money," he replied. "No one knows if Rory's going to end up with it or not. It's going through the courts right now. If the kid's rich—" he shrugged "—there'll be a huge fight among the relatives. If he's poor—" he shrugged again "—they'll be trying to dump him as fast as they can."

"I don't believe it," Cilla said, aghast. "That's *horrible!* Where's the—the government in all this? Someone should be looking out for that child. He's an *orphan!*"

Jeremiah picked up his last French fry and held up one hand to signal the waitress that they'd like more coffee. "The government will take over if the relatives don't keep him. I'm sure he'll end up a ward of the court when this is finished. Might already be, for all I know."

Cilla digested the information Jeremiah had so casually imparted. Poor Rory. No wonder the woman he called Evelyn didn't appear to care for him. He was only a meal ticket to her—if the courts awarded him the sweepstakes money. A big *if.* And if they didn't... Cilla shuddered to think of the effect it would have on the boy. Losing his mother and father and sister, and then being discarded by his remaining family, tossed aside like an old shirt no one wanted.

She felt cold and quite calm as she finished her sandwich. She'd try to make the poor child's life pleasant. She had an obligation, a duty to do what she could. No one ever knew the good a stranger, a teacher, for instance, could have in a child's life. Luckily he'd taken a notion to go to *her* school. The second cousin's throwaway remark made sense now, about the boy making up his own mind that he wanted to go to Blue Owl. He must have access to some money of his own, perhaps from his parents' estate, which would account for the school fees being paid ahead of time.

His caregivers were keeping him happy, in case he got the big money in the end. Besides, this way Evelyn Bell was clear of him for a half day from Monday to Friday.

"Hey!" Jeremiah reached across and rested his large hand gently on hers. "Don't worry yourself, Cill. There's nothing you can do about it."

He'd shortened her name. He'd turned it into an endearment, a soft, personal sound. And the touch of his hand—warm, comforting. Friendly. It made her want to throw herself on his shoulder and bawl her eyes out. For Rory. The poor motherless kid. It brought out every shred of human feeling she had, and she'd always had plenty, according to her great-aunt Martina. Somehow she knew that Jeremiah would offer his shoulder, too, and maybe even put his arms around her until she was finished. Then he'd probably give her his handkerchief. He was that kind of guy.

They received the separate bills they'd asked for. Cilla paid Jeremiah's bill and he paid hers. The cashier looked at them as though they were nuts and Cilla nearly laughed out loud. She decided against trying to explain. For some things, there were just no explanations. No excuses. No reasons.

Just none at all.

The playground equipment was nearly assembled by the time they called it quits at half past seven. Cilla was freezing by then. The sun had dropped, and the coolness in the fall air made her wish she'd brought a jacket. She caught herself about to invite Jeremiah to her place for some hot chocolate and a take-out meal. She reminded herself that this was not a date—it was a work bee.

"Tomorrow, same time?" Jeremiah asked, tossing his tools into the back of his truck. "I don't think we've got more than another two hours here."

"You're taking this pretty seriously, aren't you?"

"You bet I am," he replied. "I make a deal, I keep it." It was an admirable quality...she supposed.

She sighed. "Okay." She nodded. "Nine o'clock?" She dreaded the early start, especially on Sunday.

He grinned. "Let's make it ten, give you time to get your beauty sleep. We'll be done by noon."

Cilla was relieved. Then she wondered if he had plans for a late night himself. Did he have a girlfriend?

Did it matter?

She intended to call her parents this evening. Also, she wanted to call Mary and ask her to pick up some sheet music from a store in Calgary and mail it to her. Calgary was only a little more than an hour's drive away, but lately it had seemed to be on another planet. Was she getting cabin fever, stuck out here in this small town?

Maybe it was time for a trip to the city. Her sister Jeanne's wedding plans would be humming along by now. Much as she was relieved not to be part of the mad planning that must be going on, one crisis after another, she missed being included.

The next day Jeremiah finished even before he'd predicted. With a casual wave, he got in his pickup and left. He didn't even look back, but why would he? The playground equipment was marvelous and Cilla knew the children were going to love it. What had she expected? *She* was the one who'd been worried about making too much of this relationship.

Clearly, he didn't have the same problem. Business as usual, for him.

Next week, she decided, she was definitely going to Calgary. See a movie, go out. She could use a change of scenery.

CHAPTER NINE

MAN, IT WAS TOUGH to drive away like that. He kept her in his rearview mirror until he couldn't see her any longer. Then, when he turned the corner onto River Street, he caught a glimpse of her looking after him, standing in front of the rickety old hardware building, in the shade of that monstrous maple that should have been taken down years ago. TransAlta lopped off branches every second spring, so the foliage wouldn't interfere with the power lines, but the old tree kept coming back. Like Amanda Dexter, the leathery old lady rancher out toward Longview: it just never quit. The maple had to be fifty feet high, maybe sixty. He remembered it from when he was a kid, remembered hiding up in the branches, playing hooky in second grade. A whole colony of gray squirrels lived up there, had done so for decades.

Blue Owl School. It was a weird name.

Where in the world had she dreamed up the idea of starting a preschool out here in Glory?

He'd swear she had no friends, except that he knew his sister-in-law thought a lot of her, and since the charity auction had twice invited her to the Rocking Bar S for dinner. She'd refused both times.

What was *with* her? Why was she so stubborn? What did she think was going to happen if she accepted something from someone, had a little fun? She'd turn into a toad?

It had taken all the discipline he'd built up over his thirty-two years not to *do* something while she was around. Touch her. Pull her into his arms, even just a kidding, goofy move.

Well, he had touched her, hadn't he? He'd touched her hand in the Glory Café, an impulsive gesture when he'd seen how badly she'd taken the news about the Goodland kid. For a minute there, he'd thought she was going to burst into tears. She had a soft heart, all right, hidden beneath that Ice Princess exterior.

Was that her secret? A soft heart? One day, she'd share all that softness with a man. The man who had the key to what moved her. He was starting to wish he might be that man. He'd gone after her for the challenge. Now, he knew a little more about her, about who she was—and he was interested.

She licked her fingers when she ate a cinnamon bun, just like everyone else. She had a cagey little smile she didn't think he'd noticed. He'd noticed. She liked Tilly's pups. She even liked Tilly, never mind all that talk about cats and birds.

And he liked her. A lot. He sensed how tender she was, and how much pride she had, doing everything herself or trying to. He knew all that prissy talk about not wanting a relationship with anyone, because she was too busy, was just a way of hiding. From what? Her own feelings? As if a person planned out a life like that, week by week, year by year.

Any fool could see she was lonely.

But did any fool want to *do* anything about that? And was he that fool?

Jeremiah frowned and paid attention to his driving for a while. They hadn't settled on any other jobs for him. He didn't feel easy about that. He'd bargained on five, maybe six, days with her and he intended to make sure he got them, no matter what. Today hadn't been a real half day. Just a couple of hours before lunch. Maybe he'd call and see if she wanted to take the Goodland kid riding some day. Rory could ride Shorty—that horse could walk and doze at the same time. Every kid liked horses and dogs and ranches.

She'd appreciate that. She felt sorry for the kid. And, when it came right down to it, so did he. The Goodland boy was in a mess.

Jeremiah had a lot to deal with today. For one thing, that architect—Reta—was coming out to the ranch with more plans, even though he'd tried to put her off, telling her he had another commitment. Jeremiah sighed and turned the pickup toward the Diamond 8.

EVELYN BELL HAD no problem with his suggestion. But then, she wouldn't. After a short silence on the phone, Cilla agreed, too. Her voice was different—breathless, warm. You could tell she thought it was a terrific idea and that he was a terrific guy for thinking of it.

Check.

When they'd decided on a time—the following Saturday afternoon—Jeremiah said he'd pick up Rory. Cilla insisted she would, pointing out that it made more sense for her to do it, since she was already in town. The Bells lived on the east side of Glory, near the tracks, in an area of small bungalows, weeds and postwar, run-down duplexes, while the Diamond 8 was to the west.

That jinxed Jeremiah's strategy to take the kid home first and then drive Cilla back to her place, taking the long way around. Who could tell what might happen? He was sure hoping something would. But, at the same time, what she'd said made sense and he wasn't quite ready to play his hand. He was already worried about what she'd say when she found out he'd had more than a little to do with the "donation" Bea Hoople had made. Bea had had some—well, what you might call *encouragement* from him. He owed her. She'd done him a huge favor.

Jeremiah went through his preparations half an hour before Cilla was due to arrive on Saturday. Picnic lunch with treats for the kid—check. Shorty saddled with the child-size saddle he used when his niece visited—check. He wasn't fooling himself that they were going to do any real riding today so hadn't ordered any other mounts saddled. After all, the kid was only about four or five and had probably never been on a horse before. But he was setting the stage for *next* time. And next time, he had no plans to have Rory Goodland along.

House tidied up, in case she came in for a minute, had to go to the bathroom or something—check. Yard mowed, last mowing of the season, leaves raked up so it looked good—check. He'd had Morris Jack, who was back on payroll, do that this morning.

Everything was fine. Jeremiah realized he felt a little nervous. He ran one hand over his jaw. No need for a fresh shave. His shirt was new. He had on deodorant, clean socks. He took a few steps toward the driveway and glanced back at the knoll where the owners planned to build. He had to admit the place seemed a little bare without a ranch house to center the yard. Barns, sheds, equipment garages, feed silos, corrals, a bunkhouse and a cookhouse—it all looked fine. Just missing an important element, the house where the rancher lived, with his family.

The owners could be right. He might have use for such a house someday. Jeremiah winced. He felt as if he'd just taken a bucket of ice-cold water in the face. Marriage? Kids? He was really *thinking* like that these days?

He shook his head. No way. Maybe it was time for a night of poker with the boys. That ought to cure him of the notion.

No chance to think about that scenario now,

because he saw Cilla's car turn into the drive at the far end of the line of cottonwoods. She drove a midsize, unpretentious car. A Toyota. Couple of years old. Dark. Blue maybe. Yeah, probably, considering her preferences.

"Hi!" She looked terrific. She was wearing jeans and a gray sweater and had her hair down for a change, a scarf or kerchief or something over it. She wore sunglasses, which made her look big-city glamorous. Of course, as far as he was concerned, she could have been wearing a potato sack or nothing at all—any old way she was a knockout.

He walked toward the car, checking his impulse to give her a hug. He leaned down and opened the passenger door.

"Hi, Rory," he said. The boy seemed kind of scared. "All ready for a big day?" Rory nodded solemnly, making no move to unbuckle his seat belt. "I bet you'd like to see Tilly's new pups, right?"

The boy's eyes lit up, and he nodded and undid his seat belt. He slid out of the car. He was a cute kid. Reddish-brown hair, freckles, green eyes. Little-kid jeans with elastic in the back. Little suspenders with alligator clips on the front of his jeans.

"Hang on, Rory, I've got something for you

here," Cilla said. She was at the back of the car, fiddling with the trunk.

She pulled out a small cowboy hat and the boy's eyes grew huge.

"For me?"

"For you," Cilla said, stepping forward and settling the hat firmly on the boy's head. She smiled down at him. "Is it okay like that?"

"Oh, wow! *Thank* you, Teacher—"

"Now, you remember what we talked about in the car, Rory?"

"I'm s'pposed to call you Cilla," he said, blushing. "Right?"

"Right!" She patted him on the shoulder, then turned to Jeremiah. "Hello, Jeremiah. Thanks for this—" She waved one hand toward the pasture and the snowcapped mountains west of the ranch. "It's a wonderful idea."

"Cilla." His voice nearly failed him. For a moment he felt fifteen again, about to meet his first date. But he quickly recovered. "Hey, you're looking good."

The boy had walked on a little ahead of them, toward the pasture on the far side of the lane, where the horses grazed behind the fence. Jeremiah could see he was bursting with pride over that new cowboy hat. He'd practically hooked his thumbs in his elasticized denims and strutted as he walked. Jeremiah grinned. One of the ranch dogs approached cheerfully, sniffed the boy's backside, then fell into stride beside him, wagging a softly plumed tail.

"Rory won't really be riding, will he? I don't think he's ever been on a horse."

"We'll see how it goes." He glanced down. "What's in your bag?" She was holding a bulky canvas carryall that she'd retrieved from the trunk of her car when she'd produced the kid's hat.

"Sandwiches and stuff. Fruit. I thought we could have a snack later, before we leave. I don't know how much lunch Rory had at home. He's been pretty excited about this, Evelyn tells me. I think she's glad to get rid of him for the day, though. Have you ever been to their place?"

"No. But I know the area." Jeremiah digested her news. Well, they were on the same track. He'd ordered a picnic lunch from Marshall. Now they'd have two.

Cilla gazed after Rory, who'd stopped by the pasture fence to pet the dog. "Poor little kid. I'm sure it's just fine, but they seem so—so squeezed in there. She showed me her granddaughter. It's her oldest daughter's baby, about six months old. Evelyn seems pleased as punch. Her daughter is sixteen. The boyfriend lives with them, too. It's a tiny place. I just can't—"

"Hey." Jeremiah stopped and put his hand on her arm. She looked at his hand and turned to him, her face full of questions. "Listen, honey, you can't fix everything. That's just the way it is sometimes—"

"But Jeremiah! It's so—so sordid."

"Fine. You call it sordid. They probably call it, I don't know…cozy. Everyone doesn't have the same background you do, Cilla. You know that. So leave it be. Evelyn Bell is doing the best she can with what she's got."

"But they're *using* Rory! They see him as some sort of potential cash cow and—"

"They need the money," he said simply. "Think about it." He wanted to shake this woman. Didn't she realize people just did what they had to? Even her? Even him?

She seemed to accept that and walked beside him for a few steps, brow furrowed.

"Where did Rory live before the…the accident?"

"They rented a house over behind the municipal hall. Small place. Anyway," he said and stopped again, "let's forget the whole situation for today. Huh? Let's just show the kid a good time."

"You're right, Jeremiah," she said softly. Then she nodded her head briskly and took a deep breath. "Yes, you're absolutely right."

"Hey, Rory!" he called and the boy looked at him, eyes bright. "Come with me, I'll show you the pups."

"Whoopee, mister!" Rory reached for his hat and threw it experimentally in the air. He tried to catch it but missed and the dog snatched it up and brought it to him. He laughed.

"Oh, Jem," Cilla whispered. He felt her hand clutch his arm just by the elbow. "I've never seen him *laugh* before."

Rory was completely enthralled with Tilly's pups. He squatted beside the box Jeremiah had transferred them to, on the back steps of his bungalow. Unlike some kids who couldn't seem to stop poking and chattering, Rory stayed quiet, calm. Tilly, not the most demonstrative of dogs, even licked his cheek once, to his surprise and delight. The pups were still very small, with their eyes only starting to open, little milky-blue slits in their grizzled faces. But they were nearly twice the size they'd been when they were born.

Cilla knelt beside Rory and Jeremiah stood off to the side, leaning against the upright of the small porch, observing them. They made a pretty picture. Almost mother and son, or aunt and favorite nephew. Jeremiah wondered why a good-looking woman like Cilla Prescott hadn't been snapped up by some man yet. Was she one of those career women, married to a job? Was that why she wasn't interested in a relationship? He hoped not. It wasn't as though she did the kind of work where she'd have no time for a husband and family. She could be a wife and mother and a teacher, too.

Jeremiah took a deep breath, shocked at the direction his thoughts kept wandering. "Okay, let's go see Shorty, shall we?"

They spent an hour with Rory in the saddle, taking turns leading the elderly pinto sedately around one of the paddocks. Shorty, a retired cow pony, accepted his new rider with equanimity. He flicked his ears at a few flies and swished his tail from time to time, but other than that, he remained in his usual half stupor.

But he could have been Silver and Rory the Lone Ranger as far as the boy was concerned.

"Wow, look at us now!" Rory shouted, hanging on to the horn with both hands. The boy had drummed his heels against the pinto's side long enough for his actions to finally register and, with a snort of protest, Shorty had increased his shuffle to an amble.

"You're doing great, cowboy!" Jeremiah called. He laughed to himself. Man, kids were fun sometimes. He remembered Marigold learning to ride. Cal had her on a horse before she was two, and by the time she was past her third birthday, she was a fairly competent rider on her little Shetland. For her fourth birthday, Cal and Nina had bought her a Welsh pony, Amber, who was now Marigold's inseparable companion.

Cilla had been leading the gelding around and now she looped the reins up and handed them to Rory. He took them carefully. Shorty kept walking in the circle he'd been tracing for the past forty-five minutes. Jeremiah knew that nothing could happen to the boy; Shorty was just too reliable and too slow. All Rory could do was maybe fall off, which probably wouldn't happen, anyway.

Cilla stepped toward him. "You think that

was a good idea—giving him the reins?" she asked nervously. "I mean, we're responsible for him. If anything happened—"

"Nothing's going to happen, Cilla," he said. He liked the way she'd said *we,* included him. "Relax. Shorty would fall down and start snoring before he'd bolt. I've been through wasps' nests on the trail with that cayuse, and all he did was blink and twitch a little."

Cilla laughed. He wanted to come closer, put his arm around her. Give her a hug. Maybe even more. But they weren't on those terms.

Yet.

"You ready for something to drink? Tea? I've got a pitcher of lemonade in the fridge and some pop. Marigold likes pop."

"Maybe lemonade." She looked at him for a few moments. Her eyes were soft. "This day is very special for Rory." Her smile was delicious. "And for me. You're a good man, Jeremiah Blake. A *very* good man. Did you know that?"

Hold on, he *did* have an ulterior motive here. He started to reply, then swallowed. *A good man*...if she only knew. Sure, he'd wanted the kid to have a nice time, but his main reason for being out here today had nothing to do with Rory Goodland and everything to do with her. He was as devious as they came….

"I'll go get that lemonade," he said firmly, deciding to ignore her remark.

"No, let me," she protested. "I'd like to use your bathroom, anyway."

"All right." He was glad he'd tidied up. "I'll bring Rory back to the house in a few minutes for a break. Before Shorty works up a lather." He grinned and winked. "There's a table outside. We can use it if you think it's warm enough. Or sit on the porch."

It was mid-October, but the sun was still warm in the early afternoon. The sky was a hard, painted blue, a classic Alberta fall sky. They'd been blessed with a decent growing season and what looked to be a long Indian summer this year. It was his favorite season—no bugs, and most of his year's work done. Just fall roundup to come. That was on his mind these days. A couple of his neighbors had called, hoping to coordinate their gather with his, but he hadn't confirmed any dates yet. He had to, though; he couldn't continue this preoccupation with Cilla Prescott.

Just a few more days, he promised himself.

He watched her walk away, with a wave to Rory. The boy waved back, risking only one hand on the saddle horn as he did so. Jeremiah grinned again. "Rory! You want to learn to toss a rope?"

"Oh, mister! Can I?" The boy nearly let go of the horn altogether in his enthusiasm. Jeremiah walked toward him, and put his hand on Shorty's bridle. The horse stopped instantly and threw his weight onto one hip with a big sigh, obviously bored out of his equine skull.

"Sure." Jeremiah lifted the child off. He didn't weigh much more than half a sack of oats. "Why not? If you're going to be a real cowboy, you've got to start practicing now."

CHAPTER TEN

JEREMIAH'S HOUSE was low-key, clean and comfortable. It was very much a man's place, though, with large furniture, a huge bed with a duvet on it covered in a Navajo-type print—she peeked in his bedroom on the way to the bathroom—and, interestingly, a small home office in one corner, complete with computer, printer, phones, the works. The kitchen, compact and efficient, was at the other end of the long low-slung building, and the walls were lined with framed photographs of old-time ranch buildings and activities, possibly from the early days of the Diamond 8. She remembered that he'd told her he lived in a harness shed that had been converted to a dwelling.

She didn't know what she'd expected. Something less homey, less comfortable, perhaps.

When she'd used the bathroom, she went through to the kitchen to retrieve the pitcher of lemonade from his refrigerator, and paused at the kitchen table, where plans for the proposed house were spread out. She began to study the building, a sprawling, ranch-style plan, and picked up a pencil to sketch in a few changes lightly. Make the mudroom larger. The pantry should be off the kitchen, not off the dining room, and there ought to be room for a freezer in there. Who wanted to run down to the basement for a loaf of frozen bread?

She chewed the end of the pencil, frowning over the placement of the laundry facilities a long way from the bedrooms, where most of the dirty laundry was generated, then jumped as she heard a shouted "Hey!" and a door slam.

Jeremiah grinned, standing just inside the central door that opened directly into the living area. "Where's the lemonade?"

"Sorry. Just inspecting your house plans. I've suggested a few changes," she said pertly, going to the cupboard to collect three glasses. "I got carried away. I'm sorry."

He looked surprised. "I'm glad you did. Reta's been after me to go over it and make some changes. I'll tell her the job's been done."

"You're not serious," she stated flatly.

"I am," he returned, rummaging in the

fridge and pulling out a basket. "Here's Marshall's contribution. Now, where's that lunch you said you brought? Don't know about you, but the kid and the cowboy are starving."

WHEN CILLA GOT HOME that evening, the phone was ringing. She lunged and caught it just as the caller hung up. *"No!"*

She deposited the remainder of the lunch she'd so carefully packed that morning on the counter and put the perishables in the fridge. They'd eaten the peanut-butter-and-jam sandwiches she'd brought for Rory, and two of the olive and cheese and tomato-stuffed focaccia. She'd brought back the juice boxes. The Diamond 8 cook had provided an absolutely delicious plum crumb cake, which Jeremiah said was his specialty, and potato salad and ham and pickle sandwiches on kaiser rolls. Then there'd been the lemonade. It had been a completely satisfactory afternoon.

Cilla sauntered into her bedroom and hummed as she peeled off her T-shirt and stepped out of her jeans. She reached for the bathrobe she'd tossed across her bed that morning. A *more* than satisfactory afternoon. She fluffed her hair halfheartedly—what a mess—and inspected herself closely in the dressing table mirror. Except for the hair, she looked okay. Fresh. Windblown. Apple-cheeked and bright-eyed. She hadn't looked *or* felt that way for ages.

Of course, when was the last time she'd spent a couple of hours leading a horse around or poring over somebody else's house plans or sitting on a porch step having a picnic with a sweet young boy and a charming, attentive man? She never had.

And all that fresh air. That had to be good for a person.

Still, a shower was next and then a look at her agenda to see what she'd planned for to-morrow. She'd thought of going to Calgary, but after such a lovely afternoon, driving in city traffic and gossiping with her mother and sisters was the last thing she wanted to do with one of her precious weekend days. Was she getting *that* used to small-town life?

The phone rang again. This time Cilla managed to grab it on the third ring.

"Hello?"

"Hi, Dad!" Cilla hadn't talked to her father in quite a while. Now why had she thought, for a split second, that it might be Jeremiah?

"I'm glad I caught you in. I tried all after-noon." Her father sounded a little hurt that she hadn't been standing right there to take his call.

"I was out—"

"Big date, huh?" He chuckled, which rather annoyed Cilla.

"No. Just an afternoon with one of my students. We went out to a ranch near here, and a very kind cowboy showed him how to swing a rope and let him ride a little. I led the horse around, mainly."

"Sounds like fun," her father said. Cilla could tell he couldn't imagine anything duller.

"It was. So? What's up?" It wasn't like her father to call without having some news.

"Well, honey, I got to thinking that you'd probably forgotten all about that opening at the Miramar next Friday evening. The one your mother's cousin is doing, the young fellow from Hamilton? You remember? Your mother's worked so hard on it. He's arriving Tuesday."

Cilla groaned inwardly. Of course, she'd forgotten. She had a few other things on her mind these days besides an exhibit by a distantly related second-rate artist who'd managed to snag a one-person show in Calgary—with the very visible support of her parents, patrons the local art community didn't care to offend. And she'd promised her mother ages ago that she'd attend, as Ilsa Prescott was desperately worried no one would show up and it would go badly for her cousin.

How in the world did she let herself get mixed up in these things? Cilla wondered.

"Yes, I remember, Dad. Herman someone or other, wasn't it?"

"Hans. Hans Leitmann. Your mother says he's doing very well with his sculpture these days, so—"

"She told me," Cilla interjected. She flopped onto the sofa and put her feet up.

"Yes, well, I thought maybe you'd like to have someone accompany you to the opening, someone who's up on that sort of thing—" *Oh-oh, here it comes....* "I met a young fellow at the club the other day and we got to talking and I thought of you. I think you'd like him. He's some kind of computer expert, started up his own company. In his early thirties and quite a decent golf handicap—"

"Dad, I'm bringing someone," she lied. *Oh, please, let Jeremiah agree to go with me to a dead-boring event like Mother's second cousin's gallery opening....*

"You are?"

"You don't need to sound so surprised, you know," Cilla said, smiling. "I'm perfectly capable of rounding up my own escort."

"Oh, I know that, sugar. I just, er, well, I thought this young fellow would be an interesting companion for the evening. I thought maybe I'd be doing you both a favor! Ha-ha." Her father's laugh sounded a little strained to Cilla's ears.

"I appreciate that you're doing your best for me, Dad. But just because I'm not married yet doesn't mean I'm on the shelf," she teased. "I may never get married, you know. Lots of women don't."

"Shelf!" Sid Prescott harrumphed. "There aren't many young men who are good enough for *my* daughters, I guess I don't need to remind you. Say, what's this young man of yours in?"

"A promising profession, Dad," she said, wishing her sisters could hear them. "He's in, uh, some kind of management. Outdoor things."

"Sales, I suppose. Management, eh? Well, that does sound promising. We'll look forward to seeing you, sugar. Will you come over to the house beforehand? I know your mother's having a few people in…."

"No, we'll see you at the gallery, Dad. Thanks for calling. Say hi to Mother."

Oh, my. *Now* what had she done? All she could hope was that Jeremiah would see her through this latest silliness. She could use one of the days he still owed her, if she had to. He'd only done two, what with the half day last Sunday and then today with Rory. And then, there was the riding expedition she'd said she'd think about after this fall roundup, in early November, before Jeanne's wedding. He'd suggested they go up the mountain to check on some line cabin. A day trip. She also figured he could put the storm windows on the school. The landlord would supply them. It was only a couple hours' work, but she was having trouble thinking of things for him to do to use up Bea's donation. She hadn't seen the older woman since the auction and expected to run into her on the street any day; Bea would certainly quiz her on how useful Jeremiah had been.

The gallery thing would work out. Jeremiah had a sense of humor, and as Mary had said, he'd clean up well. Cilla hoped he had a suit; there was no way she could take him in jeans and a string tie. Mind you… Cilla smiled when she thought of bringing him into "society"—big and brash and bold as all outdoors, a genuine Alberta cowboy.

She was definite on the string tie, though. If he didn't have a suit, she'd help him buy one. She refused to show up at some galley opening with yet another of her father's Promising Prospects. It was becoming embarrassing.

Jeremiah Blake would have to do.

THE WEEK WAS a difficult one. Thankfully Jeremiah had agreed to go to the opening with her, after hesitating for only a minute or so. It turned out he had a suit, plus a couple of sport jackets. Not all that surprising, she supposed, since he obviously had to attend business meetings now and then. She'd felt silly asking about his wardrobe, but decided there was no reason to feel uncomfortable. It was strictly a favor, not a date, and would be considered part of the time Jeremiah owed her.

Then, on Wednesday, little Jake Webster, one of the three-year-olds, was feverish and uncomfortable shortly after he arrived at school. He threw up an hour later, and Cilla called his mother to come and get him. His mother, Sheila Webster, had ominous news.

"Oh, I'm so sorry, Cilla, I should have

thought," Sheila said worriedly. She was a woman in her early forties; Jake had been born well after her twins, who were now in junior high school. "I forgot that last weekend we were out visiting, and my friend was telling me she thought her little girl was getting chicken pox. I didn't check with her to see if her daughter got it. Maybe that's what Jake's coming down with. He hasn't had it yet."

Great. How many of the children had had chicken pox? Probably not even one. In other words, her entire school, at least the three-year-olds, had been exposed to it. Cilla called the public health nurse and had her worst suspicions confirmed. Chicken pox was "going around," and it had a seven-to ten-day incubation period. The most infectious period was *before* the symptoms showed up, which confirmed that her children could have been exposed as long ago as last week. Which meant they'd probably all be coming down with it in the next week or so.

Cilla couldn't believe it. Events seemed to be conspiring against her. Of course, there was nothing she could do about the chicken pox, a common enough ailment at this age, but it was just one more problem that had landed in her lap. What about the renovations that had cost more than she'd anticipated? What about the drafty old building that was impossible to keep warm? The sloping floors? The cramped office space? The bathrooms with their eternally leaking faucets? The fact that she'd lost one of her five-year-olds to kindergarten recently? Maybe she wasn't meant to start a preschool, at least not here in Glory, in this old hardware building. Maybe she should've waited until she could find a better place to rent or even buy.

But just thinking of the setbacks she'd already experienced made Cilla all the more determined to succeed at what she'd started. She'd had some luck, too; she couldn't forget that. She'd been able to buy playground equipment with the charity money. She'd had help from Jeremiah and his crew and, lately, from him personally as a result of Bea's generous gesture. The parents had been supportive, helping out whenever she called on them. Plus, she felt she had a mission of some kind to do what she could for poor Rory Goodland.

Things could have been far worse.

By Friday, Cilla was exhausted. Two more of the three-year-olds had come down with what they now knew was definitely chicken pox. Marilla Grandpré had found spots on her tummy when she'd gone to the bathroom and Cilla discovered her showing all the other children her spots during quiet time. Otherwise the child seemed fine—no nausea, no fever. Cilla called her mother, and Jerri Grandpré came immediately to pick up her daughter.

That left four in the morning class. By three o'clock, Cilla was more than ready to call it a day. Two of the four-year-olds hadn't shown up that afternoon, and phone calls home from the parents let her know that the reason was, indeed, chicken pox. At this rate, she'd soon have no school left.

In some ways, it was a break for her—she could get caught up on other things—but it wasn't for the poor mothers at home, often with other siblings who'd end up with chicken pox at the same time. Luckily, it rarely had complications in otherwise healthy children, so once the spots had run their course, they'd all be back.

Cilla tidied up the schoolroom after the last child had gone home and quickly swished through her daily bathroom-cleaning routine, spraying the sink and mirror and towel bar with a disinfectant solution and wiping them thoroughly. She diligently followed the health ministry's guidelines for day care centers and preschools.

Then she washed the dishes, and while they dried, she mopped the floor. Normally, a preschool would have a janitor hired to do this sort of thing, or a parent committee. Cilla was stuck between the two types of preschool—she wasn't making enough money to employ a janitor and she wasn't a nonprofit, parent-run preschool that could really depend on volunteer hours. She was nonprofit, so far, that was for sure. But she didn't feel comfortable asking parents to help out. Each month they paid school fees that would normally cover such costs. So that left her doing the cleanup.

Cilla rinsed the mop and stowed it in her tiny broom closet. She quickly cleared her own desk and locked the drawers. And the windows. There wasn't much to steal in here—as Jeremiah had painted out—but it was habit. A good habit, in her opinion.

She couldn't stay much past five o'clock. Jeremiah was coming for her at seven. She had to admit she actually felt excited about the evening ahead. True, it wasn't a date. It was an obligation. But, on the other hand, she knew her mother's friends and acquaintances would be drop-dead curious as to who her escort was. Jeremiah was a very handsome man. And Cilla intended to be mysterious.

Yes, it could be an interesting evening.

JEREMIAH KNOCKED promptly at five minutes to seven. He drew in a large breath and held it briefly. Would he pass? He glanced down—charcoal dress pants, a tweed sport jacket, a dark gray crew-neck sweater. He couldn't abide a tie. If Cilla insisted he wear one, he had a folded tie in his pocket. But he didn't think a tie would look that great with a crew-neck sweater. He could thank his sister-in-law for the duds. Nina had said he was a businessman as well as a rancher, so she'd taken him shopping a year ago and made him buy all kinds of things he didn't think he'd ever wear.

He reached out to knock again and the door flew open.

"Oh! Hello. Come in for a minute. I thought I heard a knock…." Cilla gazed at him, wide-eyed and gorgeous. She had on a fuzzy white soft-looking sweater, with beads or some kind of shiny things sewn into it, over a black skirt. Earrings, shiny hair swinging past her shoulders…

Jeremiah stepped in, aware that she was

casting a critical eye over his own attire. He drew himself up. "Well, Teacher. Will I do?"

"Very nice." She nodded. "You'll do."

Well. So much for that. Jeremiah kept his hand on the doorknob. It was clear she was almost ready, just searching for some last-minute thing. Probably a jacket.

"Am I permitted to mention how beautiful you look this evening, Miss Prescott?" Jeremiah raised an inquiring brow.

"I do? Well, yes, I suppose you are allowed," Cilla said hurriedly. He heard the glimmer of a smile in her voice. "Just this once. Is it cold out?"

"Not bad. Better take a jacket, though." She was nervous, he could tell.

This whole evening was a stroke of luck. He'd never have asked her to go to a formal evening event; she'd have turned him down flat. But this was different—she needed him. He was fine with that.

"Okay, let's go," she said. She had a short jacket, which she pulled on over her white sweater. She shook her hair out. "Ready?"

He held out his arm gallantly and she very pointedly didn't take it, rummaging in her purse for her house keys. They walked onto the outside landing and she locked the door behind her.

"It's not a date, you know," she said severely, frowning at him as he turned to go down the stairs ahead of her.

"Oh, I know that," he said lightly. "I didn't think it was."

He'd brought the Chevy pickup, with the full intention of offering to drive her car if she preferred. He didn't have a car himself. He'd never felt the need for one—until now.

"You want to take your Toyota instead?"

She smiled, considering. Then he saw a devilish glint in her eyes as her gaze met his. "No, let's take your truck."

Jeremiah breathed a little easier. Ah. She was a woman after his own heart...still.

The gallery was in a previously industrial part of Calgary near the Saddledome. It had undergone gentrification in the past five or six years, but there were still a lot of abandoned brick walk-ups, tumbledown frame houses and vacant lots overgrown with weeds. The Miramar was housed in part of a large brick building that had once been a tannery. The high ceilings and open ironwork and ductwork inside lent a modern look. But the building's industrial origins were undisguised—high ceilings, huge paned windows, steel everywhere, both painted and rusty.

Frankly, it wasn't Jeremiah's kind of place. But the gallery itself was welcoming, with thick carpets on the floor, specialized lighting, tables laden with tiny, complicated hors d'oeuvres and stemmed glasses. There were plenty of patrons already, guzzling the drinks and hoovering up the sandwiches.

Jeremiah thought he recognized a few Seth Wilbee types, although better dressed and probably not living in shacks.

"Cilla, darling!" A tall, fine-featured woman with steel-gray stiffly coiffed hair enveloped Cilla in a miasma of perfume.

"Mother," Cilla said, emerging from a cloud of sea-green chiffon. "I'd like you to meet Jeremiah Blake."

"Jeremiah? What a lovely old-fashioned name! I'm delighted to meet you. Delighted!" She clasped his hand with surprising strength and turned her head, searching the crowd. "Oh, Si-i-i-idney! Come here, Sid, dear. Cilla's arrived with her young man…Jeremiah Blake!"

Jeremiah gave Cilla a pointed look. *Her young man?* She was beet-red. He tried to remove his hand from the death grip Cilla's mother still had on it, then gave up. Her father arrived, pushing through the crowd. He was a hearty-looking man with flushed cheeks and an expensive haircut.

"Blake?" He thrust his hand forward and Cilla's mother finally released Jeremiah. "Sid Prescott," he said, clasping Jeremiah's hand. "Good to meet you. We had no idea, her mother and I, that Priscilla had a young man out there in that town where she's set up her little school. How are you?" He kept shaking Jeremiah's hand. "How *are* you?"

Jeremiah gazed helplessly at Cilla. She was still extremely embarrassed. Served her right.

"Fine, sir. And you?"

"Oh, very well. *Very* well." Cilla's father concluded his extended handshake, and Jeremiah promptly stuck both his fists in his pockets. For safety. "Cilla tells me you're in management—some kind of outdoor business. Is that right?"

"You could say so, sir." He shot an amused glance at Cilla. "Beef and beef products." Well, they *were* outdoor, weren't they?

"Beef? Is that so? Well, well. There's money there. We all eat beef here in Alberta, don't we? Except for the vegetarians among us, of course. Like that, you know, that lady singer from Consort. Ha-ha." He laughed heartily.

Jeremiah smiled. "K.d. lang? Well, she's a fine singer regardless of what she puts on her plate, isn't she, sir?"

"Ye-es. Oh, definitely. Ab-so-*lute*-ly." Sid Prescott spotted someone else he wanted to talk to and excused himself with a quick peck on his daughter's cheek. Ilsa Prescott had latched on to a young man with carrot-colored spikes of hair and a lot of metal glinting in his ears and nose. The artist, no doubt. She had his right hand in both of hers, Jeremiah noticed. Poor guy.

"So," he muttered, smiling down at Cilla. "Your young man?"

"Oh, stop!" she whispered back. "I only told them that so they'd get off my case. Father's always trying to match me up with someone he knows. You have no idea how annoying it is—"

"Well, I don't mind. If you don't," he quickly added, then put his left hand on the small of her back to guide her toward the drinks table. "I've been called worse. Priscilla's young man. It's got a certain charm, wouldn't you say? Jeremiah and Priscilla. Just an old-fashioned couple." He hummed a little as he picked up two glasses and handed her one. He raised his. She blushed.

"To us," he murmured, eyes on hers, enjoying every minute of her discomfort.

She ignored his toast. "Shall we go have a look at the sculpture?"

Cilla's mother's cousin was an artist in the "found" or "environmental" art category, Jeremiah learned. He welded things. Things that ordinarily weren't welded. Like bicycle parts. And empty tin cans. And pieces of discarded machinery. Jeremiah thought he recognized a tie rod and a universal joint housing in one assembly. Transistor radios had somehow been glued to antennae from old television sets. Pots and pans had been used in various ways that had nothing to do with cooking.

He paused by one sculpture and regarded it somberly, Cilla beside him. An older lady stepped up in his other side and began to comment. "Mmm. A comment on DNA, isn't it?" They were all looking at a collection of bent and battered trash-can lids welded together in some sort of spiral arrangement.

"Mmm," murmured Cilla diplomatically. *Coward,* Jeremiah thought.

The elderly lady went on, "Now, I wonder

what an observer's first idea would be on seeing something like that?"

"Mmm, yes. Interesting," Jeremiah murmured back. "Oh! My first idea, for instance?"

"Yes. What just *sprang* into your mind when you saw that sculpture for the first time?"

"You want my honest answer, ma'am?" Jeremiah asked. He felt Cilla tug frantically at his elbow but ignored her.

"Oh, yes, of course! Your honest answer," returned the woman. "Mmm?"

"Well, first off, I'd wonder where my trash can was and if it still had its lid. Then I'd wonder where he got all those trash-can lids—"

The lady emitted a tiny giggle. "Well, you've got a point there, young man. I must tell Charlie!" She clattered off.

Cilla tugged at his elbow again. They moved toward the sculpture with the tie rods incorporated. Cilla was smiling. And she wasn't moving away from him. She was allowing him to touch her, to tuck her hand under his elbow, to lean down and whisper.

"You're insane, you know that?" she said. "Completely insane."

"I am? That lady didn't think so," Jeremiah protested.

"Well." Cilla dropped the topic and looked around.

"How long do we have to stay here?" he whispered. Maybe he could get her away and they could have coffee together, in some quiet piano bar. He inhaled appreciatively. Was she wearing perfume? Or was that just *her?*

"Another half hour or so. At least. Who's that woman over there?"

Jeremiah looked. "What woman?"

"The one in the blue dress. The pretty one staring at you."

Jeremiah felt his blood chill a degree or two. He cleared his throat. "That's C.J. The woman I nearly married. I, uh, I guess that's her husband she's with. I never met the lucky guy."

"Oh, Jeremiah. I'm so sorry." Cilla's voice had lowered noticeably.

He patted her hand and smiled. "Hey, I'm the lucky guy here tonight, eh? I'm the one with the belle of the ball, right? Even if it's just a business arr—"

"But the way she's staring at you! Someone ought to go over there and tell her to mind her manners." Cilla actually sounded quite annoyed about it. As though she might march over and do just that.

"I've got a better idea, Cill."

"What?"

Jeremiah paused and looked at her. He hadn't really meant it. But now she was gazing up at him, so curious, so innocent, so eager and willing to help. She *cared* that he might have his feelings hurt by seeing his ex-fiancée like this. She really did. He was sure of it. He took her glass and set it on a nearby sculpture.

"This." He curled his arm around her shoulders, pulled her in tight and lowered his mouth over hers.

CHAPTER ELEVEN

CILLA COULDN'T believe it! Jeremiah was *kissing* her. Kissing her behind a potted palm—literally. In an art gallery. And it was no friendly peck on the cheek.

It was a full-fledged, delicious, dynamic, exciting, knee-jelling, first kiss. But in *public* like this! What would people say? What would they think?

She began to protest slightly, then gave it up.

"Oh, my!" she gasped, finally managing to pull back, her chest heaving. "What do you think you're *doing?*"

He grinned. He still held one arm tight around her. He kissed the tip of her nose, then turned, as though he did this every day of the week, public or no public, and led her casually toward another of the sculptures. "You know what I was doing," he answered. She didn't like the gleam in his eyes. Amused. Triumphant. "Kissing you."

"I realize that, but why?" Then she bit her lip. Suddenly, it dawned on her. "It was because of that—that woman, wasn't it? You wanted to let her know you weren't exactly pining away, didn't you?"

"That woman?" He gave her a strange look. "Yes. That's it. Partly. Now, tell me what's going through your head when you see this piece, Miss Prescott." He stood apart from her and crossed his arms over his chest, rocking back slightly, as though intent on the monstrous piece of welded-together garbage in front of them.

"My hair dryer," she murmured, taking his elbow possessively and hoping the pretty woman in the blue dress was still watching them. "In fact, I'm wondering where my hair dryer is. The one I had in high school."

He laughed and patted her hand. "You're getting the hang of this stuff, Cilla."

They stopped at the buffet table, and the woman in blue, with a man—presumably her husband—in tow, approached them before they could leave. Jeremiah seemed surprisingly relaxed and oblivious, but Cilla was aware of every move the woman made.

"Jem Blake!" the woman exclaimed. "I didn't expect to see *you* here!"

Cilla took a gulp of her drink and stood closer to Jeremiah, feeling a rush of emotion she could only interpret as protective. Protective? Of *this* man? All sinew and bone, sheer male perfection, more than six feet tall and 185 pounds in top physical condition? He hardly needed her to stand up for him.

"C.J.! How are you?" To Cilla's shock, he stepped forward and kissed the woman's cheek. "Your husband?"

He offered his hand with a smile, and the other man shook it briefly. "Neil McNab. Very pleased to meet you, Blake. I've heard a lot about you—"

"All bad, I'm sure," Jeremiah returned smoothly with a grin. He turned to put his hand on Cilla's shoulder. "This is Priscilla Prescott. My fiancée."

Cilla nearly swallowed her tongue.

"Your fiancée! Well, that's good news. I'd hoped you weren't still pining after Carol Jean," the sandy-haired man said with what sounded to Cilla like a forced laugh.

"Nope," Jeremiah said, with an apologetic grin toward the woman he'd called C.J. "Got over Carol Jean a long time ago. No offense, C.J.!"

She smiled glacially. "How do you do,

Priscilla? I'm very pleased Jeremiah's found someone—"

"Oh, it didn't take him long," Cilla broke in. "I'm his fourth—or is it his fifth—girlfriend since you. And we're not actually engaged—" she shot a poisonous look at Jeremiah who feigned chagrin "—although we've discussed it. Right now, I'm far too busy to contemplate such a change—"

"Oh? And what do you do?" asked the woman he'd nearly married.

"I'm a preschool teacher. I have a preschool in Glory," Cilla said, pasting what she hoped looked like a serene smile on her face. "Blue Owl Preschool," she added inanely.

"How...nice." A condescending smile from that C.J. person. "Your own business?"

"Yes, my own." How much longer could this ridiculous conversation go on? She was seething inside. The woman made "preschool teacher" feel like a suds swabber at the local laundromat.

Jeremiah must have read her mind. "Come on, darling. There's something over here I want to show you." He nodded to Carol Jean and her husband. "Nice to see you, C.J., Neil."

They moved off. Cilla was still seething. She didn't know how Jeremiah could be so pleasant to someone who'd obviously dumped him. Even if it was several years ago. He had to be still upset about it, he *had* to be.

"I don't see how you could have…have smooched her cheek like that!" she said in a furious undertone. "I thought she had a lot of nerve, coming up to you the way she did. And that husband! What a—a fool! I—I—"

Jeremiah laughed. "He seemed very nice."

"Nice! She deserves him—"

He put one arm around her. Then he put both arms around her. He rumbled with laughter. "Cilla, Cilla," he said, shaking his head.

"I'm sorry," she snapped, pushing her hands against his chest. "I fail to see what's so funny. And I also don't appreciate being introduced as your fiancée. Do you realize that might get around? How would you like *that?*"

"I'd like it," he said, more serious now. "Listen. I'm tired of this, you know, just *business* stuff. I think we both know this isn't just business anymore. We're friends now, right?"

She nodded cautiously. "I suppose so."

"And I'm a healthy single man and you're a healthy single woman, with no attachments, right?"

She nodded again, narrowing her eyes. What, exactly, was he getting at?

"I'm quite aware that you're too busy for any kind of relationship. You've told me that."

"Uh-huh."

"And I accept it. I understand your concerns. I like a woman who knows her own mind."

"So, what's your point?" She still didn't trust him. Not entirely.

"My point is, I am very attracted to you. In fact," he ducked his head nearer hers and whispered, *"I want to kiss you again and again."* She felt herself turn red again. "I'm sure you're aware of that, too. But I'm not sure I'm willing to wait until you change your mind about a relationship. Who knows when that could be? I need to think it over. Do you understand what I mean?"

Cilla refused to say anything. Nor would she nod her head. But her heart soared. She'd been so sure the attraction was mainly on the other side—hers. She was prepared to deal with that. But what did he mean about not waiting until she changed her mind?

"However—" He shot her a very devilish grin. "I really liked kissing you back there, behind the potted palm. There's, uh, another green thing right here and—" He nodded in the direction of a nearby six-foot weeping fig. "Another kiss might help me make up my mind. What do you think?"

"Well…" She hesitated. "Maybe just this once."

She'd barely answered before he was kissing her again. Cilla gave herself up to the kiss. She kissed him back. Why not? And she was pretty sure the woman in the blue dress was nowhere around.

Jeremiah Blake was kissing her because he *liked* kissing her….

So there.

JEREMIAH MADE a point of avoiding Glory and the Blue Owl School for a week. He was rattled. Rattled, jarred and entirely out of sorts. Irritated, annoyed, short-tempered with his employees. He wasn't sure anymore what he thought about the new teacher, and he wasn't going to find out without a lot of reflection. On his own. Alone.

It wasn't fair to lead her on. And that was what he was doing.

He'd copped a kiss. He'd copped a couple of kisses. And they were even better than he'd guessed they'd be. She was a warm, passionate, loyal, proud woman and he liked her very much. He more than liked her.

But he was in no position to go any further than he'd already gone. He wasn't prepared to talk about love. Because at his age, love meant other things—marriage, kids.

She'd said she wasn't interested in a relationship. He'd said he respected that—and he did. And he'd also said he wasn't prepared to wait. At the pace things were going between them, there was no way he *could* wait until she changed her mind.

All of that was true. But could he go back to being good old reliable Jeremiah Blake, putting up storm windows and delivering a load of sand for the playground? Jeremiah Blake at your service, ma'am?

He had roundup later this week. A chance to think. Couldn't have asked for better timing.

He told her that when he went to town to put on the storm windows. It was just after school, on a Thursday. He'd planned to head out with a crew of cowboys the following day, at first light. They'd need at least a week to gather all the Diamond 8 stock, separate them out from the other brands, send off the old cows to the packing house, settle the rest on their winter ranges, pasture the bulls, take care of any veterinary problems, ship the steers that were still on the place, do all the thousand and one housekeeping jobs that a rancher had to do to take care of his stock and get ready for winter.

Then there was the business of the new ranch house. They'd planned to break ground by the middle of the month, maybe even get the house built if the snow came late. He'd have to call Reta, tell her to go ahead with the changes Cilla had made. She'd noticed things about the plans that he hadn't seen, and her suggestions made sense. A staircase moved here, a bigger mudroom there, a place for a freezer…a larger en suite in the master bedroom.

Jeremiah tried to be as cool as he possibly could when he stopped at the school to do the windows, as he'd promised. He wasn't sure she noticed. She was there, supposedly helping him, handing him things and generally getting in the way. She acted as though nothing had changed since last weekend, as though those kisses had never happened.

What was the matter with women?

"Jeremiah, did you hear me? I said that Rory asked me if he could come and visit next Saturday, because Evelyn and her family are going somewhere, and I told him he could spend the whole weekend with me. Isn't that great?" She was enthusiastic about the kid coming to stay. A five-year-old.

"Sure, that's great." Jeremiah grunted as he lifted a storm window into place and braced it with his knee. He was on the stepladder and Cilla was beneath, looking up. He held out his hand for the hammer.

"This? The pliers?"

"No, the hammer."

"I've got a ton of things planned for him already," she said, passing him the hammer. "We're going to bring the hamster home that Friday. And we're going to the grocery store. I have no idea what kids like to eat. You must know, you've got your niece visiting you all the time. What do they like?"

"Oh, anything. Anything that comes out of a box or a can. Alphagetti, I don't know. Beans."

"I'll ask Nina." She had a faraway look in her eyes, a kind of light. He wished he'd put it there—not Rory Goodland. Man, was he so far gone he was jealous of a kid now? What *was* this?

"By the way, Cilla, I'm heading out on

roundup tomorrow morning, early. I won't be here next week to do any odd jobs you might—"

"Ice cream! Kids like ice cream. And what about activities? There's not a lot to do in this town, now that the pool's closed for the winter but—"

"Cilla!"

"Yes? You want the screws now? Which ones?"

"No. I wanted to tell you I won't be here next week. If you've got some jobs that need doing, you'll have to call on someone else."

"Oh." She looked bewildered. Lost, even. That was some satisfaction. "Where are you going?"

"Roundup. I told you, remember? I'm going out with a crew first thing tomorrow. I'll be gone at least a week."

"Oh." She didn't actually say anything for a while, just handed him screws and tools when he needed them. "Are we—are we still going out on that horseback ride? Up to that line cabin or wherever?"

Man. She hadn't forgotten that. He glanced at her quickly. "You want to?"

"Well, I do if you do," she answered, shading her eyes as she peered up at him. She didn't look all that sure of herself. He felt like a jerk. After all, who'd talked her into the idea in the first place?

"I'm still game. We'll talk about it when I get back."

"Um, I need to ask you something else—I don't know if I mentioned it, but my sister's getting married in November."

Oh-oh. Here it comes. "Yeah, I think you mentioned that."

"Well, would you consider going to the wedding with me? It would be like that gallery thing. A few hours. Dinner, dance, a bit of socializing. You'd have to dress up. That would—well, that would pretty well clear your obligation, wouldn't it? It'd be about the full five days, then."

Jeremiah considered. He didn't want to send the wrong signals. He wanted to back off for a while, think this through. "You got anybody else you could ask? Just in case. I can't promise anything just now," he added hastily, when he saw her face pale.

"Oh, sure. Listen—" She handed him another screwdriver. "Let's just forget it. I'll go with someone else. That's not a problem."

Hey, wait a minute. "How about I let you know when I get back from roundup," he amended hastily. Who was she thinking of asking besides him?

She didn't say anything.

"I'll let you know then, okay?" He didn't like the look in her eyes. Stubborn. And he wanted an answer. "When I get back?"

She shrugged. "Okay. If I line up someone else, though, I'll just have to think up some other thing for you do to do. To work off your last day. I mean. Maybe you could help with the Christmas concert."

Back to this stupid *business* she kept pretending they were doing. Didn't she know it was beyond that now? Way beyond that. Which was the whole problem.

Jeremiah climbed carefully down the ladder. "Look, Cilla—"

She regarded him warily. He'd never felt more like taking her into his arms and holding her, pressing her soft body against his. Kissing her. He'd never felt this overwhelming urge before to kiss a woman goodbye and promise he'd be back. Just like some hero in a war movie.

"Take care, eh?"

"I will, Jeremiah." Her eyes rested on the short brown grass at his feet. "Don't worry."

He hadn't said he was *worried,* had he? But

he wasn't going to comment. "And the kid. Take care of the kid."

"Oh, I will." She smiled wanly. "We'll have lots of fun. He deserves it, poor little guy."

"Yeah."

There was an awkward silence, and Jeremiah took a deep breath and tipped his hat forward a little. "Okay. Bye for now."

He got in his pickup and started it. He put it into gear, then hesitated as she moved toward the vehicle. She rested one hand on the side mirror.

"What—what do you do on roundup? I mean, for a whole week?" Her face was framed in the open window. He could see a couple of freckles on her nose that he hadn't noticed before.

"Well, you know." Jeremiah shrugged. "You go out with a bunch of cowboys and look for your cows that have got scattered all over hell's half acre during the summer. You find 'em, drive 'em back. Eventually end up at the home ranch."

"Where do you stay?"

Stay? Why at the Hilton, Miss Cilla! "Oh, we sleep out. In bedrolls under the stars. We eat campfire food, drink campfire coffee, have a few laughs, tell a few lies. Chew some tobacco. It's hard work."

"Any women go along?"

Jeremiah grinned. "Why? Worried?" He couldn't resist.

"Don't be silly. I just wondered."

"Sure, a few do. If they're good riders and good with a rope, we'll take 'em along. We're equal opportunity out there, you know." He winked and she flushed and stepped back.

Jeremiah eased his foot onto the gas. He wasn't going to see her for more than a week. Or talk to her. He steeled himself not to look in the rearview mirror, but just before he turned onto River Street, he allowed himself a quick glimpse. There she was, still standing under that big tree, watching him drive away.

If he could have stood on the brakes and raced back for one hug, one kiss, he would have. Or maybe…never left her at all.

But it wasn't like that with them. And it very likely never would be. For crying out loud, they had no possibility of a future, he and she. She didn't want a relationship. He didn't want a relationship. And they were practically from different planets—she didn't even know what a roundup was.

But they *had* a relationship, didn't they?

GETTING INTO the high country was one of the best things about a cowboy's life, Jeremiah had always thought. The Rocking Bar S, where he'd grown up and where his brother, Cal, now ranched, backed onto the Rockies. So did the Diamond 8. The Diamond 8 had more than five thousand acres of deeded land and almost as much again in government grass leases. He shared a few of those leases with some of his neighbors, and the big job each fall was to gather up all the stock and separate out the brands.

With that much ground to cover, a week was an absolute minimum, and that was with a crew of eight of his own cowboys, plus however many his neighbors sent out. Every coulee had to be inspected for wily cows that might be hiding out in the bottoms. Every valley had to be searched, every patch of timber scoured.

He'd been pretty distracted this past month or so. It wasn't like him. Luckily, he could count on his foreman, Ned Strange, and the number-two cow boss, Pete McGinty. There wasn't anything about roundup that they didn't know. Between them, they'd spent more years riding the range than he'd had birthdays.

Marshall Downing was going out with them this year, which was a plus. At least they'd get decent grub. Last year they'd used a cook from the Double O, Adam Garrick's spread, who was crankier than all-get-out and wasn't much of a cook, to boot. Marshall didn't drive the chuckwagon, the way the cookie would have done in the old days, but he had a camp kitchen set up in a van and brought the supplies to the predetermined meal-and campsites. They'd spend two nights at the old Wolverton camp, up near the tree line. It consisted of a log bunkhouse and a cookhouse, pretty rickety now, with the wind blowing through the chinks, but the chimney was still sound. That was always the high point of the fall roundup. Lots of tall tales and stories from the past. A little music if someone had brought along a mouth harp. Some rank jokes if there were no women present. Jeremiah loved it.

He thought of that gallery opening he'd gone to last week with Cilla. Was that really the kind of thing she enjoyed? Man, he couldn't believe it. One of those a year was more than enough for him. Overdressed people with more money than sense. Those piddly sandwiches and mushy stuff on crackers.

You had no idea what you were putting in your stomach. Nope, he preferred simple honest food and the unpretentious company of cowboys.

The first day out, Jeremiah covered nearly ten miles on his gelding, Buck, which made for a hard day. He'd partnered up with a first-timer, Trevor Longquist, and had brought along a younger horse as well as the gelding, one he'd picked up when Noah Winslow sold off some of his brother's horses. A little mare with a lot of heart, name of Nellie. He'd never worked cows with her before, and was curious to see how she'd manage. Buck was getting on, he was nearly fifteen now, and it wasn't fair to push him hard on a roundup, the way he would a younger animal. He knew the gelding would fret, though, at being left behind, so Jeremiah had brought him.

They were a good team, he and Buck, and he'd looked forward to a hard ride. He'd had Buck for ten years, ever since he'd bought him off a hazer at the Strathmore Rodeo for two-thousand dollars. Jeremiah had a good-fitting saddle, one of his older ones, fitted with a scabbard holding his trusty 30.06, the rifle Cal had given him when he graduated from high school. There were occasionally cougars or bears in this part of the country—not that a cougar was much of a threat to the stock this time of year, but they could be murder on the calves when they were born. And bears were generally no bother, although it always made sense to be prepared. He had his favorite horse under him, a blue sky above and the whole of God's creation around him. Nothing could be finer.

Yet every night as he lay under the stars, listening to some of the boys still hooting around the fire, enamel mugs filled with coffee, he thought of Cilla. He remembered every tiny little thing he knew about her. Thought back to every time he'd touched her hand. The time he'd kissed her. He got warm just thinking about the way he'd kissed her, the way she'd kissed him back.

She'd become a part of his life somehow, even though neither of them was expecting it. If she only knew how much he'd had to do with Bea's so-called donation…man, she'd kill him. And as for him, he'd gone after her in the first place because she'd said "hands off." Nothing woke him up faster than a challenge. No way was some other single guy in Glory getting to first base if *he* couldn't get there.

Then, suddenly, before he'd even realized it, he was on second.

But…when had things changed? And *had* they really changed? Marriage? Kids? Slippers? Dinner waiting? Nope. Not for him. The prospect scared him. And yet…

Could it be that he'd fallen in love with Cilla Prescott? Against all the odds?

He had nothing against kids. He got a lot of pleasure out of his niece's visits. And he'd enjoyed the afternoon with Rory. The boy had actually managed to snag the snubbing post once, the target Jeremiah had him pitching the rope at, and the joy on his face had been worth all the time and trouble. It made Jeremiah want to really teach him something about being a cowboy. Roping, riding, the works.

If he had a son—or a daughter—he could do that. Poor Rory. He wondered how the court case was going to turn out. He'd heard from his buddy, Lucas Yellowfly, one of the lawyers in town, that the case would be heard very soon, maybe even that month. The prize organizers were fighting it, saying that since the winner hadn't actually claimed the prize before being killed—that was Rory's father they were talking about—the money still belonged to the organization. It was kind of a technicality, but Jeremiah could see their point. He could also see the point Rory's relatives were making, and why they wanted to get their hands on some of that money.

No, kids were not a problem.

And he liked women, all right. He liked women just fine. Cilla's outburst to C.J. that she was his fourth or fifth girlfriend since she'd dumped him had nearly made him laugh. It wasn't true—and of course Cilla had just invented it on the spot—but he'd done his share of dating. A girlfriend? Not really. Not since C.J. Most of the others had been a few dates here, two or three months there. Dana Willetts, the most recent, had been some kind of record, nearly six months.

To tell the truth, he was getting tired of that. Maybe his sister-in-law was right. Maybe it was time he settled down, quit stringing lines with different women he took out. A woman like Cilla didn't deserve a line. A woman like Cilla deserved something better. She deserved love. She deserved an honorable offer of marriage.

By the time they'd gathered the herd and were turned toward home, Jeremiah had thought the thing through—as far as he was going to think it through now.

He wasn't finished with Cilla Prescott. He was coming around to the notion that he might just be in love. If he wasn't in love now, he was close to it. He was itching to see her again. Six nights on the range, three of them with below freezing temperatures, made him rethink the advantages of having a woman warming his bed on a permanent basis. Waiting for him when he got home. A woman he loved.

He'd take her to her sister's wedding. He'd organize a trip up to the line cabin, probably the very next weekend, if that worked out for her. They had to go before the weather turned for good, or they'd have to wait till spring. He wasn't waiting till spring to get her alone and finally spend some serious time with her. Nor was he going to any more gallery openings just for a kiss and a squeeze.

He needed to get a fix on the situation, feel her out a little more, see if she might be in a position to return some of his feelings. Now or soon. The very idea that she might *not* be scared him. That was why he'd been shy of this whole marriage and love business—he didn't like the shaky feeling it gave him. The uncertainty. As if he was on trial. Or falling, somehow, and not sure there was anywhere to land.

When they said goodbye to the Double O cowboys, who were taking their herd south at the fork in the Sheephorn, he'd made up his mind for sure. How could he miss a woman like he was missing Cilla if she didn't mean something to him? Something real? He couldn't *wait* to get back.

Cilla Prescott was definitely a possibility, he decided. A very good possibility. The best one he'd come across in his thirty-two years. He was only on second base and he decided it was time to try stealing third. No matter what happened, he wasn't quitting until the inning was over.

Even if it meant marriage? Sure, even if it meant marriage and slippers and supper at six o'clock every night and all that cornball stuff Cal seemed to like so much.

So she'd never heard of roundup or knew what a beefalo was? That was why there were dictionaries.

CHAPTER TWELVE

"Is this your mommy?"

Cilla glanced toward the sofa in the living room. Rory Goodland was leafing through a photo album she'd had on the coffee table.

"Does she look like she could be my mommy?" Cilla asked, hoping to keep the subject light. His own family had only been dead for just over a year.

"No," Rory said soberly, studying the picture carefully. "She looks more like a grandma."

Cilla smiled and came into the living room, wiping her hands on a tea towel. She'd just finished up the few dishes they'd used for supper. She'd suggested the Grizzly Drive-in, a Glory landmark, but Rory had chosen it for Saturday's lunch. Tonight they'd ordered pizza instead. Hawaiian, not Cilla's favorite by a long shot.

Cilla had told Rory he could rent any video he wanted, and he'd picked *The Sword in the Stone,* an old Disney video.

"Well, that's my mom," Cilla said. She stood by the boy. "And that's my dad, there, the one in the funny hat." The pictures were some that had been taken when the elder Prescotts had traveled out to Vancouver and back to visit one of Cilla's aunts.

"He looks like a real nice grandpa," Rory pronounced, closing the book and putting it down beside him on the sofa. He swung his heels. "Where am I going to sleep?" he asked. "Tell me again." His eyes were mischievous. He knew very well where he'd be sleeping.

"In my little room here." Cilla walked to the doorway of the small room she used for a home office. She had a love seat in it that pulled out into a single bed.

"Here? By myself?" Rory stood at the door. She'd already shown him this room. He seemed to like having her show it to him, with the fresh flowers in the vase on the desk, a folded towel and washcloth for Rory to use and the photographs of Cilla's family and friends on the wall. It was almost as though he couldn't believe that this room with all its attractions was for him. Him alone.

"Is that towel really just for me?" He'd seemed amazed when she pointed out the towel and glass and supplies she'd organized for his use. This was the second time he'd asked her about the towel.

"Yes, all for you."

"And this little soap?" With one small forefinger he reverently touched the guest soap shaped like a shell that sat atop the towel and facecloth.

"All yours." He seemed so charmed by the soap that Cilla had decided it was very unlikely he'd actually use it.

The boy's small nylon carryall with the broken zipper stood by the bed. The carryall had come to school with him that afternoon and Evelyn had said she'd be back from her trip Sunday evening, if Cilla got tired of the brat and wanted to return him early. Otherwise, she'd pick him up from school, as usual, on Monday afternoon.

Cilla had been horrified that Evelyn Bell would say such a thing right in front of not only Rory, but all the other children. Rory had seemed not to care, though. He'd waved politely when Evelyn left. Maybe she talked to him like that all the time.

"You ready for the movie, Rory?" Cilla asked, going back into the small living room. The apartment was sufficient for a single person, but she'd have to find something a bit bigger if she intended to stay in Glory. One of the big pluses was that it came furnished. Or as furnished as the tenant required. If necessary, Cilla's landlady was happy to store anything her tenant didn't need in her basement. Cilla had the idea she preferred it that way, less wear and tear on her possessions. Cilla had kept the kitchen furniture, but had moved in her own bed and the love seat Rory would be sleeping on, as well as her desk.

"No." Rory stuck his hands in his pockets as he peered into the bathroom. "Not yet. I want to look around a little more. I like this place. It's sure cool."

"What time do you go to bed at home?" she asked. She didn't mind how long Rory took to check out her apartment. She didn't really expect to enjoy the Disney movie herself. She hoped she didn't fall asleep. The popcorn held more interest.

"I go to bed pretty well when I want to," Rory said, his brow furrowed. "Whenever my cousins go. They're real noisy so I can't go to sleep until they do." He referred to Evelyn's children—and granddaughter—as his cousins.

"And when do they go to bed?" Cilla continued.

"Oh, about—" his eyes wandered "—about ten o'clock. Or midnight—" He shot her an uncertain look and Cilla realized he probably couldn't tell the time yet. "I go to bed a little before they do, so I can think about things by myself. They come in when their TV show's over. They watch that wrestling stuff, but I don't like it. It scares me," he said simply, gazing up into her face.

He was so trusting. So sweet. Cilla loved him already. But this was dangerous—she couldn't fall in love with one of her students. It was unprofessional.

And ten o'clock was a ridiculously late hour for a boy of not quite five to go to bed.

"I think you should be in bed by nine when you're at my place, don't you?"

"Oh, I want to! You've got books and stuff to look at."

"Do you look at books at home when you're in bed?"

"No. We don't have any books, 'cept some comics and some old magazines and I've already looked at all those."

Another shocking state of affairs. How was a young boy, obviously an intelligent young boy, supposed to exercise his mind? He couldn't read yet, but he could look at pictures. And he could be read to, by an adult who cared. Obviously, Evelyn Bell didn't care much.

"So. Where do *you* sleep?" Cilla persisted. That tiny bungalow she'd seen didn't have room for a small family to spread out, let alone the number of people who seemed to live there, including the sixteen-year-old daughter's boyfriend. "Where does everyone sleep?"

"Evelyn and Bill have a room. Do you know who Bill is? He's Evelyn's new boyfriend. And then Cindy and her boyfriend share one of the rooms. Their baby sleeps in there with them. Somewhere, I don't know exactly," he confessed, looking perplexed. Perhaps he'd never thought about all the sleeping arrangements in the place he now called home.

"And what about you?"

"I share a room with Wilbur and Bernie. I hate Bernie, he's mean. But he sleeps on the cot and Wilbur and me sleep in the big bed. Wilbur kicks, but at least he's not mean."

Cilla didn't want to ask what he meant by *mean;* she didn't want to know. She didn't want to get drawn into this poor child's life. She just wanted to provide a place for him to come occasionally, the way he'd done that weekend. She was thrilled that he liked her enough to just come out and boldly ask if he could stay with her. The alternative—going away with Evelyn and her brood or staying in the bungalow with his older cousin and the boyfriend and the baby—must have been worse.

"Okay, so that's most of your cousins. What about the rest?"

"The girls sleep in the living room. So they can't go to bed until everybody quits watching TV. But Cindy and Evelyn and Bill have TVs in their bedrooms."

"Do the girls sleep on the sofa?"

"Elizabeth does. Mary Jane sleeps on the floor. In the summer, they get our room and me 'n Wilbur and Bernie sleep in a tent outside under the tree. Sometimes we let the dogs in there to sleep with us!" He seemed thrilled. Then he added in a loud whisper, leaning toward her, "But we don't tell Evelyn. She'd get mad."

Cilla shuddered. What a household. What about homework, routine, schedules, order? What about a little space to have some privacy? She could imagine the chaos in the one small bathroom each morning. Or maybe they didn't bother with morning bathroom routines. More than once, Cilla had seen Evelyn pasting down the boy's unruly hair with a comb just before turning him over to her for the afternoon. At least she tried that much.

As Jeremiah had said, perhaps she was just doing the best she could with what she had.

Jeremiah. She missed him. It had been more than a week already. He knew she was having Rory this weekend but he could have called. Let her know he was back.

Now, come on, Cilla—why would he do that? You've made it pretty clear that there's nothing but a business arrangement between you. Those kisses two weeks ago at the gallery—that was just something that happened. It meant nothing. Besides, she was now quite convinced that he'd been cooler than usual when he put up her storm windows. No flirting, no fooling around. Maybe he was wishing he could get the whole thing over with these days he "owed" her, once and for all. Maybe he was getting tired of her. She still hadn't seen Bea to thank her in person….

She wished she could've spent an afternoon with Jeremiah and Rory this weekend, the way they had on his ranch. She wanted Rory to know that other adults cared about him, as she was sure Jeremiah did. Sometimes that made all the difference to a child like Rory. He might not have had the best home life, but knowing other adults cared could make a huge difference to the way he regarded himself and other people.

Rory had already asked about Jeremiah several times, and when she'd replied that Jeremiah was out on "roundup," Rory had nodded quietly. He, at least, seemed to know what that was.

"My uncle Phil used to be a cowboy," he'd announced proudly. "He used to go out on roundups. Before he moved to town. *Pow! Pow!* Uncle Phil used to shoot bears and stuff with his special cowboy gun. Pow!" Rory had galloped around the coffee table, illustrating his uncle's technique.

Cilla suggested the boy get into his pajamas before they watched the movie, and he seemed to think this was a hugely novel idea. He immediately disappeared into her office and closed the door behind him. Cilla went into her own bedroom and got into a nightie and slippers and a bathrobe. Why not? They'd have a quiet evening in front of the television, eat popcorn and go to bed early.

She could use an early night. She hadn't

slept all that well this week. Whether it was because the boy was coming to stay with her or the disruption the chicken pox had caused in her school or even knowing that Jeremiah was away… On Friday, she'd had two four-year-olds in the afternoon class. Two! The morning class was gradually getting back to normal, but she still had several kids who'd missed school all that week. If they didn't show up on Monday, she'd call home and see how they were. Rory, oddly, was the one child who'd had chicken pox before. Probably caught from one of his many cousins.

They finally settled in front of the television. It was half past seven. Rory was entranced with *The Sword in the Stone.* Even Cilla found herself gradually drawn into the story. It was a Disney production she'd actually never seen. At one point, Rory said he had to go to the bathroom and Cilla put the movie on pause and got up to get the second batch of popcorn.

"Ready?" Cilla asked when he came back, her hand on the remote, the popcorn on the coffee table in front of them.

"Can I ask you something?" Rory didn't meet her eyes.

"Sure, honey. You can ask me anything you

want. You can talk to me about anything at all, anytime. You know that."

He raised his big green eyes to hers. "Can I sit on your lap? My momma used to hold me on her lap all the time. Please."

Cilla's heart nearly burst. Poor motherless boy. With that awful Evelyn Bell looking after him—she didn't care *what* Jeremiah said. "Of course you can, Rory. Here." She patted her lap and he climbed up onto her knees. He settled in with a big sigh. Cilla turned on the movie and put her arms around the boy.

She didn't have to worry about falling asleep before the movie was over. But Rory fell asleep almost immediately and as soon as she realized it, Cilla turned off the video. She sat there for a few moments, feeling his bony little body against hers, all elbows and ankles. His hair stuck up in poorly cut bunches. His freckles stood out as he slept, his face pale and peaceful.

Cilla realized that tears were running down her cheeks. She managed to get to her feet with the boy in her arms and carried him into the office. She tried to lay him down on the bed so he wouldn't wake, but he did, a little, and sleepily thanked her as she tucked him in, a smile on his thin face.

Cilla walked out and shut the door softly behind her. She couldn't let that child go back to Evelyn Bell. And *Bill,* the new boyfriend. How many boyfriends had there been since Rory came to live with them? She just couldn't send him back there! All of a sudden, she began to hope the court case would go badly for Rory's relatives. Then they'd turn him out, as Jeremiah predicted. Which meant he'd most likely become a ward of the government and go into foster care. She'd take him in. If she couldn't get him as a foster child, she'd—she'd adopt him! She'd marry Jeremiah Blake and they'd *both* adopt Rory! He'd have a mother and a father who cared, who read stories to him, who—

Yeah, and you're living in a storybook yourself.

Cilla washed her face and brushed her teeth and took two aspirins. Her head was killing her. Any more ideas like that, and she'd have more than a headache, she told herself wearily.

She'd have a family.

THE LIBRARY WAS OPEN on Saturday. So after they hit the Grizzly Drive-in for the biggest, messiest, most delicious cheeseburger Rory said he'd ever eaten—much of which ended up on the upholstery of her car—they drove to the library.

Cilla didn't have the heart to say anything to Rory about his dripping burger. He was so pleased to be taken to the drive-in, which was apparently quite a local landmark. And Ma Perkins, the legendary owner of the drive-in, actually leaned down, peered in Cilla's open window and said, "Hi, Rory! How ya doin', kid?" Rory shyly returned her greeting.

At the library, they spent an hour looking through the children's section, and Cilla took out a stack of picture books she thought Rory might enjoy. After dinner that evening, she planned to read to him. Some of her fondest memories of her own childhood were of her parents reading to her at night, and then when Mary began school, of her sister reading to her, as well. Even though the words came haltingly at first, Mary was so proud of herself. And Cilla had been proud, too, that she had a sister who could read. Perhaps that was when she'd made up her mind to become a teacher, to bring the joy of reading to other children.

In the afternoon, they went to the park

down along the riverbank and Rory collected all kinds of fall leaves that had blown onto the ground. It was already the third of November. No snow yet, but the park was filled with the yellows of larches and poplars, the reds of the maples that had been planted at the turn of the century, the browns and golds of the oaks. Later, while Cilla prepared dinner for them both, Rory knelt on a chair at the kitchen table and laboriously pasted his autumn leaves onto some unlined paper Cilla had found for him.

"I'm gonna give this picture to Evelyn." He held up a page, gaily decorated with leaves, plus some drawings he'd made. "She's gonna put it on the fridge, I bet!"

"That's lovely, Rory. I'm sure she'll like it." Actually, Cilla *wasn't* sure. But she admired the boy's optimism and determination. He cared for Evelyn, even though it sometimes seemed she didn't care for him. But perhaps she did. Maybe things weren't always as they appeared.

"And this one's for Elizabeth!" He held up another. A river of glue ran down from the maple leaf pasted in the middle to the bottom of the page. "She'll really like this one. Elizabeth's big. She's in grade five already."

Rory worked away for another fifteen minutes or so. Cilla watched him, unobserved. He hummed, he put his tongue out of his mouth, first this way, then that, concentrating. He chose crayons carefully, considered, then put them back to choose other ones. Then, just when she was ready to ask him to clear up because she needed to lay the table, he held up two more pages.

"Guess who these are for?" He grinned, eyes dancing.

"Who?"

"This one's for you." He handed her a paper covered from top to bottom with poplar leaves, a few oak leaves in for contrast.

"Oh, Rory! It's lovely." Cilla held it up against her fridge. It was going to look wonderful there. "And who's the other one for?"

Rory kept it facedown for a moment, then produced it in triumph. "Ta-da! This one's for Jeremiah. See—that's you and that's me and that's him!"

He pointed to childishly drawn horses and people. The man was on a horse and leading another horse. The woman was on foot, leading a horse with spots on it—definitely Shorty—and a boy was in the saddle. Rory, of course. The boy was just as large as the man and woman, and the arms and legs came directly out of the heads. A typical four-year-old's drawing. The horses were walking on carefully pasted leaves.

"Rory! This is beautiful." She glanced at him. He was grinning proudly.

"I know," he said, nodding, accepting her compliment with simple grace and honesty. His eyes were shining.

"Jeremiah's going to love it. I can hardly wait until he sees it." This gave her an excuse to drive out to his ranch. Maybe they'd do that tomorrow. After all, even Jeremiah could understand how important it was that the boy deliver his gift.

The phone rang the next morning before Cilla was out of bed. She hadn't heard anything from Rory's room yet.

"Hello?" Her voice was hoarse with sleep.

"Too early for you, Sunshine?"

"Jeremiah!"

"I missed you. Did you miss me?" The deep voice had a bantering tone, but was dead serious underneath. It sent shivers down her skin.

"Missed you? It's only half past eight. Why did you call so early? Why didn't you call before? When did you get in?" She tried to still the racing of her heart by summoning a sense of outrage. It wasn't working.

"I just got in yesterday afternoon. It took a little longer than we'd planned. I called you as soon as I could."

"Was it—fun?" She didn't know what to ask. These things must be hard work, but were they also fun?

"Oh, sure. Listen—are you free this afternoon?"

She frowned, thinking. They'd planned to go fishing, off the Horsethief River Bridge. She knew nothing about fishing—and wasn't crazy about learning—but Rory had been determined that he was going to show her how to catch a fish.

"I've got Rory here with me, you know."

"Yeah, I know. How's it working out with the kid?"

"Great. Jeremiah, you've got to see the picture he's done for you."

"Picture?" He sounded puzzled. "What for?"

"For your fridge," she explained patiently.

"My *fridge?*"

"It's something kids do. It's called fridge art. Surely Marigold's given you some."

"I guess so. I just tacked it up on the bulletin board in the barn. So—what about it? You free?"

"Rory's going to take me fishing—"

"Fishing? Man, that kid's talented!"

"You don't know the half of it," she said severely. "Now, about this afternoon. We could run out and deliver the picture and say hello later, say about four."

"I've got a better idea. Why don't we *all* go fishing and then I'll take the two of you out to supper somewhere. In my red truck. Rory would like that. I'll even let him blow the horn. Pop's Diner? You ever been there?"

"No." Cilla's mind was whirling. "Okay. I'll ask Rory. If he wants to do that, I'll call you back."

There was a pause at the other end. "It's up to the kid, huh? What about you—do *you* want to see me this afternoon?"

"I—I'd rather not say," she said hurriedly.

"I know what that means," he returned in a low voice. "It means you do. And you know what that reminds me of?"

"Wh-what?" She was almost afraid to ask.

"I did some thinking out there on the mountain. I made up my mind. You and I have business to finish, right? Then, when the business part's done, we can move right along to the pleasure part." She heard the grin in his voice. Pleasure, indeed! "I'm taking you to your sister's wedding, as long as I don't have to get dressed up in some monkey suit—"

"You mean a tux?" She couldn't resist.

"Whatever..."

"What if I already asked someone else to take me?" she teased.

"You'd just have to un-ask him."

"Just like that?" She couldn't wipe the smile from her face.

"Yep. Just like that. And, listen, I've got everything figured out for next weekend. We're going up to that line cabin on the Whisky Creek before the weather turns. A day trip. We'll start early, and you can ride Shorty. Don't worry about a thing, Cill. I've taken care of it all."

CHAPTER THIRTEEN

THE NEXT SATURDAY, they left the ranch before eight in the morning. When Jeremiah had said early, he'd meant early. He wasn't worried about the long day in the saddle; he was more concerned about the weather.

It didn't look great. The sky was steel-gray and an ice fog hung over the river, down in the valley, which was just starting to freeze up. They'd been lucky so far, but winter was definitely on the way.

The cold wouldn't bother the horses. In fact, it might mean a more comfortable ride for him and Cilla, too. Sometimes heat was harder to take than cold; you could always put on another sweater or vest. He'd impressed upon Cilla that she had to dress properly. Riding boots, he'd told her, or at least boots with some kind of heel. Sneakers were not acceptable riding gear. An extra sweater in a saddlebag, extra socks, gloves if the weather stayed cold once the sun had come up properly. A hat. Sunscreen, in case they needed it, which didn't seem likely.

As for him, he was more than prepared. Ever since the time his horse had injured a leg and he'd had to sleep out in a late-February snowstorm, when he was sixteen with no bed-roll, no jacket, no gloves, no food—Jeremiah had always traveled prepared. Anything could happen on the trail, and often did. Only a fool went out expecting no problems.

He knew he could count on Cilla to follow his instructions. Not only was she beautiful and passionate and warmhearted, she was sensible. He appreciated that. A lot of women, in his experience, were not.

Plus, she was on time. Early, in fact. He'd just finished checking the horses for the fifteenth time, it seemed, when he heard Pete shout, "Woman driving up!"

That would be Cilla. Jeremiah left the horses inside the barn and walked out into the dull morning.

"Are you sure you want to do this? It's freezing!" she asked, coming up to him, rubbing her gloved hands together. She wore jeans and sensible hiking boots with a heel, a jacket over a turtleneck sweater, and carried a knapsack.

"If you do." He squinted at the sun, which was barely over the horizon and invisible behind the cloud cover. "I expect this to burn off in a couple hours. The forecast's for clear weather. I'm game if you are."

"Definitely. Anything you can do and all that," she answered, smiling. Since the afternoon they'd spent with the kid last Sunday, he was feeling a little easier. He'd sorted out some of his feelings on the roundup, and he was focused now. He wanted to know if they had a future. He was going to act as though they did.

She seemed more relaxed with him, too. She seemed to finally trust him. She'd obviously appreciated the time he'd taken to help the kid with his fishing rod, borrowed from Cilla's landlady. It was Second World War vintage, from the look of it, and Cilla said her landlady had told her it had belonged to her husband. Edo Vandenbroek had died years ago—Jeremiah had never known him—so the rod went back quite a ways.

They hadn't caught anything. Jeremiah knew there were a few jackfish in the river, maybe a pickerel or two, but they weren't biting. That hadn't spoiled the kid's enjoyment. Nor had it spoiled Jeremiah's. He and Cilla had sat on the riverbank and talked. About high school and traveling, about what they liked to eat on picnics and whether he was ticklish. He swore he wasn't. He couldn't get enough of the glint of the sun on her hair, or her laugh, or the trim turn of her ankle in her tennis shoes and white socks, or the softness of her hand when he grabbed it to help pull her up. The day could have lasted forever. He felt like he'd been waiting for her all his life—waiting all his life to court her. There was no rush. He could take his time, enjoy the simple pleasure of being with her. Let things happen slowly, naturally, between them—if they were going to happen.

It had been one of the nicest afternoons of his recollection.

Now, if he could just get her through the next ten or so hours. The high country was worth seeing, even on a poor day. He'd brought binoculars and a camera. He hoped they'd be able to make it up to the line cabin with some hard riding this morning, have their lunch there, then take a more leisurely pace back. If worse came to worst, they could shelter in the cabin, primitive though it was.

The first hour went well. As Jeremiah had expected, the sun burned off the fog as it rose, and the scattered cloud cover gradually thinned. By the time they got to the first saddleback, about four miles from the ranch, the sky was relatively clear. Jeremiah stopped on the ridge and turned his gelding to wait for Cilla, making her way slowly and carefully behind him on Shorty.

He took off his jacket, rolled it up and tied it behind the cantle. Then he reached into one of the bulging saddlebags and pulled out a bottle of water. He twisted off the top and took a deep swig, wiping his mouth as Cilla arrived and stopped near him.

"Drink?" He held it out to her and she accepted it with a smile. She seemed too out of breath to talk. She regarded the open bottle, hesitated only a split second, then raised it to her mouth. He watched as she swallowed, her mouth where his had been only seconds before. It was an incredibly exciting feeling. *Man, what next?* he thought in disgust. *You'll be asking if you can carry one of her gloves, so you can tuck it in your shirt pocket next to your heart.*

He took the bottle she handed back and screwed on the cap. Then he bent to stow it in the saddlebag.

"What's all that stuff you've got in there?" she asked.

"Food." He looked up from fastening the buckles. "First-aid stuff. A few oats for the horses. I told you I was prepared, didn't I?"

"What's the gun for?" She indicated the 30.06 in the scabbard on his saddle.

"It's a rifle, Cilla. A medium-caliber hunting rifle. Comes in handy sometimes. I don't expect to have to use it. How do you like the view?" he asked, changing the subject.

The valley spread out wide and distant below them. The Horsethief River wandered through here, quite a few miles above the town of Glory. In the distance he could see where the Sheephorn joined up with the Horsethief, and, farther down, where the Elk joined in. He handed her the field glasses.

"I think I see something," she said, her eyes glued to the glasses. "Are there any antelopes out here?"

"Give it to me," he said, putting the binoculars briefly to his eyes and then giving them back to her. Buck raised his head several times impatiently, jangling his bridle. "No antelopes. Those are mule deer you see. Or maybe whitetails. But the whitetails stay down on the prairie more. The mule deer range as high as we are now."

"Oh." She returned the binoculars. "It's a thrilling view, Jeremiah. I had no idea there'd be such scenery up here."

Scenery. This woman was going to take a bit of educating, that was for sure. And he was just the man to do it.

"Ready to ride?"

"Ready!" she sang out and kicked Shorty in the ribs. The pinto grunted and, heaving a big sigh, began to amble after Buck. Jeremiah could tell that Buck was feeling exasperated with his barn buddy. Shorty didn't keep up with many horses on the Diamond 8. He was stubborn, slow and would probably have made a better pack animal than a riding horse. He was reliable, though. Solid as the Rock of Gibraltar. That was what counted.

But they weren't going to make the line cabin by noon at this pace. He was getting hungry already, and he was sure she was. Breakfast had been a long, long time ago.

The next hour was mostly climbing, and they had to take it slow. At one point, they had to get off the horses and lead them across a rock slide. Jeremiah didn't remember this from the last time he'd been up here, more than a year ago. It must have happened last winter.

"Careful," he warned Cilla as she prepared to lead Shorty across the slide that he and Buck had already crossed. But he didn't have to worry. Shorty was as surefooted as a mountain goat. He picked his way slowly across the slide, not jarring even one rock. Buck had sent a few skittering down the slope. Jeremiah breathed a sigh of relief when they both reached his side.

"Now what?" Cilla asked cheerfully. She looked hot. Her face was flushed and she'd stowed her jacket in her saddlebag, as he had. He wanted to touch her cheek. Push back a lock of her hair. Kiss those soft lips.

"Uh, I'm thinking maybe we could stop for lunch soon. You hungry?"

"Starved. I could eat a bear!"

"I think the expression is 'eat a horse,' honey." He grinned.

"Shh!" She frowned and put one finger playfully to her lips. "Don't say that. Shorty might get upset."

"Okay." He shook his head, laughing. "Another half hour. I know a good place to eat. Out of the wind and not that far from the cabin."

They pushed on.

They arrived at the place Jeremiah had in mind just before noon. The clouds were building up again in the southeast, and he'd revised his plan for the day now. He was thinking maybe they should head back after they'd eaten. Getting to the line cabin was no big deal. It was just the destination he'd chosen; there was no other reason to go there.

Jeremiah staked the horses and let them browse a little on the dried mountain grasses. Shorty snuffled around, then stood under a tree, slack-hipped, and dozed.

Cilla watched as Jeremiah worked.

He spread a spotless checked cloth on the grass in a sunny spot. Molly McClung's delicatessen had provided everything, right down to the plastic glasses. He set out a series of plastic-topped containers, followed by a chilled bottle of ginger ale, the bottle wrapped in a cool, moist chamois cloth to keep the temperature low, hardly a problem today. A thermos of hot chocolate might have been a better choice. Out came plastic cutlery and sturdy paper plates.

Cilla was suitably impressed. "Where did you get all this? Did Marshall prepare it?"

"Nope. Marshall's cooking is more along

the lines of coffee cake and roast beef. I, uh—" He glanced at her briefly. "I got this from the deli in town. Remember your charity auction? I got a friend to bid on this for me, the catered meal for two. I decided to have them make it up as a picnic lunch and I made an early run into town this morning to pick it up."

Cilla laughed. "Oh, what a good idea!" She came forward. "Can I just sit down? Anywhere?"

"Wherever you want." Jeremiah waved expansively. He passed her the bottled water; she dribbled it over her hands, then wiped them on her jeans. He exhaled with relief—she didn't seem to remember anything about the catered lunch on offer at the auction. It was one of the items he'd got Bea Hoople to bid on for him….

"Oh, by the way," she said, sitting down where she could see the whole valley spread below them. "I ran into Bea this week—you know, that nice lady who donated you to the school?"

"Oh?" Jeremiah nearly spilled the soda he was carefully pouring into the plastic glasses.

"She was very friendly. We had a nice chat. She wondered if I'd used up all my days yet.

Asked to be remembered to you specially." Cilla took a plate and began dishing up some of the offerings laid out on the cloth—potato salad, cold fried chicken, a noodle salad, some radishes….

Cilla went on, "She said something I found rather odd. Said to tell you 'good luck with your project.'" Cilla bit into a chicken leg hungrily. She chewed for a minute, swallowed, then looked directly at him. "What did she mean by that?"

Jeremiah cleared his throat. He'd had a few seconds' warning while she got started on the chicken leg. Now might be the time to tell her about the crucial role that Bea had played in his "project."

"Oh, well." Cilla shrugged. "I guess she meant something to do with your roundup. Or maybe your new house. This is great!" She waved the drumstick at him enthusiastically.

Mmm…maybe this *wasn't* the time to tell her. Jeremiah was glad Bea had left it at that, hadn't spilled the whole pot of beans.

"Aren't you going to have some food?" Cilla looked windblown and pretty. Her red shirt glowed against the russet and gray of the autumn grasses. Her eyes were bright and sparkling, from the exercise. Riding wasn't just sitting on a horse; it could be hard work.

"Oh, I'll get a bellyful, don't worry." Jeremiah began dishing up food from the containers. Molly had really outdone herself. There was even blackberry cheesecake, his favorite. And cold cherry cobbler—a favorite of Cilla's, he'd discovered in their conversation last Sunday. He'd specially ordered it and hadn't opened the box yet.

He sat down a few feet from Cilla, where he could watch her. He handed her the plastic glass. This was no campfire cuisine, that was for sure. A guy could get used to this....

He raised his glass. "To you, Cilla. You're a wonderful woman. And a fine sport."

"Thank you, Jem." She smiled deep into his eyes and he felt a sudden urge to tell her he was in love with her. Just tell her, right there and then. Just the sweet, natural way she'd used his nickname made him happy. Everything about her made him happy....

She put her glass down and Jeremiah took a swallow from his.

"Can I get your opinion on something, Jeremiah?" she asked.

He took another mouthful, lifting one eyebrow to invite her confidence. "Mmm?"

"I'm thinking of trying to adopt Rory Goodland—hey, what did you do that for?"

Jeremiah had choked and spit his mouthful onto the grass. *"What?"* He coughed. "Cilla! You're not *serious?*"

"Of course, I'm serious," she said, frowning. "I wouldn't just say something like that."

"*Adopt* him?" Jeremiah was astonished. "What for? I mean, the kid's not even available for adoption. What are you talking about? You're not married, you're working full-time—"

"What does that have to do with anything?" she asked, her brown eyes snapping. "Being married, for instance?"

"Well—a lot," he answered lamely. She *couldn't* be serious. He picked up his fork.

"I don't like that Bell woman. Eveyln. I don't care what you say," she said urgently. "She doesn't look after him properly. And—and one of those cousins is mean to him. He told me. Bernie's his name. He said Bernie was mean."

"*Mean?*"

"Yes, and there's no order around that place. The girl's boyfriend lives with them and—and the children go to bed whenever they want. He says his cousins watch that disgusting wrestling show—can you imagine? *Children?* And—"

"Mean." He took a mouthful of noodle salad, chewed and swallowed. "Let me get this straight. Some kid's mean to him and he doesn't have a regular bedtime, so you're going to adopt him. What do you think you are, the SPCA?"

"Jeremiah Blake," she said ominously. "Will you just listen to me? I don't see why I couldn't. I've got my own business. I have an income. Prospects. A family—"

"What family?"

"Why, my mother and father. And my sisters, that's family." She looked daggers at him, eyes narrowed defiantly.

He nodded. "Okay." Somehow he didn't think Social Services was going to see it that way.

"If the judge doesn't give him that prize money, his relatives could very well turn him out—you said so yourself."

"Turning him out is one thing, adopting him is another," Jeremiah muttered. The wind had come up a little.

"Speaking of that prize money, how much are we talking about here, anyway?" Her face was troubled. He couldn't believe it. She was absolutely serious about adopting this kid.

He drained his glass. "Half a million or so."

"Half a million dollars! What was it, a lottery?"

He nodded as he checked the southeast with an experienced eye. Whatever was blowing up was coming their way fairly quickly. "Listen, let's talk about this later. I'm thinking maybe we should head back. We could go to the line cabin another time when—"

"Why?"

"Well, look at that bank of clouds over there. We could be getting some bad wind. Maybe rain."

She rolled her eyes. "You're not going to quit over a little wind, are you? A little rain?" she scoffed mutinously. This wasn't going to be as easy and straightforward as he'd thought. "How much farther to the line cabin, anyway?"

"Another mile or so. About another half hour, but it's fairly rough going. We'd have to cross the creek."

"Well, let's go. A mile's nothing." She got to her knees and began gathering cutlery and plastic dishes. Jeremiah wondered if he should ask how she knew a mile or so was "nothing," then decided he'd keep that question to himself. Maybe that cloud would blow over.

"We can pack the rest of the stuff we haven't eaten and get up there. We can always eat the leftovers back at your place later." She smiled and he forgave her everything.

His place later. Now *that* was an idea that had possibilities. He was glad she'd mentioned it. If only she hadn't brought up that nonsense about adopting Rory Goodland. He'd never heard anything so crazy. Sure, the situation was a mess. He felt sorry for the kid, too. But he didn't go so far as to want to *adopt* him, did he? The kid had family. He had people who were looking after him. Relatives.

Man. She was bound to want to talk about it again, probably down at his house. They'd just argue. And the last subject he wanted to argue about when he had her alone was a kid. Rory or any other kid.

"Okay. Let's pack up here. But don't say I didn't warn you if we have to ride through a blizzard on the way home."

"I won't. Don't worry. I'm a big girl, Jeremiah. I can handle a little rain." Then she grinned and added cheekily, "If *you* can."

It was all he could do to restrain himself.

He wanted to haul her into his arms and kiss her. He could hardly wait until the idea occurred to her, too. When it did, he'd be ready and waiting.

The next half hour was a struggle. By the time they'd reached the creek, the heavens had opened and they were soaking wet. The creek was strewn with boulders and Jeremiah had to lead the way up the narrow, twisting streambed for several hundred yards until he found a place where they could safely cross. He could barely see in the blinding rain, lashed every which way by the wind.

This was absolutely crazy. This went against all his instincts as an outdoorsman. They should have gone back an hour ago, as soon as he'd seen those clouds blow up. You didn't go exploring in weather like this, dipsy-doodling about, especially not in November. You were asking for trouble. He should've just told her straight out, plain and simple, no matter what she said. He should've insisted they turn around and go back to the Diamond 8, pronto. He was the expert, not her. He should never even have come this far; all the way to the lookout where they'd had lunch. He was so anxious for her to see the country he loved that he hadn't stopped to consider the possible danger of getting stuck out here in a storm. There was no excuse for it. None at all. They should have turned back two hours ago, when he'd first noticed the clouds, before the rockslide.

The storm was moving up a notch now and they'd have to wait it out and hope it slacked off in an hour or so. At least there'd be firewood in the line cabin, and a roof over their heads. They couldn't head down the valley in this. The footing was too treacherous for the horses. He shuddered just thinking of crossing that rockslide again.

Plus, it seemed darker all of a sudden. Maybe that was just because they were in a forested area. After all—he looked at his watch—it was still early. Just past one in the afternoon, hardly dusk.

Jeremiah urged Buck forward, until they reached the place where he thought the horses could make it across. Then he stopped and patted the gelding's steaming neck and waited for Cilla to join them. Cilla on Shorty had been a dozen or so yards behind them the whole way. He'd stopped once or twice, to see if she could keep up, and then ridden ahead, confident that she could.

Where was she? Jeremiah peered into the darkening forest. "Cilla!"

He listened, but all he could hear was the soughing of the wind in the trees and Buck's heavy breathing.

"Cilla!"

His heart lurched painfully as he heard the crashing of branches from behind a copse of alders. That was all they'd need now—to surprise a sleeping grizzly. Bears liked to bed down in clumps of alders and willows. But black bears would be in hibernation by now, and any grizzlies would have made for the higher elevations. There wasn't much feed to keep a bear awake and interested at this time of year. He'd never seen a grizzly on the Diamind 8's range, but that didn't mean anything. Grizzlies were solitary creatures that stayed away from civilization if at all possible.

Shorty broke through the clump of trees and Jeremiah shouted in anger born of fear, "What's the hold up? Don't you know I'm waiting here for you? I thought you'd gone the wrong way—"

"I'm here, aren't I?" she shouted back. She patted the pinto's thick neck. "So where's this cabin?"

"Other side of the creek. We can cross here. The far bank's fairly high, so dig your heels in and hang on. The old boy's gonna have to climb a little. I'll go first."

"Okay!" she yelled back. It was cold, and Jeremiah swore there was a little ice in that rain. Sleet.

"You okay? Shorty all right?" Something made him hesitate.

"We're fine!" She lifted the reins in both hands, as though to urge Shorty forward. Jeremiah had tied the reins together when they started out to make it a little easier for her. She'd ridden before, but he wouldn't call her an experienced rider. "Go!"

Jeremiah gathered his own reins in his left hand and slapped Buck's withers with his right palm. "All right, Bucko. Do your stuff," he muttered, and dug his heels into the horse's flanks. Buck responded with a burst of energy, and after clattering over the rocks in the creekbed—the water only went up a few inches past the horse's fetlocks—he lunged up the bank. Nothing to it.

Jeremiah slowed Buck at the top and was beginning to turn back toward the creek to watch Cilla cross, when he heard a sound that struck sheer terror into his heart—the unworldly scream of an animal in pain.

Shorty!

CHAPTER FOURTEEN

HE WHEELED Buck around.

He couldn't quite make out what was happening. Shorty plunged and reared, riderless. Cilla was off the horse, down on the bank, half in the water. *What the—* Then his heart froze in his chest. He saw a low-slung grayish-brown animal the size of a large dog at the edge of the creek, under Shorty's hooves. A cougar! He grabbed his rifle and leaped off Buck in one motion.

At first, he couldn't see her in the spray of water and mud—then he saw her. At almost the same instant, he saw the cougar, a small one, raking her leg with its front feet and reaching for her arm with its teeth bared. Cilla screamed. *"Jeremiah!"*

Shorty leaped in terror. Jeremiah raised his rifle, then lowered it. He didn't want to risk injuring Cilla. Or worse…

He scrambled down the bank, yelling, and landed a solid kick on the animal's hindquarters. The cougar turned, snarling, and Jeremiah aimed in the space of a second and got off a quick shot. The report of the rifle mingled with Cilla's scream and the smell of gunpowder. Jeremiah's ears rang. The cougar fell right in front of him, legs twitching, jaw working uselessly. On its chest was a huge patch of red.

"Cilla! Baby, are you okay?" Jeremiah dropped his rifle in the muck and ran to her. She reached for him, sobbing, and he grabbed her shoulders and pulled her out of the stream. She was hiccuping with fear and shock.

"I—I don't know," she cried. "I don't know. What happened?"

"Lion. Mountain lion went for the horse, I guess. I didn't see it happen. How's your leg?" He could see blood, and her jeans were torn. Despite her protests, he carried her up the bank. Buck had dragged back a good ten feet or so from where he'd left him, but had remained standing over the dropped reins as he'd been trained to do.

Where was Shorty? Jeremiah's heart hammered in his ears. He wiped the rain from his eyes and searched the nearby bush and small open space for the pinto.

"Shorty!" There was no response; Jeremiah

hadn't expected any. Even at the best of times, it was doubtful the pinto would respond to his name. They were in a fine mess now. No second horse, and Cilla injured, he had no idea how badly. Maybe the pinto had stopped once he was clear of the creek and the cougar. Maybe he'd come back. He wouldn't want to leave Buck. Horses were social creatures.

Cilla's arms were strangling him. She was shaking so hard her teeth rattled. "Here, honey. Get onto Buck. Can you hang on? I'll lead him. It's not far to the cabin now—"

"Jem…that creature. Is—is it dead?" she whispered. Her eyes were huge. He nodded and she burst into tears. He lifted her into the saddle.

"Hang on to the horn. Whatever you do, Cill, don't fall off." She nodded dumbly, tears streaming down her muddy face, shoulders shaking.

He began to lead Buck toward the cabin. The horse was spooked and kept stepping sideways and throwing his head up. His ears flicked back, then forward, then back again. Either he was picking up some scent from Shorty or…more likely he couldn't get the smell of lion out of his nostrils.

Jeremiah was shocked. He knew there

were cougars in these mountains, but generally they were timid beasts. They might go after a young deer or a newborn calf or even, rarely, an injured animal that was bigger, maybe a half-grown elk. But to attack a full-grown horse? That was unheard of. A horse and rider? With all the noise there'd been, the two of them calling back and forth? It wasn't natural. There had to be something wrong. Some reason for such bizarre behavior.

Rabies. Jeremiah's blood ran cold. After he'd taken care of Cilla, he'd go back and get his rifle and check the animal out.

Her sobbing tore at his heart. Fury rose in his throat and nearly choked him. This was his fault! All of it. If he'd done what he should have and put his big boot down and told her they were going back to the ranch after lunch—even before lunch—none of this would have happened. If he'd taken his responsibilities seriously, a woman he cared about, more than he'd ever cared about anyone before, wouldn't have been hurt. He still hadn't examined her leg, except to see the tattered fabric of her jeans and the blood beneath. He still had no idea of the extent of her injuries, never mind anything like rabies.

The cabin loomed around the last stand of

mountain ash, most of their leaves gone now, leaving only the scarlet berries. He'd never seen anything so welcome in his life. It wasn't far from the creek, less than a hundred yards, but it had seemed an eternity.

He dropped the reins and reached up for her, then changed his mind. "No, you stay there, honey. Can you hang on for another minute or so? I want to check out the cabin first."

"No! Take me with you!" she pleaded.

"Cilla! Snap out of it," he said firmly and the tears rolled down her cheeks again, streaking clear patches through the mud. She was probably in shock. Who wouldn't be? "Just hold on to the saddle. I'll be right back. Buck's fine."

He left her and went to the door of the cabin and pushed it open with some difficulty. The rusty hinges squealed in protest. He wiped cobwebs out of his face as he stepped inside. The cabin was small and gloomy, with only two tiny paned windows admitting light. There was firewood in the box by the stove, though, and he'd noticed some stacked under the eaves, as well. The one rough bunk at the far end was stripped bare, only bedsprings showing. The cowboys never left mattresses up here because the mice destroyed them from one season to the next. A tattered-looking blanket hung on a rafter. He had no idea who'd left it behind.

Well, beggars couldn't be choosers. They were lucky the cabin was here at all.

More than lucky.

Jeremiah hurried back outside and went around to lift Cilla down. She came willingly, collapsing in his arms. He grimaced. Man, what it took to get her to do what you wanted once in a while! Then he cursed himself for his own dark humor.

The cabin held a table and two chairs, a washbowl with an empty bucket on a wooden stand, plus a dented enameled basin and pitcher. The water had to be hauled from the creek. There was a piece of mirror, no more than three inches by seven, taped up to the log above the sink, maybe for some cowboy to shave with, although he'd never known anyone that particular when out line riding. The bed took up the far end of the shack, and the stove, a rectangular cast-iron model, evenly rusted, stood in the center. To the right as you came in the door, over the table, was an assortment of wooden boxes nailed to the wall; they served as cupboards. There were some glass jars in them, with sugar, tea, coffee, matches, dried beans—stuff that wouldn't be eaten by mice or damaged by freezing.

It was rudimentary, but Jeremiah knew a cabin like this could feel like a fancy hotel after two weeks spent sleeping out in all kinds of weather, mending fence or chasing cows.

The first thing to do, after he'd glanced at her leg, was to get the fire going. Then bring in some water. They'd need clean water to wash the wound. He set her down on a chair and strode over to the cupboard to retrieve a coal oil lantern. Lucky again—there was fuel in it. He turned up the wick and put a match to it.

Light! He held up the lantern. Cilla's face was strained and tired. She was wet, cold, shivering, bleeding. Shock was probably a bigger danger than her injuries. He had to get her warm. He took a quick look at her leg. It didn't seem that bad—probably a superficial wound.

"Listen, Cilla. I'm going to get this bed ready, and then I'll move you over there, okay? We need to look at that wound more closely and you need to get out of those wet clothes. Your leg's stopped bleeding. I don't think it's too serious." He was making that call based on the fact that there was no blood on the floor beneath her boot. Obviously, it had clotted already.

Cilla rested her two elbows on the table and buried her face in her hands. He could see her shoulders shaking. That was okay. Shivering was good, too. So was crying. All those things would help maintain her body temperature. A chill combined with shock could be lethal. He had to get the fire going.

He strode over to the bed and picked up the piece of plywood that stood against the wall. That was what the cowboys used as a base for their bedrolls and air mattresses. He didn't have an air mattress, but he had the blanket someone had left. And his saddle blanket.

"Cill?"

She raised a teary face. He reached down and lifted her into his arms and held her tight against him. "Don't worry, honey. Everything's going to be fine." He kissed her forehead, her muddy cheek. "I'll take care of you. Okay? We've got a stove. I even brought my cell phone so we can let people know where we are."

"Oh, Jeremiah!" She rubbed her wet face into his jacket. "I'm so sorry, this is all my fault, if I hadn't been so *stubborn* back there—"

"Shh. Never mind that. It's my fault for letting you talk me into it. I should've laid down the law…." He checked to see how she'd taken his remark. She'd smiled weakly, which was a good sign. "Now, see if you can get out of those wet things, your jacket and stuff, and wrap this blanket around you. I'm going to start the fire, then I'm going to look at your leg and wash your face and do what has to be done."

The wind was howling outside. Poor Buck! It hadn't even crossed his mind that the horse was still standing out there, waiting patiently. He'd been so worried about Cilla.

That rattled him. There was no excuse for a stockman's neglect of his animal. A horse could mean the difference between life and death out on the range. You took care of your horse first, no matter how tired or hungry you were. *Always.* It was an ironclad rule.

Ducking against the onslaught of the wind, which was definitely carrying sleet now, he led Buck to the small shelter that stood behind the cabin, a shelter with a small pole corral around it. It was designed for any cowboy's horse, no matter who used the cabin. There was some of last year's hay under the roof, and Jeremiah had brought oats in a saddlebag. He'd give Shorty's share to Buck. He was beginning to have serious doubts that the pinto would be back. He'd probably high-tailed it to the Diamond 8 and was already halfway home.

He heaved the saddle onto one of the pole rafters in the shelter. Then he carried the saddlebags with his supplies, food and first-aid kit, into the cabin and, finally, he brought in his saddle blanket. It was wool and it was thick. Even if it was a little damp, it would be warm and would help soften that wooden mattress she was going to have to rest on.

He'd go and get water in a little while—they still had bottled water. It was time he had a look at her leg.

Cilla had struggled out of her jacket and was shivering uncontrollably under the blanket. She still had her wet sweater on. He quickly poured what remained of the first bottle of water into a tin saucepan and put it on the stove. The fire roared, and welcome heat was beginning to penetrate the cabin.

"Let go," he said, pulling the blanket from her grip. "We've got to get the rest of these wet clothes off. Now, stand up, Cilla. Come on, stand up!" He had to be firm, even rough, with her. There was much more at stake here than maidenly modesty. She wasn't thinking straight.

"Okay, don't worry, I'm not going to look. Well, not any more than I have to..." He heard a weak attempt at a laugh, which was the best news he'd had. "These jeans and this sweater *have* to come off."

Cilla cooperated and stood on her good leg, leaning against him. He unbuttoned her jeans and worked them down over her hips. What in the world did she have on underneath? It looked like something his aunt Weezie might wear on a cold winter's night. Bloomers, apparently, that went from waist to knees. He felt the fabric between thumb and forefinger. Wool, he'd swear. Just like his winter long johns. That was good; she'd be warm in that, wet or dry. It turned out she had something similar under her sweater, a light wool undershirt.

He'd forgotten to take off her boots. He made her sit down again, then bent to untie the laces and pulled them off, first one, and then the other.

He whistled and held up the second boot. "Will you look at *that?*" The thick leather was scarred from the cougar's attack. Either teeth or claws had drawn deep grooves in the ankle portion. *Grooves that could have gone into her flesh.*

Cilla peered at her boot, uncomprehending.

"That could have been you, Cill. Your foot. Good thing you had proper boots on."

She made a small sound, somewhere between a moan and an acknowledgment. She seemed woozy. He had to get her warmed up as soon as possible. He glanced at the stove. The saucepan was steaming.

"Okay. Let's see that leg." Jeremiah wrapped the blanket around her again, leaving only her injured left leg exposed. He moved the oil lamp closer.

She had two lacerations on her calf, lacerations that ended where the top of her boot had been. They weren't deep, but they'd bled profusely. *That's good,* he thought. Copious bleeding would clean out the wound. Who knew what kind of infection could set in from this kind of thing? She'd have to have a doctor look at it as soon as they got home.

Home.

Where was that? He lived in a converted harness shed, and she lived in rented quarters on the second floor of an old house. But the way he'd felt out on the range last week, missing her, home was just about anywhere she was. That was a dangerous thought. A very dangerous thought. He still had no idea how *she* felt.

"It's not too bad, Cilla. Probably hurts a lot, but he didn't get very deep. I'm going to put some iodine on it, and a bandage."

She nodded. She looked terrible. Jeremiah rooted through his saddlebag for his first-aid kit. Then he opened the second bottle of water and poured some into another saucepan. He'd make her some tea—hot, sweet tea. That would help.

He took a cloth from a stack on the cupboard shelf and dipped it into the steaming water, holding it up for a few seconds to let the heat escape. Then he wrung it out lightly and dabbed at her wounds. She winced. The cloth probably wasn't doing much good, just helping to clean off the dirt. He opened the bottle of iodine from his first-aid kit and poured it on generously, then positioned some sterilized gauze bandages over both lacerations and taped them down.

"Here, honey," he said, sitting on the bed beside her. "Let me wash your face." He folded the cloth, clean side out. “You’re a mess.”

She smiled and closed her eyes and let him wipe off the worst of the mud streaking her cheeks and chin. He saw her lips tremble slightly as he dabbed at her face; he hesitated…and kissed her. Gently, once. Then again.

She opened her eyes. They were dark with emotion. And pain. “Thank you for taking care of me, Jeremiah.” Her voice was hoarse. “I—I don’t deserve it.”

“Don’t be foolish. Of course you do. Now, lie down and I’ll make you some tea. Milk? Lemon? Crumpets?” He smiled.

“Lemon,” she murmured, leaning back. “And a crumpet.”

He threw a teabag into a tin cup and poured in the still-simmering water. He stirred two heaping spoons of sugar into the mug of strong tea and handed it to her. “Here you go. Tea with lemon. Crumpet coming up.”

She took a sip and grimaced. “Ugh.”

“You need the sugar, Cill. Drink up, and you’ll feel better. Guaranteed. I’ll see if I can find some painkillers, in case that leg starts to hurt worse.”

Jeremiah suddenly realized he was feeling really tired. Now that the urgency and action of the past two hours was over, he had to figure out what to do next. There was no question of trying to make it back to the Diamond 8 today, even if Cilla was in any condition to attempt the ride, which she was not. They only had Buck. And even if they'd had both horses, the weather wasn't letting up. If anything, it was getting worse.

The icy rain was hammering on the cabin roof. The sky looked grim. It was nearly as dark as evening, and yet according to his watch, it was only around three o'clock. The temperature had dropped again. Ten degrees, at least, in the past two hours. They'd be lucky if they could make it out tomorrow. If they couldn't, Cilla Prescott had better acquire a taste for boiled beans.

He threw a couple more sticks of wood on the fire and glanced at her. She'd raised herself on one elbow on the hard bed, obediently drinking the tea. She looked a little better already. More color in her cheeks.

He had an idea. He started to shrug his jacket back on.

"Where you going?"

"Out. To check on Buck."

"Oh. Okay." She began to add something

else, but seemed to think better of it. He knew she was frightened, and that was perfectly natural in this situation.

He liked to think she was worried about him, too. A little, anyway.

"Be right back." He stepped out into the wind and shut the door firmly behind him. He went around the side of the cabin and scooped up an armload of firewood. It was wet, but would dry quickly enough inside. He wanted a good supply in the cabin. He made several trips, apologizing for letting in the cold air each time he opened the door. She was well wrapped in the blanket, though, and the little stove was now sending out a blast of heat.

Then he made his way to the horse shelter, turning up his collar and walking sideways, to avoid the sleet in his face. He shivered. Man, this was some November blow.

Buck greeted him with a whinny. The horse seemed relatively comfortable in the makeshift shelter. Jeremiah pulled a bale of the old hay down from the loft and broke it open, kicking a couple of flakes in front of the horse. Then he gathered up as much of the remaining hay as he could carry and headed back to the cabin.

"Hay!" she said, sitting up, when he burst in.

"Or—" he pushed the door shut behind him with his hip "—eiderdown. A mattress. Depending on your requirements, ma'am."

She giggled, and he'd never heard a more welcome sound.

"Can you get up?" He dumped the hay near the wall farthest from the stove. They'd have to be careful about sparks. They had enough troubles without a cabin fire.

"Here." He helped her stand, then keeping the blanket around her shoulders, supported her as she hopped over to the table and sat down on one of the rickety wooden chairs.

He went back to the bed, rolled up the saddle blanket and set it on the floor. He spread hay on the plywood, then another layer, then another. "What do you think?"

"Looks wonderful!"

"Bet you never thought you'd say that about a hay mattress, did you?" he teased, grinning at her over his shoulder.

He fluffed up the last layer and carefully spread out the saddle blanket. Then he helped her back to the bed. She stretched out, still wrapped in the blanket. He covered her carefully. Her eyes were bright but not feverish.

"Thanks, Jeremiah."

"You owe me."

"All right. I do."

"Just answer me this one thing, Cill and you won't owe me anymore."

"What's that?"

"What the hell's that *thing* you're wearing? It looks like a pair of chopped off long johns. Bloomers?"

"You told me to dress warmly. You said we should be prepared—"

"But what *is* that?"

"I guess you could call them bloomers." She smiled. "Well," she added quietly, "we used to wear this skiing in Switzerland. Wool and silk. Keeps you warm."

Jeremiah felt like a fool. "Listen. If you're okay for a while, I'm going to go back to the creek and get a bucket of water and retrieve my rifle." He didn't mention the cougar, but he planned to have a good look at it, too.

"Oh." Her eyes were huge again. She appeared comfortable, though, in that bed of hay. He was glad he'd thought of it.

He checked the fire. Still burning well. "I'll try and call Pete or Marshall back at the ranch on my cell. I hope the batteries are okay."

He rummaged again in his saddlebag and pulled out the cell phone. He punched in the number at the cookhouse. He could usually count on Marshall being in, especially at this time of day.

There was no ring and Jeremiah noticed that his phone had a "no service" message. They must be out of the range. Behind a hill or something. He'd take it with him to the creek and try there. He'd try until he got through to someone.

"Cill?"

"Yes?" She sounded sleepy.

"You'll be okay?"

"Mmm."

"I'll be back as soon as I can. Say, half an hour. An hour at the most."

"And if you're not?" she asked drowsily.

He picked up the water bucket to take with him. "Don't come looking for me, whatever you do. That's an order."

He didn't trust her. She was being awfully cooperative and her foot was injured, but he still figured her for someone who had a hard time following instructions. His instructions. And there was no way he wanted to be out there searching for her if she took a notion to follow him.

"Got that?" He had his hand on the door, ready to dart out.

"Yes, sir." She saluted.

He gave her a look.

She just giggled.

CHAPTER FIFTEEN

JEREMIAH'S RIFLE LAY in the mud by the creek. There was mud on the polished walnut stock and a big glob of mud right on the trigger guard. He carried it to the top of the bank and stowed it at the base of a tree. Man, he thought, wiping his hands on his jeans, he had to clean it up as soon as he got back to the cabin. As it was, he'd probably have rust spots. And the barrel would have to be cleaned. He wouldn't be able to trust the rifle if any debris had entered the barrel. He couldn't believe he'd thrown it down like that! He'd never done that—ever.

Tossed down his rifle, allowed Shorty to get away without even trying to go after him. And then leaving Buck to stand there in the rain and sleet. He'd never neglected an animal in his life.

What had got into him? Cilla Prescott? Yes, he realized, that was *exactly* what had happened. Every lesson ever drilled into him—feed your horse before yourself, look after your rifle, close gates, catch a runaway horse—had dropped right out of his mind when he'd seen Cilla down in that water. Cilla had to come first. That pinto thrashing over her—his hooves were iron-shod. He could have killed her! The cougar—

Jeremiah went back down to the creek. The cougar lay in a heap where it had fallen, looking like no more than a moth-eaten fur rug. Jeremiah half knelt and turned it over. It didn't weigh much. Skin and bones. Starving. Yet why had it gone for the horse and rider? Jeremiah studied it more closely. The animal had a broken lower jaw, partly healed—off-kilter. It wasn't something it had received in a kick from Shorty, or any time recently. There was a thick mass of scar tissue, with open, raw patches near the cougar's ear. It had obviously been in some kind of fight, been injured, possibly broken the jaw, and since then, had clung to life. A seventy-pound cougar that should have weighed twice that had to be pretty desperate to go after a horse and rider.

Poor thing. Jeremiah let it flop back down, then thought better of leaving it there and carried the animal into the woods a couple of dozen yards. They'd have to cross that creek again and he didn't want either Buck or Cilla to see it. Buck, of course, would pick up its scent; that couldn't be helped. But Cilla didn't need to be reminded so graphically of what had happened.

Speaking of Cilla…

Jeremiah felt in his inner pocket, inside his jacket, and pulled out his cell phone. His back to the wind, he punched in the number for the cookhouse down on the ranch. Still no service! He checked his watch. He'd been gone half an hour already. He didn't entirely trust that woman. If he was more than an hour, he was afraid she'd be getting up and hobbling out to look for him.

He left the rifle where it was and hiked up the creekbed to a ridge, where there was a jutting rock escarpment. It was a good ten-minute climb and dangerous because of the footing. The sleet and rain had turned to a mixture of snow and rain now. If the weather got much colder, they'd be in for a bad day tomorrow, trying to make their way back to the ranch.

At the top of the rise he had some luck with his phone. He heard the faint voice of his cook. "Marshall!"

"Boss! What you callin' for?"

"I'm stuck up here at the line cabin. Bad weather. Shorty get back?"

"Shorty?"

"Yeah. We lost him. He got spooked and took off."

"No sign, boss. I'll tell Pete to watch out for him. You got the woman okay?"

"Yeah. She hurt her leg, not too bad, though. Tell Pete we're at the Whisky Creek line cabin and I can't get through on my cell from there. I'll call at ten o'clock tomorrow—ask him to stand by." He didn't want to tell Marshall about the cougar, not yet. He didn't want to upset Pete at this point, either, not unless he ended up needing help to get Cilla off the mountain, which wasn't likely.

"Ten-four. Bad weather here, too, boss. Sleet."

"Over and out, Marshall."

It was an old farewell line from the days of one-way radios.

At least that was done. Jeremiah climbed carefully down, clinging to roots and clumps of grass. There were already patches of ice on the rock. He picked up his rifle at the creek, where he'd left it, and faced into the wind to head back to the cabin. He was soaked to the skin. He hoped Cilla had kept the stove going.

Jeremiah grinned to himself. He felt like a real old-time mountain man. Where ya been, Jem boy? Been a-huntin', shot me a varmint, goin' back to my li'l ol' cabin for a plateful of grub and an armful of lovin' from the li'l woman. Well, the plate of grub, anyway, he thought, smiling. And the woman was there, all right.

The loving part—that was a crap shoot.

But Jeremiah was an optimist. When *hadn't* it been a crap shoot?

CILLA WOKE slowly, to the small sounds of pitch exploding in the stove and the complaints of logs resettling in the fire, as well as the surreptitious sounds of someone trying to be quiet in the kitchen area.

Why was it that when people wanted to make no noise, the sounds they made seemed even louder?

She yawned and raised one hand to push the hair from her face. She must have dozed off for a while. She felt warm and cozy in her nest of hay, but her left leg was throbbing. It hurt more now than it had when he'd bandaged it.

She hadn't had a good look at it yet. She wanted to believe him when he said it wasn't that bad. She wanted to believe *everything* he said. He'd saved her life.

Cilla reminded herself that she was just feeling vulnerable. And grateful.

"Jem?" Her voice sounded raspy.

"You awake?" He moved something, probably a chair, in the small kitchen and walked toward her. "How you feeling, Cill?"

"Better." She ran one hand through her hair again, then blinked and tried to sit up. "Still raining?" She frowned.

He waved one hand toward the stove and she saw his jacket and a vest hanging on a line she hadn't noticed before. Her jeans and sweater and jacket were there, too. "I got soaked again. It is not a pretty day out there. Can you hear the wind?" So that was the noise coming from outside, and down the chimney.

"Mmm. Did you get through to the ranch?" Gradually, Cilla had begun to feel more alert.

"I talked to my cook, Marshall Downing. He's going to pass the message on to Pete. Hey!" Jeremiah looked directly at her, suddenly concerned. "Was there somebody I should have called for you? Anybody expecting you this evening?"

She shook her head. "I had no plans for

the long weekend." Monday was Remembrance Day, traditionally a day off for schools and government employees. She was quiet for a moment or so, thinking of what she'd had planned. This was like being in another world. Just the two of them. And the cozy cabin. "Just catching up on some work, I guess." She yawned.

"Hungry?" He smiled at her.

"Starving!" She sat up a little more, then grimaced.

"How's the leg?"

"Sore. Hurts quite a bit," she admitted. "Maybe I'll take one of those painkillers you mentioned. We've still got the picnic stuff, haven't we?"

"You bet. You didn't think I ate it all myself while I was waiting, did you?" He got up and walked back into the kitchen area, returning with two painkillers and a glass of water.

She downed the painkillers, then swung her legs out of the bed.

"Hey, where you going?"

"To wash." She held up her hands.

"Well, hold on. I'll help you." He put his hand under her elbow. She hobbled beside him. He was close, very close, and there wasn't that much room in the cabin, anyway.

She was a little embarrassed about her bloomers and undershirt.

She washed in cold water at the dented basin, dried her hands, then allowed Jeremiah to escort her back to bed.

"Okay?" He let her go, a little prematurely she thought. She sank down on the hay mattress.

"Fine."

He went back toward the kitchen and she swung her legs onto the bed and covered herself with the blanket. The hay was actually fairly comfortable and had the most glorious smell. Grass, lazy summer afternoons, the buzzing of crickets… Maybe that was why she'd dozed off so easily.

Jeremiah returned, bringing her a plate of food. "I'll get a chair and eat right here beside you."

Cilla waited until he'd dragged a chair along, carrying his own plate, and handed her some cutlery. He settled down beside her, too close beside her. She glanced up at the various articles of clothing hanging near the fire. She wondered if her sweater was dry yet. Not that she was cold.

"Mmm. This looks good." There was a breast of fried chicken on her plate, some more of that delicious noodle salad, potato salad, pickled asparagus, radishes, a bean salad and a pita bread. She ate hungrily, tearing off pieces of the chicken and stuffing them into her mouth.

Jeremiah ate in silence for several minutes, too. They were both famished. It had been a long day—and it was far from over.

"You think we'll be stuck here for a while?"

He nodded. "Overnight."

"We'll be able to go home tomorrow? On one horse?"

He shrugged, a casual, masculine movement. Utterly graceful. Her eyes were drawn to his shoulders, the sinews in his arms….

"Probably, but it depends on the weather. It's ugly out there right now. I hope it warms up." He paused. "We can make it with Buck. It'll be slow going and I'll have to walk some. But I've done that before—Cilla?" He stopped, his fork halfway to his mouth.

"What?"

"You're sure staring." He shoved the forkful of noodle salad into his mouth and smiled as he chewed slowly, regarding her with eyebrows raised, a glint in his eye.

"I've never seen such a magnificent man, that's all," she murmured, returning the raised eyebrows. *She couldn't believe she'd said that.*

He stopped chewing. "Magnificent?"

"Yeah. You're a good-looking guy. Above average. You must know that."

He resumed eating, pushing the last of his potato salad into the middle of his plate. "I've heard something like it before."

"So, any sign of Shorty?" High time this conversation got back on track.

"Shorty? No! That pinto's back at the Diamond 8 by now. Never knew he could run like that."

She shook her head. "One minute we were picking our way across that creek, the next—" She closed her eyes. "I don't know what happened, Jem. All of a sudden he reared and there was this horrible sound, like someone screaming…."

"That was Shorty," Jeremiah said. He put his empty plate on the floor and reached over to check the stove. The fire glowed on his face, red and black, when he raised the lid, then closed it again. "A scared horse sounds like that. It's eerie."

"Eerie, all right. And then—everything happened so fast. That cougar was in my face and I could see its eyes, just cold, cold yellow." She shuddered and held the blanket to her chest, her food forgotten. "Then I guess you shot it because there was a noise, the gun, I guess, and—and then you pulled me out." Her voice had sunk to a whisper. Jeremiah was watching her strangely.

"Did you remember me yelling at you?"

"No, I don't remember anything about that, just being scared. I thought I was going to die...." She stared at him. Tears stung behind her eyes.

Jeremiah looked at her for a long time. Then he took her hand. "I checked him over, Cill. I was worried because I've never heard of a cougar going after a horse like that. I thought, well, I thought it might be sick—"

"Do you think it was?"

"No. Starved is more like it. It'd been in some kind of fight or accident a couple weeks back. It had a broken jaw and quite a few injuries, weighed half of what it should have. Starved and desperate. Desperate enough to go after a horse and rider."

"Poor, sad creature," she whispered. "And poor Shorty!" she said, thinking of the amiable pinto both she and Rory had ridden.

"Poor Shorty!" Jeremiah's eyes widened

as he looked at her. "Probably the first time he's had both eyes open at once in ten years."

"Oh, Jeremiah!" She started to giggle, covered her mouth with her hand, tried to stop—all she needed to do now was get hysterical. "He's—"

"No kidding. That horse has never been a hundred percent wide-awake since I've owned him. Pete figures he was born snoring." He grinned.

"Stop it! He's not that bad." She passed him her plate and he took it, then stood there looking at her with mild concern.

She lay back on the bedroll and allowed herself to laugh. Really laugh. For the first time in a very long while, she realized.

Poor Shorty!

Jeremiah left her, taking both plates with him. She laughed until her stomach hurt, and then she sat up and watched him. He was rummaging through one of his saddlebags again.

The painkillers, the food, the heat, had gone to her head.

What a man. What a fantastic, generous, funny, wonderful, handsome man. Thankfully Bea had given her the opportunity to get to know him a little. She'd been so stubborn, so determined not to socialize with any men while she was in Glory. At least not until she'd got Blue Owl up and running.

What if she'd missed all this? All this—this adventure!

That reminded her...she needed to take a look at her leg. She sat up and pushed back the blanket and raised her left knee. The bandage started just above her ankle and went halfway to her knee. She touched it gingerly. Sore.

Jeremiah had returned, looking mysterious.

"What?"

He grinned and produced a plate from behind his back. "Cherry cobbler!"

"Jeremiah!" She searched his face. He was obviously pleased with himself. "Where in the world did you get this?"

"Same place I got all the rest. Molly's. She packed some blackberry cheesecake for me." He went into the kitchen area and came back with another plate. "See?" He held it up. The dessert looked a little scrambled, but not bad.

"You remembered," she said, suddenly serious. She recalled the laughing conversation they'd had last Sunday when Rory had been fishing off the Horsethief River bridge. A favorite dessert was a minor thing, she supposed, but that wasn't the point. He'd made a special effort to please her, and Cilla was deeply touched by that. "That's so…so sweet of you," she whispered, feeling overwhelmed.

She ate the portion of cherry cobbler—which was delicious—right to the last crumb. Then she leaned back and sighed.

This was perfect. Everything was perfect. The meal, the dessert, the man. The cabin was beginning to take on a rustic, charming aura, where at first it had just been gloomy and damp.

If her leg hadn't throbbed so much, everything would have been *completely* perfect.

She watched Jeremiah as he carried the plates to the table and tidied up the cartons he'd taken out of his saddlebags. Tomorrow they'd head back to the ranch and back to their regular lives. Blue Owl School. Jeanne's wedding. Rory. His ranch work. This adventure would become a distant memory. A time out of time. But right now it was perfect.

CHAPTER SIXTEEN

JEREMIAH took a deep breath and walked toward her. He sank down into the chair he'd used during their meal and took her hand in both of his. "I think we need to talk, don't you?"

"Maybe."

"Listen to me." He glanced down at her fingers. "We don't have a relationship, right?" His gaze was razor-sharp.

"We don't, do we?" she said, her voice very small.

"Have a relationship?"

"Yes."

"No, we don't. That's what you said. That's what you want. Right?" He leaned forward and kissed her. His lips touched hers so gently the sensation seemed to blend with the hiss from the firewood in the stove, with the soft glow of the oil lamp.

She felt a silence descend. A silence that was intense, rich—not empty at all. She heard only the random sounds of the fire. The very air seemed sweet. She felt every other consideration float away, until her world was reduced to this cabin, this situation, this man….

Then he leaned forward again, still holding her hand in both of his.

"I think we do have a relationship, don't you?" he asked softly, lifting one strand of her hair. "I mean, let's not be, well—stubborn about this." He stroked her hair, hair that desperately needed washing after the mudbath she'd taken in the creek. Hair that hadn't seen a brush or a comb since early that morning.

That morning! It seemed a week ago, a year….

"We do," she said fervently, wondering why she'd ever denied the obvious. "You're right, we do."

"Is that what you want? A relationship with me?" he asked, almost absently, still fingering her hair, stroking her cheek now with the side of his thumb.

"Yes," she whispered. "It is what I want. *I do.*"

He locked eyes with her for a full minute. Then he took a deep breath. "So do I, baby. So do I." His voice was intense. "This is something I've been wanting for a long time, Cill. In fact—" he stopped, as though thinking better of what he'd been about to say.

"It is?" She was confused. Thoroughly confused.

"Ever since I saw you way back in August, I made up my mind to 'have a relationship' with you, as you call it."

"You did?" She was beginning to sound like a bad echo.

"Uh-huh." He caressed her fingers, sending small shivers through her spine. "I confess, I saw you as a challenge."

"A *challenge*—"

"At first," he interrupted with a look full of meaning. "At first, Cilla. Then things changed. I started to, well, I started to like you." He gazed into her eyes again, then added, "Even more. Much more." His voice deepened, grew husky. "The truth is, I'm in love with you, Cilla. I'm totally, completely in love with you. Against all my better judgment. It worries me. Because I've never been a forever kind of guy. I think I am now."

He kissed her again, and she put her arms around his neck, clinging to him. He felt so strong, so safe.

"You're mine, Cill. You're mine. I love you."

CILLA HAD NO IDEA what time it was, except that she was hungry. And the cabin was cold and very bright. Morning? Obviously the stove had gone out during the night and neither had noticed.

She didn't want to think about the new day yet. About what they had to do today. All she wanted was to be right here, in this cabin.

Jeremiah Blake. A Glory man. A cowboy. A man who spent half his time on a horse and the other half in the company of semiliterate men who chewed tobacco that came in little round cans with Copenhagen or Skoal written on the side. Men who'd never read Shakespeare or heard of Bill Gates. Men to whom music was a honky-tonk guitar or a harmonica, and who thought Willie Nelson was the best singer who'd ever drawn breath. Men who knew more about how to shoe a green horse or break in a rope than they knew about a woman's heart.

Jeremiah.

He'd said he loved her. How many other women had he said that to? C.J.? Who else?

But it was true; Cilla knew it was true. She wanted to weep. He was such a wonderful, open, honest, caring man. Too confident to pretend. Too strong to concern himself with things that didn't really matter. He was the most wonderful man she'd ever met. She wondered what her parents would think of him, Ilsa and Sid. Or her sisters, Mary with her oilman and Jeanne about to be married to the fat little Italian entrepreneur who made panty hose or ceramic tiles.

Jeremiah Blake. A man who lived in a converted harness shed and liked it. A man whose eyes lit up when he saw a dog, any dog. A man who always said thank you and, sometimes, please—a man who'd never had to beg for anything in his life.

She loved him, too. How could she *not* love such a man?

How could she *love* such a man? The knowledge scared her to death.

"You awake, Cill?" He called out from his bed roll on the floor across the room. His eyes were warm.

"I'm awake," she answered softly, smiling. He was beautiful. He was looking at her as though he thought she was the only woman on earth.

"How's the leg?"

"The leg?" She frowned, concentrated. "Still sore."

"I'm not surprised."

"Jeremiah?"

"Yes, honey?" He raised his head and braced himself on his elbow.

"Do you think it snowed?"

"Snowed?" He bounded up and strode toward one of the windows. "Will you look at this? An ice storm!"

Taking a blanket with her, Cilla hurried to the window. She would never have imagined anything so beautiful. Every twig, every branch, every blade of grass, every rock was translucent with ice. She breathed deeply. "Oh my...have you ever seen anything like it?"

He nodded grimly. "Once or twice. If this doesn't melt, we're in deep—uh, trouble up here."

"Trouble?"

"Unless you're crazy about beans." He laughed and lazily scratched his chest. It was a very relaxed, very male gesture. "We've got water. And we've got a little pita bread left and some pickles. But other than that, it's beans, baby. Just beans." He grinned at her.

The sky was mercilessly blue. Surely, the sun would warm things up and the ice would melt.

She shivered and tiptoed back to the bunk, noting that her leg wasn't throbbing as much as it had the day before. She'd have to take another look at it. Maybe put more of that first-aid ointment on it.

"I'll get a fire started."

She'd never felt so content in her life. Even if they were stuck up here for a whole extra day, with only the prospect of Jeremiah Blake for company and nothing but beans to eat. She was happy.

CHAPTER SEVENTEEN

JEREMIAH MADE IT to the rock where he'd managed to call the ranch on his phone. It was treacherous going, but he moved slowly. All he needed was a broken leg. He knew he should take extra care; he hadn't had much sleep the night before. They'd talked and talked, keeping warm by the fire.

She was some woman. He'd had no idea this would happen. He had to tell her about Bea and his interference at the auction. Cilla wasn't the type to hold a grudge. Especially not now. Not when everything was turning out so well.

He'd nearly asked her to marry him. He had nearly taken a step that meant no return. Not that he wanted to go back. Just that he'd made no secret of his feelings. And she hadn't said she returned them. Not in so many words. She *had* to feel the same way he did. She was just getting used to the idea.

He had to believe that. He couldn't imagine a future without her in it.

Marriage. He took a deep breath and dialed the ranch cookhouse number. Marriage—why not? It was time. If he could come home to Cilla Prescott's arms every night, he'd happily give up his bachelor ways. They weren't all they were cracked up to be, anyway.

He was late calling the ranch. He'd told Marshall he'd call Pete at ten; it was nearly eleven.

"Jem? That you?" Pete sounded worried.

"Yeah, it's me. How's the weather down there?"

"Terrible. Haven't had any word from town yet. We've had quite the storm, trees down everywhere. The road's a slick of ice."

"Same here. What's the forecast?"

"Supposed to warm up this afternoon."

"Maybe." Jeremiah cast an experienced eye at the sky. Not a cloud to be seen directly above, but there were some small gray clouds drifting on the horizon to the southwest.

"Yeah, maybe. Whaddya plan to do, boss? Walk out with the woman? Shorty showed up last night, dirty and tired. Poor old cuss."

"Good. I was a little concerned about him getting caught up somewhere. I'd like to try and walk out today if I can, with Buck. We weren't prepared for staying up here. Not much in the way of grub."

"Let me know, Jem, eh? When you decide for sure if you're coming? That way I can be watching for you."

"Will do." He hesitated. He wanted to ask Pete how the stock was making out, if any of the utility poles in the yard had fallen, but it wasn't really Pete's job to be taking care of that. He—Jeremiah—should have been there, down at the ranch, not romancing some schoolteacher up on the Whisky Creek. "Thanks, Pete. Over and out."

He tucked the cell phone back in his inside pocket. Their clothes had dried overnight, none the worse for wear, except that Cilla's jeans were filthy and had a ragged tear at the bottom of the leg to remind her of their adventure up here at the line cabin.

As if she needed a souvenir like that. He clambered carefully down, pleased to see wood smoke from the chimney as he approached the cabin. The smoke went straight up, which likely meant they were in the middle of a high pressure system. Those clouds he'd spotted to the southwest could be the next system moving in. At this time of year, it could get worse instead of better.

His instinct was to move out while they had the chance. Buck was fine; he'd checked on the horse quickly before he left the cabin. He'd give him a good feed now and water him down at the creek. Cilla would be no problem for the quarter horse, and they could ride double on the easy stretches.

It was just this ice. He decided that if the sun started a thaw by noon, they'd risk it. He surveyed the ground, the trees, the distant mountains. Cilla was right—it *was* beautiful. Like a fairy-tale world. But he had a whole other world—a practical world of cows and feed and water lines—that he had to get back to.

Buck nickered a welcome as Jeremiah entered the horse shelter. The gelding had finished the flakes of hay Jeremiah had left him and was looking rested, despite all the excitement of the previous day. He patted the gelding's neck and ran a hand over his back. Then he led the big palomino down to the creek. He'd leave Buck with plenty of hay so he could feed while they got ready and packed up. That way, the minute it began to thaw, they'd be ready. They'd need five or six hours to get down the mountain, barring any mishaps.

When he returned to the cabin, Cilla was cooking beans. "Say, don't you think you're being a little premature there?" he asked with a grin, pegging his hat onto the nail behind the door.

"Beans take a lot of soaking and cooking. I didn't know what was going to happen, so I thought I should get started. If we don't use them, we can leave them for the squirrels or something."

"I guess so." He looked at her. She was wearing her red sweater and her bloomers. No jeans. Maybe she thought they were too dirty to wear in the cabin. She'd obviously had a good wash and tried to do something with her hair. She'd pulled it back and tucked it into a knot at the top of her head. Her eyes were bright, her cheeks flushed.

"Don't you care about leaving today?" He was curious. On the one hand, he was pleased to see her cooking the beans and heating water. It meant she didn't mind spending an extra day here with him, if it was necessary. On the other hand, he was worried about the kind of damage this storm might have done at the Diamond 8. He was needed down there at the ranch. He should *be* there.

"I'd like to get back, yes," she answered, coloring slightly. "But I don't mind if we have to stay up here, either. Tomorrow's a holiday."

She'd put the remainder of their food on the small table for breakfast. Pita bread, a little leftover cherry cobbler, some crackers and pâté. He pulled his chair up to the table and sat down. It was strange—the two of them sitting opposite each other. How was it all going to sift out? Jeremiah reached for a piece of pita bread.

"I can see you've been baking this morning, Miss Cilla," he began, smiling.

"I have." She offered him the box with the remainder of the cherry cobbler. "Eggs Benedict?"

"I sure could go for a plateful of eggs Benedict! Thank you, ma'am," he said solemnly, taking a very small portion of the cobbler. He wished there was more food.

They ate in silence for a few moments. Cilla seemed relaxed and confident. He didn't know what that meant.

"Jeremiah?"

"Yes?"

"I've been thinking."

"Uh-huh." This could be good or bad. "What about?"

"Rory. Rory Goodland."

Jeremiah groaned to himself. Not that kid again! "Yeah. What about him? I understand the court thing is going through this week, or so I heard from Lucas Yellowfly—you meet him yet?"

"No. Who's he?" She stared blankly across the table. He hoped he'd distracted her. He didn't want to talk about that Goodland kid she was obsessed with.

"He's a lawyer in Glory. Only one worth hiring if you ever need one. His partner spends most of his time on the golf course. I think Lucas is handling this for one of the kid's relatives."

"Evelyn Bell?" Her eyes snapped and her cheeks grew redder.

"Maybe." He ducked his head and took another bite of cobbler.

"I *see.*" The sound of her voice did not augur well for Yellowfly, when she met him. Man, she sure could take a bone and shake it. And right now she had her teeth into this Rory Goodland business.

"I want to know what you think of it, Jeremiah. Your opinion matters to me. A lot," she said softly. Her eyes held his.

"Er, my opinion about what?" he asked cautiously.

"Rory! I want to adopt him. I want to start steps in that direction the minute I get back to Glory—"

"Cilla. This is a serious business. You can't just go adopting a kid who's not up for adoption and—"

"But he will be! The minute that witch finds out he's got no money. That's what I'm hoping for," she confessed, her cheeks still red. She gave him a guilty look.

"You're hoping he'll be broke, so his second cousin will throw him out…so you can adopt him," he said flatly. "When he could be fixed for life." He shook his head. "What about his future? Don't you care what that money could mean to the kid's future?"

"I suppose you think I shouldn't be doing this," she said.

"You want my honest opinion?"

"Of course I do."

"You're right I don't think you should be doing this. You're crazy to get mixed up—"

"Why am I crazy, Jeremiah Blake. *Why?*" She hammered the wooden table with the tin plate in front of her and Jeremiah realized they were having their first fight. Over what? A kid who had a decent chance of coming into several hundred thousand dollars by the end of the week!

"You've got a career, you've got a family of your own, your parents, your sisters. You're likely going to have children of your own one day—" He paused, wanting to tell her that he hoped they'd be *his* children, but not quite finding the courage. This wasn't the best time to propose. "The last thing you need is to be tied down to someone else's—" He searched for the words he needed.

"Brat? Someone else's *brat?* Is that what you're trying to say?" She threw her fork down on her plate.

"Don't be ridiculous! Orphan, okay? Of course I'm not trying to say—"

"Now I'm ridiculous, is that it?" She got to her feet, fury written all over her fine features. "Last night I was someone you pretended to care about and now I'm *ridiculous!*"

"To adopt a child is a very big thing," he began again doggedly. "I know you feel sorry for the kid, but you've got to think it through. You need to consider everything. You're single, for instance. Do you think a judge or a social worker is going to decide you'll make the best parent when there are other people around, actual relatives?"

"I don't see why it should matter. Not these days. And if it does, I'll—I'll just get married!" Her eyes were bright. She seemed about to burst into tears. He couldn't believe they were having this conversation. "Someone will marry me—*you'll* marry me. You said you loved me last night!"

"Sure, I'll marry you. I'll marry you in a flash. Tomorrow, if you want. But I'm not marrying you for that kind of reason. I'm not marrying you so you can adopt someone else's kid!" He was mad now, too. He stood and grabbed his hat from the door and his jacket from the back of his chair.

"Where are you going?"

"Out." He shrugged on his coat.

"When are you coming back?"

"I don't know. In a while."

She put her hands on her hips. "This is childish, you know. You're acting like a kid yourself!"

"Fine. Pack up your stuff. We'll leave in an hour."

"What about the ice?"

"It's going to start melting anytime now.

The minute it does, we're leaving. So get your stuff together."

"Yes, *sir!*"

He went over to the bed and ripped the saddle blanket off. Then he marched to the door and left, slamming it behind him. Childish? Yeah, right! But he didn't care. She made him angry. He'd never met a more stubborn, determined, ornery woman. Or one so beautiful.

There'd never be another woman like her. Not for him. And he'd even offered marriage! But not quite the way he'd planned.

JEREMIAH SADDLED Buck in a temper. The horse grunted when he tightened the cinch and stepped sideways, flicking his tail.

"Sorry, old fellow. It sure isn't your fault, is it?" he apologized to the horse, loosening the cinch. "Not your fault I had to go and fall in love with such a stubborn woman. Poor Buck!" He patted the gelding's neck by way of redress. "Guess a love life's nothing you have to worry about, huh?"

He put the bridle on and adjusted the stirrups to a higher level for Cilla. He wanted to get out of here. If that ice would only start melting. He didn't want to camp out on this mountain tonight if it froze up again and they couldn't make it down or back up. Especially not with the mood she was in.

Adopting a kid! What kind of a harebrained idea was that? Sure, he felt sorry for Rory Goodland; he thought the boy was just great—for a kid. And Jeremiah agreed he'd had a lot of rough breaks, but... He had a sudden thought. She was just stubborn enough to try to find a guy to marry her, simply to look like a better candidate to a judge or social worker. She'd hook up with some guy her dad had picked out for her. One of the Promising Prospects she'd told him about once. She wouldn't care.

Jeremiah left the shed and peered up at the sky. Still no sign of those clouds moving in, but the wind was starting to waft through the trees again. Which made it dangerous out there. Huge icicles were dropping out of the trees. A dump of ice like that could kill you. Severely injure you, anyway.

Luckily, most of their route was through open country. But there was that patch of trees just the other side of the creek. Jeremiah recalled a clear area farther along—might be a better place to cross in these conditions. He glanced at his watch. Almost noon. He'd hike up there and check it out. He'd be back in an hour. That would give him a chance to cool off. Give her a chance, too, although she probably didn't figure she needed cooling off.

Plus, another hour would let the sun do some serious melting, or at least get it started. Then he'd have a better idea of whether to head out or stay here another night.

But the way things were going with Cilla, he figured he'd be locked out of the cabin and have to sleep with Buck.

CILLA SAT BACK in her chair after Jeremiah had slammed the door. She was getting a headache. How had they ended up fighting like this? All she'd done was ask his opinion about something important to her. Now he was stomping out and accusing *her* of being ridiculous!

Tears filled her eyes and she wiped them angrily away. What a man. What a typical man. And she'd fallen for it, hadn't she? The whole nine yards! Telling her he loved her, that she was wonderful and—and everything else he'd told her.

She'd believed him! She'd fallen for the oldest line in the book. At her age!

Get packed, he'd said—no, ordered. Next he'd be expecting her to wash his socks and leave the crossword for him in the morning paper.

If she was ever crazy enough to marry him!

Not that he'd actually asked. Not in so many words. Well, he'd marry her in a flash, he'd said, but not just so she could adopt Rory.

Didn't Jeremiah know she loved him? Didn't he know she'd marry him because she loved him or not at all? Cilla looked around—she wanted to kick something. And there was nothing to kick but his empty saddlebag leaning against the wall. So she jumped up and gave it a kick.

Then she started to laugh. There was nothing at all satisfying about kicking an empty canvas pouch that just sort of heaved itself into the air and then settled down with a tired poof.

She felt helpless. If she wasn't injured, if she even knew where she was, she could do something on her own. Take some action. She hated having to depend on him. She especially hated being mad at him *and* having to depend on him.

Ridiculous he'd called her.

She got up and wiped the tin plates clean with a paper napkin and threw the soiled napkin in the fire. It was burning merrily. She yanked the remaining clothes off the line—her clothes. Yuck. Her jeans were stiff with dirt and so was her jacket. It didn't matter; they were dry. She shook them out and started to cautiously pull on her jeans.

She'd better check her leg before they left. She sat down and peeled back the bandage. It seemed to be healing, and there was no sign of infection. She spread some of the antibiotic cream from Jeremiah's first-aid kit on the wound and covered it with a fresh sterile bandage and tape. How thoughtful of him to bring all this stuff along.

Cilla pulled on her jeans and gathered up the rest of her belongings and set them on the table. Okay, she was ready. It still hurt to walk. If she'd had any thoughts of leaving on her own—and she didn't—the ache in her leg would have scotched that. She limped to the door and stuck her head out. No sign of Jeremiah. The sun was high, though, and the air was fairly warm. What weird weather. Ice, then thaw—then what?

Melting ice from the roof dripped down steadily just in front of the door. This was what Jeremiah had said he wanted to see before they started back. So—why not start back? Where had he gone?

She hobbled around to the shelter area to see if he was there with Buck. The horse raised his head and turned toward her, ears pricked with interest. There was no sign of Jeremiah, but the horse was all ready to travel. Saddle, bridle, the works.

"Yoo-hoo!" she called tentatively. "Jeremiah! Time to go!"

There was no answer, just the soughing of the wind in the trees. The air smelled fresh, cold and fresh. The way it did after an overnight snowfall. The magic of the ice world was fast disappearing as icicles melted in the sun and dribbled onto the ground, small patches of plain old water instead of the exhilarating crystal display. She heard a sharp crack and saw an enormous chunk of ice fall from the pine tree a few yards from the cabin. Scary!

Cilla limped back to the cabin. Wasn't that just like a man? To stomp out and disappear and not tell anyone where he was going or when he was coming back. He'd been in such a rush for her to pack up. He'd said he wanted to go when it started melting. In an hour. Now it was melting and the hour was nearly up and where was he?

She sat in the cabin for another twenty minutes. Then she couldn't stand it any longer. What if he'd fallen somewhere? What if one of those chunks of ice had crashed down on top of him? What if he was lying hurt somewhere?

She remembered what he'd told her the day before about not following him. But it had been raining then. And she could barely walk. She could walk now, well enough to hobble out to find him. He *must* have had some problem, maybe an accident, or he'd be back by now. Cilla pulled on her jacket and gloves and pushed open the door. "Jeremiah?" She listened to the echoes of her voice in the distant hills, mocking her…"mi-ah, mi-ah, mi-ah."

It gave her the creeps. She made up her mind. She was going to see if she could find his tracks. That had to be straightforward enough—just follow his tracks until she came to where he was. Even a city slicker like her could figure that out.

CHAPTER EIGHTEEN

JEREMIAH STARED AT the empty cabin. Where was she?

He strode inside, noting that her scarf and hair ribbons were neatly piled on the table, and the stove was still burning. One of his socks still hung on the makeshift line over the stove. She couldn't have been gone long. She'd been furious when he left, but she wouldn't take off on him, would she? She *couldn't* take off on him, not with that leg.

Buck? He went around to the horse shelter. Buck whinnied and snorted, anxious to get moving, and Jeremiah absently slapped him on the rump.

He stood outside facing north and noticed footsteps in the rapidly melting frost. Footsteps that were definitely not his. He knelt, examining the tracks, which paralleled the earlier, largely melted ones, of his own trail. She was looking for him.

He'd been gone an hour and a half and she'd set out looking for him.

She was adding up to be more trouble than she was worth.

He started after her. He'd gone the long way around himself. Once he'd checked the creek for a more suitable crossing place, he'd continued up the mountain several hundred yards, then had swung to the west and come back to the cabin from a different direction. If he'd backtracked, he'd have found her.

What did she think she was doing going after him, anyway? Couldn't she stay put, do what she was told for once? He had no choice but follow her. She couldn't have gone far.

She hadn't. He followed her tracks through the muddy patches where the ice had melted. Under trees and in the shadow of rocks, the ice was still crystallized but it was easy enough to see where she'd walked. He saw a few places where she'd slipped, and his throat went dry. She was a fool to have done this.

Sure, he'd been mad when he left. However, he'd cooled off. Now he was mad again. But Jeremiah knew his anger was a result of his fear. If anything had happened to her…

She was sitting on a fallen log near the

creek when he found her. He heard her before he saw her.

"Jeremiah?" Her voice was high and frightened. He quickened his pace. She'd probably heard him crashing through the bush and thought he was another cougar or a bear or something.

"Oh, Jeremiah!" she said, sounding relieved when she saw him. She stood and held out her hands to him and Jeremiah immediately forgave her for scaring him the way she had.

"Cilla!" He folded his arms around her. "What were you thinking, taking off after me like that? I was worried sick when I got back to the cabin and you weren't there."

"Were you?" Her voice was wobbly.

"Yes, of course I was, honey." He held her away from him, to examine her face more carefully. "Are you okay?" She nodded. She looked drawn and tired. She'd overexerted herself coming out here, and her leg was probably killing her. "I'm not still mad. Are you?"

"Oh, no!" She buried her face against his jacket and he felt her arms cling to him. He held her even tighter. If anything had happened… He squeezed his eyes shut.

"Oh, Jem, I was terrified you'd been hurt when you didn't come back. That you'd fallen or been hit by ice or…"

"Shhh." He kissed her forehead, her nose, her lips. "Never mind all that. We're both okay. Let's just get back and get going, eh?"

"All right," she said quietly and took his hand when he held it out to her.

Neither of them said anything on the return trip to the cabin. The ice and frost were melting quickly now, and there were rivulets of water here and there, running toward the creek.

In the cabin, Jeremiah quickly packed up his saddlebags. He threw an armload of firewood into the box near the stove, to serve the next occupant of the cabin. He hauled the hay out and threw it on the ground; he didn't want it attracting mice. He did a quick check of everything—the stove was nearly burned out—and pulled the door closed.

Cilla was waiting for him at the horse shelter. He led Buck out and tightened the cinch.

"Ready?" He turned to her and smiled. She was so quiet. He was almost afraid to ask what was on her mind.

"Am I going to ride?" She looked uncertain.

"Yep. You ride and I'll walk. I found a

place up the creek where I could cross on some rocks and a log and you can walk Buck over. Then we can probably double up until we get back to the rockslide—is anything wrong, Cilla?"

"Oh, Jeremiah. I just wanted to say I'm so sorry. I've been such an idiot. I don't know why I do these things when I'm around you—I'm usually so rational. I'm usually so sane."

He grinned. Did this mean what he hoped it did? "Look, I said a lot of things I shouldn't have said this morning. I—I don't know why I came down so hard on you. I guess I'm just jealous of the kid," he said, catching her eye and holding out his hand to help her onto the horse.

"You're not!"

"I am. I want you all to myself." She put her hand on his shoulder and he lifted her into the saddle.

"I think you're wonderful. I really do," she said, looking down at him, her eyes shining. "But we're so *different*."

"We are," he admitted, checking her stirrups. Buck tossed his head a few times. He was obviously eager to get back to his familiar corral and barn. "But we're the same where it matters, Cill. You must know that."

Her eyes grew cloudy. "Do you think so?"

"Think about it. We are," he said, very firmly. "Come here." He reached up and grasped the nape of her neck with his right hand and pulled her toward him. Then he kissed her, softly, sweetly. He kissed her with all the love he felt for her, and he could feel her respond.

"Careful!" he said, breaking the kiss and smiling. "Don't fall off."

"Oh, you!"

He took the reins and began leading the gelding up the trail they'd made. Like he'd said, he'd marry her in a flash. But she had a lot to think about before they got to that point. So did he. When he arrived back at the Diamond 8, he was going to be very busy. He hoped what they'd learned about each other, what they'd experienced together, would last.

It had to last. Right now, it was all they had.

The trip down the mountain was slow and difficult. They rode double most of the way, Cilla pressed tightly against his back, sitting behind the cantle, her arms tight around his chest.

He walked about a quarter of the route. Over the rockfalls, the creek, through a marshy patch a mile or so from the ranch.

He'd never been so happy to see anything as he was when he saw the lights of the Diamond 8, visible when he emerged from the last valley. It was nearly pitch-dark, but Buck knew his way. That horse deserved a triple ration of oats. This time, Jeremiah was putting his horse first. Cilla would have to wait. She could take a shower in his house and maybe later they'd get a chance to cozy up and watch the video of *Pride and Prejudice.* He'd rented it so often on the off chance, he'd finally decided to buy it. Maybe she'd stay and watch it. Maybe she'd want to go straight home.

Either way, he was looking forward to civilization.

"BOSS? THAT YOU?" Pete's worried voice reached them as Jeremiah unlatched the gate that led to the pasture adjoining the barn.

He was heading straight for his house to drop off Cilla, then taking Buck to the barn. One of the boys there would look after him. The gelding needed a good rubdown and a bucket of grain. He'd be fine in the morning, despite his fifteen years.

"Yeah, it's me, Pete." He hadn't heard anything from Cilla for the past twenty minutes. Coming down the mountain, she'd rambled on and on about her family, her mom and dad, her sisters and who they'd married and why she wanted to adopt Rory. She'd gone on and on about why she'd become a teacher and why she'd picked Glory for her school and how she wanted to go to Rome one day to see where her hero, Dr. Maria Montessori, had worked and maybe she'd visit her sister and her new husband in Florence when she did.

Jeremiah had finally tuned her out. He was worried at first that maybe she'd lost it, that she was babbling. That she'd gone off her nut temporarily, maybe dangerously. But he couldn't see why that would be. She wasn't cold, she wasn't feverish or in shock, her leg was healing.

He decided she'd just needed to talk. And he didn't mind as long as she let him steer the course home and make all the decisions that needed to be made. A ship only had one captain, and a horse only had one rider—only one holding the reins, in any event.

Actually, he'd enjoyed hearing her soft voice in his ear as she clung to him from behind. Sometimes she'd rested her head on his shoulder and he could have sworn she'd drifted off for a few moments here and there.

She was exhausted. So was he. A solid night's sleep would be good for both of them.

"Man, am I glad to see you! We were beginning to wonder what had happened. Marshall was all for sending out a search party."

"We made a late start, Pete," Jeremiah answered. No point getting into details. "We got away later than we planned and then we just had the one horse. How's Shorty?"

"'Bout the same as usual, I'd say. That the woman behind you there?"

Pete shone his flashlight in Jeremiah's face and he squeezed his eyes shut.

"Jem?" Cilla's voice sounded sleepy. He had to get her home. Get some decent grub into her, a bath and bed.

"Yeah, we're here, Cilla. I'll take you over to my place, then I've got to take care of the horse—"

"Never mind Buck! I'll look after him, boss. You worry about the woman."

Sometimes Jeremiah wished Pete McGinty, long divorced and reputedly sworn off the female sex, wouldn't refer to all women as "the woman."

Pete walked beside him as they moved slowly toward the house. Normally, Jeremiah would have walked, too, but he didn't want to disturb Cilla, half-asleep behind him.

"What's the news, Pete? Any ice damage to the ranch?"

"A few poles down on the lane. Roof came off the combine shed, don't know exactly why. We had some wind, though. Maybe the weight of the ice. Road was a mess. Still is. Wallace hit the rhubarb on the Connors Corner coming to work this morning. Fool. I told him to take it easy. Couple hundred dollars' worth of dents to his pickup. A—a few other things I'll tell you about later."

Jeremiah wondered what *that* meant. Later. Something he didn't want Cilla to hear? "How about town? You hear of any trouble there?"

"Oh, this and that." Pete seemed nervous.

The porch light came on automatically, and Jeremiah managed to grab Cilla and help her down into Pete's care. Pete held on to her gingerly, and Jeremiah dismounted as fast as he could, just in time to catch her.

"She's got a tore-up leg, Pete," he grunted, taking Cilla's weight with his left arm. "We had a little run-in with a mountain lion up there. He took after Shorty."

Pete whistled. "No kiddin', boss!"

"I shot it. It was a mangy thing, hard up for

grub, I guess." Jeremiah turned his attention to Cilla. "You okay, hon?"

"I'm fine, Jeremiah. Just fine," she said softly, but he could see her wince as she put weight on her sore leg. "It's good to be back. Thanks for your help, Pete."

It was hard to tell in this light, but if Jeremiah had to put money on it, he'd say Pete McGinty was blushing. Cilla had a way with her; she never forgot a favor, she was grateful for any help offered or given, even though she'd never—or almost never—ask for it.

Jeremiah helped her up the porch steps. Normally, he'd just take her in his arms and carry her inside, but he thought she might be embarrassed with Pete looking on.

"Say, boss—" Pete cleared his throat nervously.

"Yeah?" His number-two cow boss wore a pained expression. "You got something to tell me?"

"Matter of fact, I do," he said and cleared his throat again. "There's bad news from town."

Jeremiah felt Cilla stiffen in his embrace. She craned her head around to look at McGinty. "What kind of news?"

"Well, it's to do with you, ma'am. The school. You see—"

"What? What's happened?" He could feel her impatience with Pete's roundabout approach. "A break-in?"

"Spit it out, Pete."

"The ice storm in town was pretty bad, I hear. That big maple on the corner, right near the school, it came down." Pete shuffled from one foot to the other.

Jeremiah felt Cilla breathe a little easier. "Oh, I thought something serious had happened, maybe to one of the children. Or my landlady or—"

"That's just it, ma'am. The tree came down on the school. Total wipeout."

Jeremiah was glad he already had a grip on Cilla. She fainted dead away in his arms.

WHEN SHE WOKE UP, Cilla wasn't sure where she was for a few moments.

Then she remembered Pete's words. The tree had fallen on Blue Owl School. She felt empty inside. All her dreams, all her hard work, all her inheritance from her aunt Martina—gone. The children had lost, too. She'd have to return everyone's money. Start again somewhere else. Where? Never mind the cash, there'd be insurance money—when would she ever find the energy to start over?

Cilla wanted to cry, but tears wouldn't come. Her eyes were hot and dry. There was only one thing to be thankful for—the school was closed for the three-day weekend. Remembrance Day! What a day to remember.

What a weekend to remember.

Cilla glanced around the room. There was just one lamp on, in a corner, casting a soft glow. She was in a big bed, a king-size bed, with a comfortable feather duvet. Earthy colors everywhere, a man's room. She was warm and cozy and clean. But she was starving. She felt like she hadn't eaten for a week.

This was Jeremiah's bedroom. Or what passed for a bedroom in his house. It was a long, plain building that had been converted into living space. She knew, from being there the day she'd brought Rory, that the kitchen and living area were at one end and the bedroom and bathroom at the other, separated by a room divider. It was a bachelor's quarters. She'd remembered poring over the house plans he'd left carelessly spread out on his kitchen table and suggesting changes to him. She wondered if he'd actually made them, as he'd said he would.

"Cilla?"

"I'm awake, Jeremiah. You don't need to whisper."

He came in and sat on the bed beside her. He looked handsome but haggard. This weekend had been tough on him, too. But he hadn't lost his whole dream, had he? His ranch had suffered a little damage, but it hadn't been wiped out.

"How you feelin', hon? You ready to eat? I put some stew on and it's hot if you want a plateful."

She managed a bleak smile.

"You fainted."

She frowned. "I—I just remember Pete saying the tree had fallen on the school and then I don't remember anything else."

"You sure gave Pete a turn," Jeremiah said, taking her hand in his.

"Did I? Poor Pete!" She turned her hand so her fingers meshed with Jeremiah's. She felt safe here, protected. She couldn't bear the thought of seeing the school tomorrow, a mess of crashed timber, broken furniture, shattered glass. She shuddered.

"I called your parents. Told them about the school, in case they'd heard and were worried. Told them no one was hurt and I was taking care of you." He smiled. "They seemed to like that idea, although your mother was all for driving over here immediately. I, uh, talked her out of it."

"Good." The last thing she wanted now was to talk. To someone who didn't know what was going on, who'd have a fit about her leg, who'd disapprove of her being alone in a man's house, who'd want to rush her back to the family compound.

She wasn't going back. She was going only one way—forward.

"Jem? I'm going to rebuild the school. I'm going to do a better job than I—"

"Hold on, Cill. You haven't even seen the damage yet."

"I know. But I'm going to see what I can salvage. Maybe it can be repaired, maybe with a new roof and—"

Jeremiah shook his head. "I talked to the owner. Gus McCready. He's tearing it down. Just as soon as you get your stuff out of there, whatever you can save. He says it should've been knocked down years ago."

She sat up straighter. "Well, why did he rent it to me then, if it was only good for demolition?"

Jeremiah gave her a serious look. He

shrugged. "Who knows? You can be pretty persistent when you get your mind made up about something. Maybe you talked him into it."

She *had* talked him into it. She remembered now that he hadn't been all that keen to rent to her, but had relented after she said she'd continue looking for a more suitable place once the school was running. She'd told him she hoped to find something by Christmas.

She'd forgotten all that.

"Oh, Jeremiah, I feel so bad about this. It's true. I meant to look for a better place. That's what I told Gus. I—I just got so caught up in what I was doing, trying to make a go of the school, that I forgot all about it. I'd put so much money into the place, fixing it up. And because I was irresponsible, I've jeopardized the children's *lives*. Do you realize that, Jem? I've put them in *danger* just because I was so stubborn." She covered her face with the palms of her hands.

"No one was hurt, honey. It's just stuff that—"

"But they could have been! Don't you see? That storm could have come up during class."

"But it didn't."

"That tree could have fallen down anytime. In a big gust of wind, anything—"

"But it didn't happen like that, Cilla. Look, you want some of that stew?"

He seemed relieved that she nodded, and got up and left the bedroom.

He didn't understand, she told herself. She'd been at fault. She'd sworn all her life to protect and defend little children, to act in their best interest, and here she'd ignored the informed judgment of others—even of her landlord—to selfishly pursue her own goal. Oh, yes, she *had* to have a preschool. She had to run her own business. She had to prove to her family that she was capable. And she had to have it all right then. She couldn't wait, not even six months, to make sure she'd found the right place.

Jeremiah seemed very subdued, too. Maybe he did understand. He brought her stew and a mug of milk and two pieces of buttered bread and put the tray on her lap. She ate everything.

"Do you want to go home tonight?" he asked, not looking at her.

"Do you want me to?" she asked in response.

"No. But I'll take you in if you're anxious

to see the school. And to sleep in your own bed tonight." He took the tray out of the room.

She thought for a few minutes. She did want to see the school, assess the damage. But she just wasn't up to it now. Too much had happened already. Besides, it was dark. What was the point?

"I'd rather wait until tomorrow," she said when he returned. "If you don't mind. But I'll take the couch tonight."

"No. I'm already set out there. Try and get some sleep. Things will look better tomorrow."

CHAPTER NINETEEN

THE MAPLE TREE that generations of Glory children had loved and climbed for so many years had a hollow heart.

It had been trimmed so many times over the decades, that rot had set in, probably at some badly pruned limb, and eventually the tree had weakened. But its demise had taken more than a windstorm; it had taken an ice storm that had deposited hundreds of pounds of ice on the old tree. It had finally succumbed to inevitability and fallen.

Unfortunately, its mighty crown had come down on the old Buffalo Head Hardware Store building, where Blue Owl Montessori Preschool had been housed.

Jeremiah followed Cilla to town the next morning to survey the damage. There wasn't a great deal she could salvage, and it turned out that the insurance company that held the landlord's policy wouldn't allow her to go onto the premises at all. It was fenced off and Cilla could only look on in anguish from a distance of twenty-five feet. Her own insurance company would replace the furniture, supplies and equipment she'd lost. She could see small chairs and tables upended, some of them crushed. She could see the elephant foot plant, its green fronds shriveled and blackened in the cold. She could see the pegs where the children hung their clothes, with one forgotten jacket hanging there. She could see several of the children's drawings taped below the blackboard.

It was the sight of the elephant foot plant with its withered foliage and the one small jacket hanging forlornly that did Cilla in. She turned to Jeremiah, buried her head on his shoulder and began to sob. It was long overdue. She'd wanted to cry earlier and couldn't. Now that she'd seen the physical evidence of what had happened to her pride and joy, this terrible mishap, she was able to give vent to the enormous grief she felt about the loss of her school.

Jeremiah went home with her. There were a dozen messages on her answering machine, which she dutifully sat down and answered, while he checked her fridge and went out to get some milk and eggs. Many were from friends and neighbors in the community. Several were from parents of her students. Two were from her sisters. There was a message from her banker, expressing his sincere regret. She wondered at that one. But returning the calls gave her something to occupy herself when there was nothing more to be done.

"You going to be okay now, hon?" Jeremiah had bought her some groceries and now he had things to do himself. She couldn't keep him here all day, holding her hand; he had a business to take care of at the Diamond 8.

"I'll be fine. It's been a shock, but—" She shrugged. "I'll just have to deal with it. It could have been worse. Someone could have been hurt."

It was small comfort, considering, but she clung to that thought.

After Jeremiah left, she sat down and made a list of all the children who'd been registered at Blue Owl. She began to make telephone calls, reassuring the parents that she was fine, that she would probably start a new school, but it most likely wouldn't be until the following year. She thanked them for their support. She'd be returning the postdated checks. Yes, she'd be looking around for better quarters. No, she decided—when so many parents asked—she had no plans to leave Glory. *Not at present.*

Mrs. Vandenbroek made her way up the outside staircase to bring Cilla a freshly baked loaf of bread, giving Cilla the chance to have another cry. The good woman bustled arthritically around the kitchen to make her a cup of Earl Grey tea. In her heavily accented English, she sympathized, occasionally wiping at her own eye with a corner of the apron she always wore.

By midafternoon, Cilla felt much better. She sensed that something had happened. Something important, but she wasn't sure yet what it was. The only parent she'd spoken to who wasn't wholly supportive was Evelyn Bell. Rory's caregiver couldn't hide her disappointment. Cilla hadn't realized until then how much Evelyn had counted on the school to get her small charge out of her hair for several hours each day. Poor Rory!

Cilla thought about what she'd discussed with Jeremiah up on the mountain, and realized she was more determined than ever to do something for the boy. She offered to take Rory for the next week, in the mornings, since it was such short notice—short notice! What? Her building being squashed?—and

Evelyn could so obviously use the help. Evelyn accepted, rather peevishly. Anyone else would have been offering to give *her* some sympathy and help. Not Evelyn Bell.

Then, unbelievable as it was, she had a long, hot bath, changed the dressing on her leg and went to bed. It was just past three in the afternoon, but she couldn't think of anything she'd rather do. She didn't have to worry about going to work in the morning, although there'd be lots of details to take care of. She wanted to forget about everything for a while and lose herself in her book—she'd moved on to Austen's *Mansfield Park*—drink hot lemonade and honey in bed and turn her thermostat way up. She wanted to relax and feel pampered and warm. To indulge herself.

Cilla allowed herself to daydream. Jeremiah was such a wonderful man. Too bad he was so arrogant and stubborn and so quick to jump to conclusions. But, she reminded herself, he was quick to say he was sorry, too. That wasn't too common in a man, in her experience.

And last night.... He'd been so comforting. So caring. Bringing her food. Making sure her leg was all right. Phoning her parents and her landlady.

Jeanne's wedding was less than a week away. She'd go to Calgary tomorrow or Wednesday and see if there were any last-minute things she could do to help her sister or her mother. She'd take Rory with her, just for the outing. She needed a change of scene. Worrying about setting up another preschool, in Glory or elsewhere, could wait until after the wedding. Until after Christmas.

Right now, though, her sister's wedding was the last sort of event she wanted to attend. Jeremiah had promised to go with her, which did make a difference. She was looking forward to seeing him dressed up in a formal suit or tux. As for herself, she just wasn't in the mood to celebrate someone else's good fortune and wedded bliss, even her sister's.

A new dress would be nice. She decided then and there that she needed one. Something that made her look slim and beautiful. Something special. Rory would help her choose. She wanted to let her mother and father know her intentions regarding the child soon. They'd need time to get used to this. A grandchild but no husband. Oh boy, her father would be dusting off every Promising Prospect in his Rolodex.

Cilla returned to her novel. The prospect

of Calgary tomorrow cheered her; it was certainly preferable to standing on the street, staring helplessly at the crushed building that had housed Blue Owl. Workers would begin to clear the site in the morning, Gus McCready had told her, now that the insurance people had been through.

The next morning, Cilla picked up Rory just after ten o'clock. She'd asked Evelyn if it was all right to take the child to Calgary for the day and Evelyn had no objections. Cilla hadn't thought she would have.

The boy helped her choose a dress—not Rory's first choice, which had been a rather overwhelming confection of pink lace—but still wonderful, a gorgeous white wool dress, cut very simply and with a full, draped skirt, boat-cut neckline and long sleeves. Rory asked her if she was going to wear an apron over it, and Cilla replied very seriously that she was not, over the helpless shriek of her mother, who'd come with them. Ilsa Prescott seemed taken with the little boy, and he with her. Cilla hadn't mentioned anything about her plans regarding Rory—not yet. But she found it comical to watch the two of them at lunch at D'arcy's, her mother's favorite society lunching place—Rory telling her solemn stories of the family from hell, his rubber-booted feet absently kicking the front of the leather banquette, and Ilsa responding with oohs and aahs and clutching Rory's hand in sympathy from time to time. Cilla wished Jeremiah could see them.

The fact that Jeremiah had been so opposed to her idea of adopting Rory, or at least becoming a larger part of his life, bothered her deeply. He'd called her *crazy. Ridiculous.* Didn't he like kids? Of course he did! He adored his niece and nephew, and had mentioned more than once how much he'd enjoyed showing Rory how to swing a rope. Surely he'd thought of having children of his own one day.

Oh, well. There was no changing people. Not even people you cared about…loved.

THE MORNING of the wedding Jeremiah called to ask if it would be all right if he changed at her apartment just before they left for Calgary. She said of course it would be fine. He had an auction he was going to in Vulcan, a small town just east of Glory, and he wouldn't have time to drive all the way back to the Diamond 8 before he had to pick her up.

Cilla made sure she was finished her bath

and makeup and in her dressing gown before he arrived. He was on time; it was just after two o'clock. Jeanne's wedding was at five. The reception would begin at half past six at the Palliser Hotel in the center of the city.

She hadn't seen him since he'd brought her home after their weekend adventure, although she'd talked to him several times on the phone. He knew she was minding Rory most days. He didn't object. Actually, he didn't say much about the child at all. She'd forgotten that Rory's future was being decided in the courts that week.

Jeremiah didn't kiss her when he came in, which surprised Cilla. But he watched her intently, as though studying every detail of her hair, her face, her dressing gown. "You look very beautiful, Cilla. As always. None the worse for wear. How is your leg?"

"The doctor says it's healing just fine. I've still got a bandage, but I think my dress will cover it." She smiled. It was wonderful to see him. She hadn't realized until that moment how very much she'd missed him. But she wanted more of him than a look. She wanted to feel his arms around her, his lips, his touch.

"You hear about the Goodland case?"

"Oh, no!" Cilla stared at Jeremiah, one hand to her mouth. "What happened?"

Jeremiah's expression was grim. "They did him out of it. Split the money. Rory gets five percent, minus costs, to be tied up until he's nineteen. Twenty thousand dollars or thereabouts, which is better than a kick in the pants, I suppose. The rest stays with the sweepstakes organizers." He looked thoroughly disgusted.

Cilla examined her own feelings. She'd told Jeremiah she'd be glad if he didn't get the money, so she could adopt him when Evelyn threw him out. But she didn't feel that at all. She felt sad that Rory had lost not only his parents and sister but any chance to settle his future with the money the family had been on their way to collect.

"It doesn't seem fair," she said quietly. "Maybe it could be appealed."

"You're not glad?" He eyed her narrowly.

"Of course not!" She held his gaze. "You must think me an awful woman, Jeremiah, if you truly believe I could be happy for his loss. He lost his whole family!"

"Come on, Cill—"

"No, I'm serious. I know I said that. But I realize now I didn't mean it. I'm very sorry for him." She searched his gaze. "Not that I think he'd have had much left by the time Evelyn Bell and her family was done with it."

"No," Jeremiah said and walked over to her hall closet to hang up his clothes. She hadn't even checked them out. Dark suit, a white shirt—did that mean he was wearing a tie? "I suppose you're right."

Cilla slipped into her dress while Jeremiah was showering. She was putting on her pearls, a twenty-first-birthday present from her parents, when he emerged from her bedroom, looking completely frazzled.

"Can you tie this thing?" he asked, holding out an untied bow tie, the kind that went with a casual tux. "And what is this with the shirt—there are no buttons in the sleeves. Just buttonholes on both sides."

She laughed. "You have to put the studs in the holes. That's what these are for—" She took the handful of studs he had in his left hand. "It's what buttons were originally, before someone got the bright idea of sewing them onto one side."

"Well, why *don't* they sew 'em on, then? Makes a lot of sense to me," Jeremiah muttered darkly.

"Tradition, my good fellow," she said. "Tradition. Where'd you get this, anyway?"

"Nina made me wear the stupid thing. It's Cal's. I don't suppose *he's* ever worn it. But Nina thinks every man should have one in his closet."

She inserted the studs into the proper places in his sleeves and tried very hard not to catch his gaze as she fastened them. She didn't dare look at him, but she was very aware that he was studying her.

"All right?" She made the mistake of glancing at him.

"Oh, baby! You look good enough to eat." He stepped forward and kissed her. Then he stepped back, a grin on his face. "I promised myself I wouldn't do that."

"Why not?"

"Why not?" he repeated, sounding alarmed. "Well, you know why not."

"Do I?" she asked coolly. "Well, I guess I do know why not." She didn't have a clue, unless he meant that whatever they'd shared was over. Finished. Maybe this was his obscure way of telling her it was finished.

They continued their conversation on the way to Calgary in her car. He drove.

"I just want to ask you one question, Jeremiah, just yes or no. No elaboration, please. Did you mean those things you said to me up at the cabin?"

"Yes," he returned promptly. Then she wished she hadn't insisted on no elaboration.

"Good," she said, hoping he was as curious as to why she'd asked as she was about his answer.

Finally, when they'd parked in front of the church, Cilla put one hand on his elbow. "Do you still mean what you said back then?"

"Yes." He paused, then smiled. "Any more questions?"

"No," she said, and got out of the car.

The wedding was wonderful. Lidio di Fabrizio, Jeanne's betrothed, was a little better-looking than Cilla remembered, and not quite as pudgy. He was clearly very pleased to be marrying her sister, who stood half a head taller. They must be in love, Cilla thought, dabbing at her eyes with her handkerchief. She could cry all she wanted at other people's good fortune. Everyone would expect tears at a wedding.

Jeremiah was solemn and followed the service carefully. He turned to look at her several times, and once handed her his large white handkerchief. She needed it; she'd nearly demolished her own small one.

Then they were walking out of the church and she was smiling and nodding at people she knew and noticing the glances of admiration Jeremiah was receiving, from both men and women. He was a man who stood out from the crowd. The formal dress didn't hurt, either. Mary winked at her and she saw their friend Kirstin, wincing in exaggerated appreciation and giving her a frantic thumbs-up.

Honestly. Some women.

At the reception, Jeremiah was the perfect gentleman. If anything, he seemed subdued. Not that he felt he was in exalted company, by any means—he could always hold his own—simply that he seemed distant, as though his mind was elsewhere.

The dinner was superb and the decor was gorgeous, the ballroom filled with beautifully dressed men and women and flowers and greenery everywhere. A fountain decorated the center of the floor, with naked cherubs and gold shrubbery—meant to appear Italian, Cilla thought. A bit over the top.

Jeremiah hadn't danced with her, although the bride and groom had danced and all the obligatory dances had taken place—the groom with the bride's mother and the bride's father with the groom's stepmother and various permutations thereof, since Lidio's real mother was dead and his father had since remarried four times. The current wife and all the ex-wives were in attendance.

"Jeremiah?" She touched his arm lightly as they sat at a table near the edge of the dance floor.

"Hmm?" He leaned toward her.

"I—I wondered if you're feeling all right?"

"Me?" He looked at her in astonishment. "I'm fine. I wondered how you were, with that leg."

"Oh, forget the leg. I just thought you were awfully quiet. You were quiet at the church, too."

"I'm always quiet in church," he said, winking at her. "I don't like to draw divine attention to myself. There's so many more who need it."

"Oh!" She laughed. She supposed he *was* feeling fine; after all, he said he was.

"Do you want to dance?" He stood and offered her his hand. "I thought your leg would be bothering you and you wouldn't feel like dancing."

"I wish you'd shut up about the leg. I can

walk, can't I? That means I can dance," she said, taking his hand. *Finally, to be in his arms...*

He was an expert dancer. But then, she'd known he would be. He guided her gently but firmly across the floor, avoiding the more awkward couples.

When the music stopped, he folded her into his arms and kissed her. When they parted, there was a smattering of applause. She blushed.

He led her back to the table and picked up glasses of punch for them both. He handed her one.

"Cheers, Cilla. To a wonderful lady."

She raised her glass. "To a wonderful man, Jeremiah."

He smiled. "I think the word was *magnificent,* wasn't it?"

She couldn't stand it anymore; she couldn't stand the teasing, the veneer of sophistication. The chat. Sure, he could do it, but this wasn't the Jeremiah Blake she knew, deep down, no matter how handsome and suave. No matter how well he'd "cleaned up," as her sister Mary had said.

She stood close to him, so she could look directly into his eyes. "Did you mean what you said, Jem? Did you really mean you love me?"

He took her glass from her nerveless fingers and set it down on a nearby table. Then he clasped her hands in his and looked down at them, intertwined. "Yes!" His hand was hard and callused and tanned. Hers was soft and white, freshly manicured.

"I love you but look at us, Cilla," he said softly. "We're like night and day. This is your world. You know what my world's like. It's completely different from this. I don't think you could live in my world."

"Jem—"

"I don't belong in a monkey suit like this."

"But you look wonderful in it—"

"I don't care what I look like. It's not me. You know, I'd rather be sitting on the back porch scratching the pups' tummies than this. I only came for you. I only came because you wanted me to. I'd only do it for you, Cill, not for anyone else. But I couldn't do too much of it, I just couldn't. Not even for you."

"Jem, I—I don't know what to say—"

"Then don't say anything. I meant everything I said to you last weekend." He raised one hand and ran it through her hair, traced the curve of her cheek with his thumb and sighed. "I keep hoping maybe you'll start to feel the same way. I love you, Cilla. If we loved each other, we could figure things out. I meant what I said, I'd marry you in a minute. No matter what. All you have to do is love me back. I'd never marry a woman I didn't love. Or who didn't love me. Not for all the gold in Fort Knox."

She buried her face against his chest and felt him put his arms around her. She felt his lips in her hair. She was vaguely aware that several people had stopped nearby and were eavesdropping as hard as they could without seeming to notice them.

"I—I think I love you, too, Jeremiah," she muttered, her face buried on his chest. "I know I do." He gripped her hair and turned her face up. She was ready to cry all over again, just like at the church. "It must be love! I've missed you so much this past week. I dream about you. I can't sleep, I keep thinking about you all the time—"

"Say it! Tell me you love me, Cilla."

"I love you. I love you. I think you're the most wonderful, maddening, understanding, forgiving man in the world."

"Will you marry me?"

"I will. I'll marry you…."

"Have my babies?" His voice was hoarse. "Lots?"

They definitely had an interested audience now, but Cilla didn't care.

"All of them."

"Live in my new house with me, sleep in my bed with me?"

"Yes! I'll even wash your socks but I won't save the crossword for you in the morning. I like doing it myself."

"Fine. You can do the crossword."

He kissed her then, a deep, passionate kiss that said it all. He loved her; she loved him. He was never going to let her down or let her go. He was going to marry her, just as soon as they could agree on a date.

That might be the problem. He'd probably be happy to drop in at the magistrate's office in Glory; she had always thought she wanted the whole nine yards at the Palliser Hotel ballroom in Calgary, like her sisters. Flowers, satin gowns, five-piece bands dressed in penguin suits, wedding cakes from Stacy's...but maybe not.

She felt his arms strong and tight around her and knew there was nowhere she'd rather be. In his arms. Whether that meant a borrowed tux or a worn-out plaid flannel shirt. Just as long as he was in it.

"I have a small confession to make to you," he whispered, "before we can get married. I want to marry you with a clear conscience."

"What is it?" she whispered back.

"You know that picnic we had up at the cabin?"

She nodded, mystified.

"I told you I bought it at the charity auction through a friend?"

She nodded again, frowning.

"My good friend, Bea Hoople, actually."

Cilla stared at him. "She's a good friend?"

"A good friend of my aunt's. I've known Bea since I was a kid."

"So?"

"And you know that weekend for two in Kananaskis that went for a high price?"

"Yes?" The light was beginning to dawn. Cilla bit her lip.

"Well, I paid for that, too. Through Bea. I thought it might make a nice honeymoon package someday."

"Jeremiah Blake! Are you trying to tell me what I think you're trying to tell me?" She tried to look severe, but she just couldn't do it. She'd *wondered* why Bea, even though she'd said she had a great-nephew at the school, had spent so much at the charity auction.

"I am. Uh, last but not least, you know that cowboy Bea bought and donated to you? Well, I paid for him, too. Through the nose!"

"Jeremiah Blake!" she squealed. "You ought to be shot. You cheated! You organized the whole thing."

"Guilty as charged," he said, grinning widely. "And I'd do it all again, if I had to. Although I wish I hadn't had to pay quite so much for myself."

She flung her arms around his neck and stood on her tiptoes. "Kiss me, you magnificent man. And then...you can kiss me again."

He did.

The small crowd that had gathered clapped wildly, but Cilla didn't even notice it. She was busy.

The five-piece band played on.

CHAPTER TWENTY

THEY TALKED NONSTOP about their plans on the way home, and later, at Cilla's apartment. Jeremiah even confessed that he wouldn't mind if she got more involved with the Goodland boy. Not if she was going to marry him and have his children. Besides, he said, he was fond of the little kid. Thought he had real cowboy potential. And what was one more, he said, if they had half a dozen of their own?

Which was exaggerating the situation considerably, Cilla told him. She was thrilled that he'd accepted her need to take care of the little orphaned boy. She couldn't explain it, even to the man she loved.

They drove to the Bells' place about five o'clock the next afternoon. Cilla had risked a phone call to Evelyn, broaching the subject of Rory's coming to live on the Diamond 8 with her and Jeremiah, just as soon as the manager's house was built and they were married. Rory could live with her in the apartment until then. There had been no talk of adoption. Cilla had finally realized that the chances of that were remote, as Jeremiah had always said.

"Nervous, honey?" Jeremiah glanced at her, then reached across the bench seat of the old Chevy pickup and grasped her hand.

"A little," she admitted and took a deep breath. She had no idea why this was so important to her, so tremendously important to her. After all, she and Jeremiah would have children, she had no doubt.

Poor Mrs. Vandenbroek. She was losing another tenant to marriage. Just as she'd feared when Cilla had signed the lease. At the time, marriage was the farthest thing from her mind. Could that really have been only a few short months ago—last July?

They approached the railway tracks and Jeremiah slowed as the truck rattled across the tracks and the frozen rutted road beyond. The part of town where Rory lived—Painter's Flats, as it was known around Glory—had no sidewalks or curbs. The roads were mainly graveled, although the access road on the west side of the flats was paved. Probably because there was a school on the opposite side.

Children ran around the streets, treating the snowy surface as just one more playing field. They had rosy cheeks and shining eyes, despite the oddly matched clothing many of them wore. Several didn't even wear boots, but slid over the snowy surface of the road with running shoes on.

Someone had tried to build a snowman during the last snowfall, nearly a week ago, with mixed success. Cilla could see a lump of snow with two pebble eyes and a drooping carrot nose. Dogs barked or lay curled up shivering on snowy stoops. A variety of cars, some running, some obviously in disrepair, were drawn up in several drives. In front of Evelyn Bell's house was a rusty pickup and a small Japanese car with a baby's seat in the back. The boyfriend's.

Jeremiah braked in front of the Bell bungalow. Cilla paused for a few seconds, trying to collect herself, then spotted Rory's small head in the kitchen window. He was waving like crazy. She smiled and waved back.

Evelyn appeared at the open door. "You want to go for a walk with the boy? He's all ready—been waitin' ever since you called."

"Sure," Cilla replied. She'd put on her gloves. It wasn't exactly winter-cold, but it was freezing and she was glad she'd worn her suede jacket. Jeremiah had on the black leather jacket and jeans he'd worn to her apartment. He looked like a cowboy—as he always did, except when he was going to a wedding.

She wondered what he'd wear to his own. Not that she really cared, just so long as he married her.

"Go get your boots on, Rory!" Evelyn ordered over her shoulder. Her hair was in need of a cut and her apron had one of its pockets torn partly off. She was wearing a flowered housedress and the appetizing aroma of something roasting in the oven wafted out onto the cold November air. She didn't invite them in.

"Did—" Cilla gathered her courage and squeezed Jeremiah's hand. "Did you happen to mention to him what we—what we talked about?" She didn't want to come right out and say it, in case Evelyn hadn't. And in case Rory was listening.

Evelyn laughed. "Oh, I talked to him, all right! He's got his suitcase already packed. Can't wait." She paused and regarded Cilla severely through a fringe of overlong bangs. "It's nothin' to do with what the judge said, y'understand? It's just that we're crowded here and I could use the break. He's my cousin Iris's kid, I got an obligation to take care of him, but if you're willin'—"

"Oh, I do understand. I do," Cilla said, her heart soaring. Clearly, Evelyn was in favor of letting the boy come to live with her. As for adoption? They could look into that later. It might never happen. At any rate, there was no hurry.

"Hi, Teacher!" Rory said, coming out onto the rickety wooden stoop. He wore mismatched mitts and a brown jacket that was at least a size too large for him. His boots were bright red. They seemed to be new.

"Rory, please call me Cilla," she said, smiling happily. Jeremiah, she noticed, was grinning, too. "There's no Blue Owl School now, you know, so I'm not your teacher anymore."

"Will there be another Blue Owl someday?" Rory asked, coming down the steps and walking confidently up to the two of them. "I miss it. I *liked* coloring there. And numbers. Evelyn says I'm awful smart at numbers."

She released Jeremiah's hand to take Rory's. "I hope to start another school," she answered him, holding his hand warmly in hers.

"That's my dearest dream. Maybe next year. We'll see what happens." She caught Jeremiah's eye over Rory's head. She knew what he was thinking—she might be about to deliver their first child by schooltime next year. Well, if she wasn't pregnant, Blue Owl would definitely be her first priority. After Christmas, she planned to find new quarters and gradually put the insurance money into new equipment and supplies.

"Where should we go?" Cilla asked the boy, looking around the neighborhood.

"I know, let's go to the big log where me 'n' my friends play Star Buster."

Star Buster? Jeremiah and Cilla exchanged amused glances. Rory wasn't content to hold Cilla's hand for long and soon he was trudging ahead of them, swinging his arms and shouting back instructions and comments and pointing out various places of interest in the community.

Eventually they came to the log. It was dusted with the previous week's snowfall, the snow that had drifted in a few days after the ice storm.

"Over there! Tracks from something!" Rory pointed to the top of the log.

Jeremiah took a closer look. "A squirrel, I'd say. And maybe a few magpies."

"Looking for something to eat, right, Jem?" The boy's green eyes sparkled as he gazed up at Jeremiah. Cilla was touched that he'd used Glory's common name for Jeremiah so easily.

"Probably. You know magpies!" Jeremiah said, pulling Rory's cap down over his eyes. "They're always hungry. Just like kids."

"Yup!" Rory happily pushed his cap back. "I could eat a—a—" he held his arms wide and stood on his tiptoes "—a *snake* right now!"

"With mustard and onions?"

"Nope. With ketchup." He smiled up into the tall cowboy's face.

They were enjoying this, Cilla thought. They had a relationship—they *could* have a relationship. That was just the kind of thing men and boys did, fooling around with caps. Talking nonsense. The two men who meant the most to her—Jeremiah and this little orphan. Rory had said nothing about the money or the court's decision. Cilla hoped he had only the vaguest notion of what that was all about. At four, almost five, it probably meant nothing to him. What mattered was the loss of his mother and father and sister.

Rory cleared the snow off the log with his hand. "Here! You sit here, Cill." He indicated the cleared space. Cilla came closer and positioned herself on the log. She squinted against the bright light. "Okay. Now what?"

"Jem. You sit here." Jeremiah stopped in front of her as he obeyed the boy and leaned down and kissed her lips softly. "I've got another confession to make, honey."

"Oh? What's that?"

"I don't *do* crosswords."

She giggled. Jeremiah continued to the place Rory had assigned. He sat down and put his arm around Cilla and kissed her again. His lips were cold.

"This is comfortable," he said, winking at her.

"No, you move over there, Jem. You're too close," Rory ordered, coming over and indicating the exact spot he wanted Jeremiah to sit. Obligingly, Jeremiah got up and sat back down about a foot away from her.

Cilla wondered what the boy was up to— and then she realized and her heart melted all over again.

Rory stood in front of them, grinning. His cheeks were already rosy from the cold. He rubbed his snowy mitts together. "Now, guess what?"

"What?" they both said at once.

"Ta-da!" Rory rushed forward them and climbed onto the spot between them. He turned around and looked up at Cilla, then at Jeremiah, then back at her again. "See? This is *perfect,*" he said, patting each of them on the nearest knee.

Perfect. Jeremiah and Cilla looked at each other over Rory's head and Cilla was sure he felt exactly the same way she did. They reached out and put their arms around each other's shoulders, cradling Rory Goodland between them. The sun was just setting, going down in a golden flood across the snowy streets, the vacant lots, the early strings of bedraggled Christmas lights. Behind the town of Glory. Behind the Rockies.

Rory was right. It was absolutely perfect.

* * * * *